# Cocaine

## Larry Jeram-Croft

Copyright © 2012 Larry Jeram-Croft
All rights reserved.

Cover image by POA(Phot) Sean Clee; @Crown Copyright 2011

**Also by Larry Jeram-Croft:**

The 'Jon Hunt series' about the modern Royal Navy:

**Sea Skimmer
The Caspian Monster
Arapaho**

The 'Jacaranda' books about the Caribbean of the modern day and Nelson's time:

**Jacaranda
The Guadeloupe Guillotine**

Science Fiction:

**Siren**

## Prologue

*1945, The Caribbean Sea*

The sleek, grey U-Boat still managed to look new, even after so long a journey. Her Captain viewed the forward part of the hull from his position high in the conning tower. This far south and west there was little chance of being intercepted by any enemy aircraft, unlike the previous weeks, where they had had to dodge almost incessant air patrols and no few surface ships as well. However, this machine with her massive battery banks and new design snorkel had easily evaded them all. The Mark XX U-Boat was the only one of her kind. Designed to replace the older Mk XIV 'milch cow' supply submarines, the whole Mark XX programme had been cancelled by Doenitz last year to make way for more attack boats to be built. However, U557 had survived and had been taken over by the SS. The Captain had only discovered this a few weeks ago when he had been summoned to what remained of U-Boat headquarters and given his assignment. The war was lost, that had been clear to many for months now but he was to command this last mission, a voyage taking some of the treasures of the Reich and her key people into exile.

The SS Colonel called from below asking permission to come up. The Captain gave a curt acknowledgement. Big submarine she might be but there was precious little room up here with the two lookouts and himself. He squeezed to one side, as the man appeared through the hatch.

The Colonel took a great breath of fresh sea air. 'My God, you only realise the stink you've been living in when you taste real air again.'

The Captain smiled. 'Imagine what it's like in an attack boat, with twice as many men, in half the space and at sea for twice the time.'

The Colonel grimaced. 'No, thank you. Frankly, I don't know how you navy people do this.'

'To serve the Reich, what else?' Privately he thought, *'you won't catch me out like that you bastard.'*

That got a noncommittal grunt from the Colonel. 'Well, the Reich is just about finished Captain, let's be honest about it. It's why we're here after all.'

The Captain kept his counsel.

Apparently not noticing the silence, the Colonel continued, 'so, we arrive tonight. Can you do it in the dark?'

The Captain shrugged. 'Day or night makes no difference, we approach submerged. I can use my periscope underwater and con us in, as long as the lights are on. We might scrape the bottom but that's hardly a problem, we won't be going anywhere afterwards.'

'Good and then we disperse as briefed.'

Two o'clock that morning and the Captain breathed a sigh of relief as he spotted the underwater guidance lights. Bringing the massive submarine to a crawl, he carefully conned her towards the transits that gave him the safe heading he needed to enter the massive underwater cavern, the cleft in the cliffs, that housed the hidden U-Boat resupply and repair facility, on the South American coast. A sudden scraping sound from hull brought a curse from one of the men on the planes. The Captain kept his council, he knew how hard it was to maintain an exact depth at such a slow speed but he daren't go any faster. Last time he had done this he was in a much smaller attack boat and everything had been easier. This machine may have been brilliant in the open ocean but she was a pig in these confined conditions.

Suddenly he saw the light he was looking for and ordered the engines to stop. The submarine glided forward a few more metres and came to a halt with a gentle bump. He then ordered more water to be let into her diving tanks and she settled slowly on the sea floor.

An anxious minute later and the rumbling sound of machinery echoed through the boat. The Captain knew it was the massive concrete door being lowered behind them and then he heard the whine of the pumps starting up. In less than an hour, the underwater cave would be pumped dry and the boat would be settled on the wooden floor pilings. A dry dock underwater, it never failed to amaze him. With such ingenuity how had the German people been defeated?

The next day was busy for everyone. The base staff and boat's crew, unloaded the submarine. The tanks that were originally designed to carry spare fuel to replenish submarines at sea had been converted to carry cargo. The Captain, along with most of crew had no idea what was in the packing crates, although from the weight of some, it wasn't hard to work out. The treasury of the Third Reich had escaped the Allies clutches at least. All day, they toiled taking the cargo up the narrow stairs and into waiting trucks on the surface. The extra passengers, the men in suits who said very little the whole voyage, had disappeared in the first truck. The Captain didn't expect to see them again.

Suddenly it was over. The submarine was empty. All that was left was for them all to disperse. Maybe some would get their families out and be able to start new lives with them. The Captain had no family. They had been roasted in the oven of Dresden. A town they all had thought safe. He felt numb as he mustered his crew and base staff for the last time. They all stood smartly to attention on the casing, waiting for his order to leave.

He didn't even hear the bullet that struck the back of his skull. Nor did he see his brains fly across, to splatter the crewman in front of him. The crewman was also oblivious, as the machine gun fire cut him down in the same instant. Some of the crew dived for cover but there was nowhere to hide. Those that made it over the far side of the hull simply fell to their deaths on the dock's concrete bottom.

The cessation of noise was as startling as when it started. The bitter smell of cordite, mixed with the contents of men's bladders and bowels filled the air. The Colonel surveyed his work from half way up the steps. He indicated to his two men to get out of their hiding places, leave the machine guns and check the crew. Several shots rang out as the wounded were finished off.

The look of horror on the faces of the two executioners was almost funny as they returned to the stairs and saw the Colonel with one of their own machine guns pointed at them. It didn't last long as he cut them down to join their previous victims in sprawled death on the dockside.

Satisfied that all was neatly cleaned up, the Colonel made his way out into the fresh sunlight. He breathed the heady scent of freedom and a new beginning. With the last witnesses to the whereabouts of the riches of the Reich disposed of, they could start to plan a new life in safety. His last act before closing the heavy metal hatch was to light the fuse of the small charge placed in the access tunnel. He walked back several metres and waited. The explosion was more heard than felt. He returned and lifted the door and was pleased to see nothing but rock and rubble. Closing the hatch for the last time, he walked over to the waiting car.

In the dark, silent cavern below, the dead lay with their submarine. It would be a long, long time before daylight and anything resembling justice returned.

# Chapter 1

'Oh my God,' the exclamation left the lips of Lieutenant Commander Jonathon Hunt, without conscious thought, as he braced himself for the impact. He was standing right at the front of the bridge of HMS Chester, the Royal Navy's newest Type 22 frigate. At five and half thousand tons and almost five hundred feet in length, it was pushing it to call her a frigate. Most people seeing her for the first time would have compared her to a wartime cruiser. However, her size seemed unimportant to Jon as he looked out of the bridge window. The bows slammed down into the next oncoming wave. He looked up and could only see a foam streaked wall of grey dirty water. The sky was completely blotted out.

His knees buckled slightly as the bow shook and started to rise. Suddenly nothing could be seen, as a great shovel full of seawater was thrown backwards over the bridge by the rising bows and vicious wind, hitting the glass with a sound like a thousand bullets. For a few seconds the bridge windows might just as well have been underwater, until the overworked windscreen wipers cleared the view again. Now, everything was blue as the bows pointed skywards for a second, before they started their inexorable descent into the next massive trough. All around the sea was almost white, with spume being blown off the tops of the waves and streaks streaming along, forced by the hurricane strength winds.

As the ship came level, the Captain called to the Quartermaster, 'steady Johnson this looks like a big one.'

The Petty Officer, who was steering the ship, wasn't using a wheel, just a small, almost toy like, joy stick. Normally the ship would be steering herself but not in these conditions. Human reactions were needed. As the ship teetered downwards again, the Quartermaster found he had full port wheel applied and for a second nothing appeared to be happening. The bow was still swinging to starboard. For a second, he thought he had lost it and was about to shout that he needed the engines to assist him, when the bows steadied. To be caught sideways in the trough of one of these massive swells would mean disaster, even to a warship of this size. They could be toppled over like a child's toy.

'So, Flight Commander, how are your little babies down in the hangar?' Asked Captain Peterson, in a conversational tone, as though nothing untoward was happening.

Jon grimaced and braced, as they slammed into the next wave. 'Well Sir, the whole Flight team are there. I don't think I've ever seen so many lashings on two helicopters in my life. The Lynx is taking it quite well but the Sea King doesn't have such strong undercarriage and its centre of gravity is much higher. That's the one we're concentrating on but thankfully all seems well so far.'

'Good, you might be amused to see this then.' He handed Jon a paper signal to read.

Jon studied it for a second and then laughed sarcastically. 'How nice of Fleet to send us a strong wind warning. We told them what was going on six hours ago.'

'Quite, but not really unexpected this time of year, in the middle of the Atlantic. I'm just surprised they didn't see the depression forming and warn us. What is the wind speed now by the way?'

Jon looked down at the anemometer dial. The needle was pegged all the way around to the stop it usually rested on when the wind was calm. The gauge only read to sixty knots. Assessing the gap to the where the needle was stuck, he made an estimate. 'Something over eighty knots Sir. Quite a breeze.'

'Indeed, but the barometer has just started back up again, so hopefully the worst is over.'

'Yes Sir and going to operate where we're going is always risky but the dangerous season is six months from now. I never expected a hurricane on the way over, in winter.'

'Nor did any of us,' the Captain was interrupted by a door slamming behind them. Paul Tarrant, the ships First Lieutenant and second in command came into the bridge, dripping sea water from his foul weather gear.

'All good on the upper deck, Sir,' he reported. 'The cutter was working loose but we've managed to get some extra lashings around her. Otherwise, we're in surprisingly good shape. A couple of bent guard rails, nothing more.'

'Good, well done Number One. At least now it's daylight we can see what's going on.'

The First Lieutenant looked over at Jon. 'No flying then Flight Commander? I'm surprised you're not in your pit, standard aircrew procedure surely?' His wry smile belied his words.

'Ah Number One, I tried that but it rejected me, literally. It's a real bugger to wake up when you're two feet off the ground and about to hit the deck.' He reached over and rubbed his sore shoulder.

'Permission to come on the bridge?' a cheery voice called from behind them. The Captain turned and saw Lieutenant Brian Pearce, Jon's Observer and second in command of the ships aviation team. 'Of course Brian, come and join the wardroom weather appreciation society.'

Brian looked forward out of the windows, just as the bow slammed into another massive wave. His feet slipped and he had to make a grab for the compass Pelorus. 'Fucking hell, this is rough. I suppose everyone is blaming me as usual?'

'Well, you are the Met man,' replied Jon and he handed the weather signal from the CinC Fleet Weather Centre to Brian, who took it in at a glance and snorted his derision. 'I'd like to get some of those bloody forecasters out here sometime and let them see and feel the consequences of them getting it wrong. Anyway, the reason I came up Jon, was to say that the Chief says he reckons that they've done all they can and he'd like to send half the lads to breakfast and to get some sleep, they've been up most of the night.'

'Yes, of course Brian, I just wonder if there's any hot food.'

'Oh yes,' interjected Paul. 'The galley's working. You wouldn't believe how good the chefs have been. It will be a simple meal and they might even be able to eat it, as long as they can keep it on their plates.'

He was interrupted by a cry from the Quartermaster. 'Can't hold her Sir!'

The Captain looked over and assessed the problem. In a calm voice he called, 'Full Ahead on the starboard shaft.'

The Quartermaster's hand was already on the throttle lever and he slammed it forward. The whine of an accelerating gas turbine engine could be heard, even over the force of the storm. The ship's head immediately steadied and the helm regained control.

'Half Ahead Starboard,' the Captain ordered, looking relieved. To use Full Ahead was an emergency order and could easily damage an engine but in this case it hadn't had time to run up to damaging power levels.

'Well gentlemen, there may be a rising barometer but we're not out of it yet.'

The First Lieutenant looked at the other two and taking the hint responded, 'Indeed Sir we'll leave you to it.'

Jon and Brian were on the way to the wardroom, when the ship started to heel. 'Here we go again,' said Brian as he was half way down the ladder and he wrapped his arm around the railing.

Jon, who was already at the bottom, also grabbed for the rail as the ship continued to roll. Suddenly they could hear the rising scream of one of the gas turbines, only this time the heeling continued. Suddenly, there was a slam and the ship rolled rapidly the other way.

'Fuck, it looks like we've been caught out in a trough. Hold on Brian, this could get hairy.'

Brian didn't answer, just looked grim as the rolling continued. Being down below in the ship, they had no idea just how far over they were but when Jon's feet slipped out from under him, it was clear they were well past forty five degrees.

'Jesus, is she ever going to stop?'

Suddenly she did with another enormous slam from somewhere up forward. Their thoughts were interrupted by the ship's main broadcast.

'HANDS TO EMERGENCY STATIONS. HANDS TO EMERGENCY STATIONS. CLOSE ALL WATERTIGHT DOORS. THE UPPER DECK REMAINS OUT OF BOUNDS.'

'Right come on,' yelled Jon as he started down the main corridor towards the hangar, grabbing for hand holds, as he tried to run along the rapidly lurching deck. All around, men were appearing running to their various stations. The main broadcast alerted them again.

'The Flight Commander is requested to go to the hangar.'

'Where the bloody hell do they think I'm going,' shouted Jon to Brian over the general clamour just as the ship took another lurch. This time it felt less severe.

Suddenly the calm voice of the Captain was heard over the broadcast speakers. 'D'you hear there? This is the Captain speaking. Sorry about that gentlemen but as you may have gathered the weather caught us out just a little there. However, we are back under control. I have gone to emergency stations purely as a precaution for the moment. That said, I want all personnel to check for damage wherever they may be and report to HQ1. Hopefully the weather will abate over the next few hours. That is all.'

They had reached the hangar door by now and Jon started knocking off the securing clips, just as someone started doing the same from the other side. When the door opened, they saw the worried face of Chief Nichols, the Senior Maintenance rating.

'What's the problem Chief?' asked Jon grimly.

'It's the Sea King Sir, the starboard oleo has collapsed.'

'Shit, show me.'

He didn't have to look far. The hangar was almost completely full with two aircraft and there was hardly any space around them. On the far side was a grey Lynx but closer to Jon was the massive bulk of a grey Mark Two Sea King. It was immediately apparent that something was wrong. It was leaning over at a horrible angle. Jon looked up at the rotor head.

'Did the rotor head hit the side of the hangar?'

'No Sir, but when the strut collapsed all the starboard side lashings went slack and she's slewed around a bit. We're tightening them up as you can see but it's bloody dangerous.'

As to make his point, the ship gave another lurch to port and the loosely secured helicopter lifted up to port until the lashings came tight and then slammed back onto the damaged undercarriage.'

'I can see why the strut failed, Chief,' observed Jon grimly and then his eye was taken by movement behind the massive wheel sponson. One of his sailors was clearly attempting to tighten a lashing and had slipped on the wet hangar floor where the sea was getting in under the gap of the main door.

Recognising his Leading Aircrewman, Jon yelled. 'Hold on there Thompson, I'll come and help.'

Before anyone could stop him, Jon started past the two sailors attempting to tighten the forward lashings and made a dash to get past the main wheel sponson, before the next wave rolled them to port again. He almost made it, when the whole aircraft lifted up. Sensing the danger, Jon flung himself down and slid past the big double tyre wheel, just as it slammed down again, missing his head by inches. Thompson had partially recovered by the time Jon got to him but there was blood flowing from a gash above his right eye.

'Hold on, Tommo, I've got it,' said Jon and he grabbed the nylon lashing from his grip and started operating the ratchet. The next time the big Sea King steadied, he was able to fully tension the strop, as were those at the front and suddenly the monster was tamed. He helped his stunned aircrewman back to the front of the hangar.

'Right, someone escort Tommo to Sick Bay please,' he called to the other maintainers present.

'It's alright Sir, only a small cut,' Tommo replied wiping a bloody hand over his face.

'Do as you're bloody well told,' Jon responded not unkindly. 'It's why we have a Doctor on board after all.'

One of the Petty Officers grabbed Tommo and helped him out of the hangar door. Sick Bay was only just down the main corridor.

Jon looked at the SMR. 'Well Chief, that's Nellie buggered. Any idea what it'll take to fix her?'

'Probably not as bad as it looks Sir,' Chief Nichols replied. 'Those struts are designed to collapse with too much load, for when you ham fisted aviators thump her down too hard. I'm pretty sure we've got a spare but there's no way we can change it until the deck is steady when we are alongside. I'm sorry but it bears out my misgivings about trying to fly that bloody great thing off a ship this small.'

'Yes, well we've all had concerns but that's the whole point. This is only a trial to see if we can realistically operate a Sea King from a frigate, in an operational environment. Chalk this incident up to the negative side. But you wait until we're hunting submarines. You're going to be surprised how effective she'll be.'

The Chief grunted half hearted acknowledgement. 'As long as I can keep her serviceable.'

Jon clapped him around the shoulder. 'We bend em, you mend em. You know the rule. Now if we're all secure here again, I'm really going to try for some breakfast.'

As they made their way lurching from side to side along the main corridor, towards the wardroom, Jon thought about the day he had been asked to command the new experimental, two aircraft Flight. His convalescence, after he had left the hospital at Haslar, had gone well, despite the strenuous efforts of his Russian girlfriend Inga, to rupture his stitches. All too soon, he was back in the familiar office of his appointer, in Whitehall, the man who held the key to his next job. Circumstances were once again different. It had been made clear to him that the story of his little foray into the Arctic ice would have to remain a national secret forever. The appointer himself, actually new little about it but it was clear that Jon could take his pick of any number of plum jobs becoming available.

'Here's something that's right up your ally Jon,' said the appointer. 'It's another ship's Flight job but with a massive difference. The powers that be want to try an experiment, using the new Type 22, Chester. She's been given a larger than normal hangar and they intend to embark a mixed flight of one Lynx and a Sea King.'

'Bloody hell, why would they want to do that?'

'Well, as you know these new towed array sonars we're starting to use, have an enormous range, especially against clanky old Russian submarines. The problem is, although they give a reasonable accurate bearing, because of the way the sonar works, the range is problematical. Sound bending in water means that the sub could be in one of a number of what they call 'convergence zones'. Unless they have a way of finding out which, it's almost impossible to accurately locate the target. The idea is they send the Sea King out with its active sonar, to find out.'

'Two questions then. Firstly why the Lynx and secondly has anyone tried to fly a Sea King from a frigate's deck before?'

'Well, as I hear it, you've already done just that, only last year.'

Jon grimaced. 'You're not supposed to know about that and anyway it was an emergency.'

'Yeah well, I have to be made aware of certain things, don't worry it's not common knowledge. But to answer the first question, the Lynx is there as the weapon carrier. The Sea King could carry torpedoes or depth charges but at significant loss of payload for fuel. The idea is they work together. The Sea King localises the sub and the Lynx kills it. Of course the Lynx also has the air to surface kill capability with Sea Skua which the Sea King hasn't, so the ship overall has a significantly increased capability with both types on board.'

'And deck operations?'

'Well Boscombe Down have done some preliminary deck clearances and it will be up to you to explore the envelope in an operational environment.'

Jon sat back in his chair, this sounded interesting. 'Who else has been selected so far?'

'Only the Sea King pilots, a couple of hot shots that have just finished their second tour on 814. The idea is that you will be Lynx and Sea King qualified and have a second Lynx pilot as well. That way, both aircraft can fly without you if necessary or you could take either aircraft. It's another facet of the experiment. As you know, we don't normally let a pilot be operationally current on more than one type.'

'Observers?'

'Not selected yet but Brian Pearce could be made available, if you wanted him.'

'How could you think of anyone else? That's if he wants to come of course.'

'Oh I think he will. I've saved the best bit for last.'

'Go on,' said Jon, responding to the appointer's wide grin.

'Well you'll have to do a Portland work up, as she's a new ship. But then after Christmas next year, she will be deployed to the AUTEC ranges for trials for six months, as well as taking over as West Indies Guard Ship.'

Jon was almost flung off his feet as he entered the wardroom. Grabbing a handhold he turned to Brian. 'Bloody hell Brian, I signed up for six months in the sun in the Bahamas and West Indies. No one told me the trip over was going to be such a nightmare.' But then he continued with an anticipatory grin. 'Still, it won't be long before the first Cocktail Party and all that Caribbean totty.'

## Chapter 2

*Eighteen months earlier*:

Paulo Mandero suddenly realised that he was bored. Lying on his sun lounger by his exclusive pool he knew he shouldn't be. Behind him was his beautiful house and before him the sea with his private beach and two yachts tied to his private jetty. Life hadn't always been this good and maybe that was the problem. He was at the top of his game now and what more was there to achieve? His thin tanned face frowned, as he contemplated his future. Yes, he could make more money but he had so much already what was the point? He sighed to himself, he would have to set himself a new challenge soon or go mad with the tedium. Maybe he should try to reduce the number of his competitors, the problem was that they could be just as dangerous as himself and starting a war was probably too risky. He would need to find an edge before he went down that route.

His thoughts were interrupted by his current girlfriend. She came around the corner of the house, a tray in her hand.

'Your drink Paulo,' she said timorously offering him the tray.

He took the drink and lay back looking at the semi naked girl, wearing just the smallest of bikini briefs, standing at his side. Yes she was stunningly beautiful but so she should be, after winning all those beauty contests. With a slim waist, long, long legs, up-thrusting breasts and blonde hair, she was all a man could ask for. In bed she would do everything he told her. And maybe that was the problem again, no challenge just a mannequin to do with as he pleased.

He suddenly stood up, spilling his drink. The girl sprang back with fear in her eyes. He saw it immediately. Normally it would excite him and he would take her off somewhere and make her pay for it. Last time it had taken weeks for the marks to fade. This time, it just sickened him. He realised he felt less than nothing for her and reaching with his right hand he grabbed a handful of her hair and forced her to her knees. She immediately reached for the front of his shorts, just like the well trained whore she really was. It was funny to see the surprise on her face, when he put his hands on either side of her head. Even funnier when her eyes opened with astonished surprise, as he gripped her head hard and savagely twisted it to one side. There was a satisfying snapping noise as she went limp and he let her already dead body drop to his feet.

He made his way back into the house calling for his head bodyguard as he did so.

'Yes Boss,' answered Manuel almost immediately.

Manuel was an old friend. If you took unquestioning obedience and enormous physical strength as the basis for friendship.

'There's a mess by the pool, get rid of it please.'

Manuel looked where he was pointing. No emotion crossed his face. 'Sure thing Boss.'

Paulo continued into the house. Suddenly he felt better, invigorated, ready for a new challenge. Getting rid of the girl was just the first step.

Turning around for a moment he called to the retreating Manuel, 'and tell the Englishman I want to see him.'

'The Englishman' was Phil Masters and at that moment he was on the bridge of the seventy five foot Motor Yacht 'Maria' moored on the jetty. On the other side was the one hundred foot sailing yacht, originally named 'Maria II' for which he also had responsibility. He was staring out to sea through the glass of the bridge windows, wondering how on earth he had ended up here.

It had all started ten years before, that fateful day when he finished the Royal Naval 'Perisher' course. The previous weeks had been spent in the company of five other candidates, showing just one man, that he had the qualities necessary to command one of Her Majesty's Submarines. It had been bloody tough, all of them on the course had come near to failing at one time or another but eventually it was over and he was called in to a personal meeting with the 'teacher' as he was known. It was then that the bottom fell out of his world, all his ambitions, the only thing he had focused his life on since joining the navy twelve years earlier. He would remember that fateful conversation for the rest of his life.

'Come in Phil, take a seat.' The man was giving nothing away.

Gingerly he took the only other seat in the Captain's cabin of the nuclear submarine that he had sweated so much blood in over the weeks.

'So, how do you think you performed?'

He thought the question rather unfair but didn't say so. 'Well, I had my bad moments Sir but I think we all did at one time or another. Overall, I hope you consider I did well enough.'

The man didn't answer straight away. He was clearly composing his thoughts. 'Phil, do you remember what I said to you after the big mistake you made on week three?'

How could he forget it? 'Yes Sir, of course and I'm pretty sure I took it to heart.'

'So, what would you say about your performance yesterday?'

Phil was nonplussed. The final exercise had been bloody hard but he had achieved the required end result and managed to obtain a successful firing solution on another British submarine. 'I thought it went alright Sir,' he responded, lifting his chin and looking him in the eye.

'So, you don't remember freezing again, just before we turned to the attack heading?'

What was the bloody man on about? 'No Sir, I don't remember anything like that.'

Teacher sighed and looked sad. 'Phil, look I'm terribly sorry but you froze again for over a minute. The fact that you don't even remember it only makes it worse. It's something we just can't tolerate in a submarine Captain. I'm sure you must see that.'

Phil suddenly felt cold. 'You're saying I've failed? Just like that, after all I've done, Jesus.'

'Look old chap, I've given you the benefit of the doubt on several occasions and you do have talent, there's no doubt of that but you have this habit of retreating into yourself when under stress. I've seen it before you know. We all do it to some degree. But despite giving you every opportunity to do something about it, you just got worse as the course went on. Yesterday was your final opportunity I'm afraid and you didn't rise to the challenge.'

Phil felt physically sick. His world was crashing around his ears. What was worse was that there was nothing he was going to be able to do about it. All his cocky self confidence had never allowed for the concept of failure. And there it was, staring him in the face. 'There's nothing I can say, is there Sir?'

'Sorry old chap, no there isn't.'

He had no recollection of leaving the submarine. He did however, recall the looks of sympathy on the faces of the other course members and that just made it worse. What the hell was he going to do now? The stigma of 'failed Perisher' was the death knell to any submariner. His career in submarines was over and he really couldn't face some sidelined job in a bloody frigate.

He resigned two weeks later and the navy let him go quite quickly. His situation wasn't that unusual. Getting work 'outside' had been easier than he thought it would be. Lucy, his wife, had a father who worked in the City and he managed to get him a job in a finance house. He had actually been fairly successful but every now and then something would remind him of his failure and it would send him into a fit of depression. It didn't go unnoticed with his colleagues or his Boss for that matter. Nor did his remedy, which was to hit the booze harder and harder. After just over a year, they 'reluctantly' let him go. Shortly after that, he returned home, after another days job hunting, to find the house empty and a note on the kitchen table from Lucy, saying she couldn't take it any longer. He almost ended everything there and then but somehow found the strength to come up with a plan, a way of making a clean break. Going to the bank, he withdrew as much cash as he could and got on the next flight to Antigua. It was the island he had spent so many happy days on as a child with his parents and where he had learnt to sail. Getting work in the sailing industry had been ludicrously easy. Being a 'retired' RN officer was an excellent way of opening doors and he soon found himself busy skippering charter yachts. It might have all stayed like that with his happiness slowly returning, when fate forced yet another twist to his life's story.

He was skippering a luxury ninety foot sloop and had just returned from a cruise to tie up on the hard, in Nelson's dockyard for Christmas. His four American customers were leaving the next day and he couldn't wait. They had tried his patience like no others. One couple were fine but the other two were the customers from hell. The wife continually complained about everything, from the food to the fact that the yacht leaned over when sailing. Her whining, high pitched voice would make even a Saint want to commit murder. However, the husband was even worse. He knew it all and continually told Phil what he was doing wrong. Whenever Phil offered to let him take over in order to be shown how it should really be done, the bloody man refused, saying he expected the hired help to get on with it. That was until that morning, when they were mooring the yacht stern to, to the jetty. The idiot had decided it was time to show off his prowess. Arrogantly pushing Phil to one side, he attempted to drive the boat sternwards between two other super yachts. Not allowing for the crosswind and the way the boat handled going backwards, the clown managed to hit one of the other yachts to cries of anger from her crew, before Phil was able to shoulder him aside and regain control. The Yank said nothing and stalked off below decks, where Phil could hear his voice and the screeching of his fat wife.

An hour later, the man appeared on the jetty and confronted Phil.

'Get our bags off and order us a taxi, we're leaving,' he ordered in a sneering tone.

'I beg your pardon, I am the skipper not your valet,' Phil responded with growing anger.

'You're paid help and will do what I require. Now do as I say.'

A red mist was clouding Phil's vision. He clenched his fists and with a superhuman effort managed to stay in control. He noticed that the exchange was starting to attract the attention of the crews of the other yachts and several passers by. A confrontation in public was not a good idea and anyway the bloody man was leaving.

'I am the skipper of this boat and I'll get one of the crew to remove your bags.'

'Not much of a bloody skipper, you couldn't even berth the yacht without hitting something. Be in no doubt, I will be reporting your behaviour and lack of skill to the charter company.'

Something snapped and before he knew it, Phil had planted his fist hard on the bastard's nose, where it crunched with a satisfying spray of blood. The fat wife had come on deck and seen it all. She started screeching hysterically, at the same time as her husband fell backwards, with a look of astonishment on his face. What then surprised Phil even more, was the round of applause that broke out from the other yachts. Clearly, they had witnessed the whole affair and heartily approved. However, Phil realised immediately as his blood cooled, that he had committed the cardinal sin and assaulted a customer. He reached forward placatingly, to help the man to his feet but had to dodge a kick and a growing stream of abuse from him and his hysterical wife. With threats of litigation and hoots of derision from the massed audience the two of them made an undignified exit. Once again, Phil knew he had buggered up his career.

'Well, my friend, I expect the Police will be here soon. Those two morons will not let that go unpunished.'

Phil looked round to see who was speaking. A slim, tanned and very well dressed man was addressing him. He looked to be in his late thirties or early forties and had a thin, almost feral appearance. The look on his face was sympathetic but for some reason it didn't seem to travel all the way to his eyes.

'I'm sorry, do we know each other?'

The man laughed and held out is hand. 'No, my name is Paulo Mandero and I own the rather nice yacht next to you, that now has a long scrape down its side. But please don't worry, I saw what happened and don't blame you for it one bit. In fact I was very impressed by the way you regained control and recovered the situation. Right up to the time you hit the fat American that is.'

Phil smiled ruefully and took the man's hand. His handshake was firm and dry. 'Yes well, I don't expect my Company will be impressed at all. And as you say, maybe the Police might have something to say as well.'

Paulo laughed. 'If it had been me, he wouldn't have been able to get up afterwards.'

Something in the way he made the remark, made Phil realise he really meant it. Just for a second he knew that this was a hard man, who shouldn't be crossed.

'Sorry, my name is Phil Masters and I guess I'm now an unemployed Yacht Skipper.'

'Ah well, maybe that's where I can help.'

That had been the start of their relationship. Paulo was in need of an expert boat handler and commercial skipper. He freely admitted that while he liked his boats, he hadn't a clue how to drive or sail them. He had fired his previous man only the day before, although he wouldn't say why. Phil found out later, it had something to do with one of the young male stewards. Paulo had seen how Phil had handled the yacht that morning and after confirming that he had all the necessary qualifications, offered him the job on the spot. Never one to look a gift horse in the mouth, Phil had accepted. That's not to say he didn't have any reservations. There was something about Paulo that unnerved him but what choice did he have? And anyway the money he was offered was far more than he would have been paid doing simple charter work. To his surprise, he never heard from the fat Americans again. The Police never made an appearance and it wasn't long before he was sailing Paulo and his beautiful, if slightly scarred boat, back to his house in Columbia. It was only some months later that he found out who he was really working for. That he was now the skipper for one of the most notorious drug producers and smugglers in the Caribbean.

Snapping out of his reverie, as his name was called from the jetty, he saw the bulk of that thug Manuel calling up to him. Acknowledging the summons, he replied that he would be right up. What had surprised him the most about the whole situation was that when he had discovered his new Boss's occupation, it hadn't bothered him at all. In fact he was enjoying the whole experience. So it was with a degree of anticipation that he made his way up to the house, wondering what he was wanted for now.

## Chapter 3

The Officer of the Watch on the bridge of HMS Chester was having trouble keeping his eyes open. No one had managed much sleep in the last twenty four hours. It was very hard to nod off, when you needed both hands holding on tightly, just to stay in your bunk. However, at last the weather was moderating. The wind had dropped to less than a Force Six and although there was still a large swell running, the ships motion was now relatively gentle. He only had an hour of the morning watch left and then he would be able get some rest. The sun was coming up in quite spectacular fashion behind them and lighting up the ragged clouds in a glorious orange and gold. The view was helping him to stay awake.

Suddenly the Marine VHF radio burst into life. 'Mayday, Mayday, Mayday, this is Motor Yacht, Daddy's Girl. We are about twenty miles due east of Bermuda, my father has fallen down a hatch and hurt his back, can anyone help.'

The voice was female and sounded quite distressed. The OOW pushed the Captain's panic button to get him on the bridge as fast as possible, before grabbing the radio microphone.

'Daddy's Girl, this is warship Chester, we are about sixty miles away from you. Can you confirm how many people are on board and provide more information about the casualty over.'

The relief in the girl's voice was obvious as she replied. 'Chester thank you, there's three of us, my father myself and my brother. My father is in a bad way, he can't feel his legs, over.'

By this time the Captain, still dressed in his dressing gown, was on the bridge but he gestured to the OOW to carry on.

'OK Daddy's Girl, don't move him and keep him warm. We have a Doctor on board and should be able to get to you quite quickly. Can you confirm your position and describe the vessel to us please.'

'We're a seventy foot Motor Yacht, our hull is dark blue and according to the chart we are about twenty miles on a bearing of two six one from the north east point of Bermuda.'

'Right Daddy's Girl, stay by the radio please, we will get back to you as soon as we have more information.' He turned to the Captain, 'I'll plot an intercept course Sir.'

Captain Peterson nodded. 'Come up to twenty five knots as soon as you have it and also pipe for the Flight Commander and First Lieutenant to come to the bridge please.'

Ten minutes later, the ad hoc planning meeting was taking place on the bridge.

'Well Jon, can we get them off by helicopter with this sea running?' asked the Captain looking out at the large swell.

'Yes Sir, the biggest problem is that Nellie is broken but we can use Eric the Lynx. However, we will need to take the Doc with us to assess this guy, as well as our aircrewman, so it could get crowded in the back. But it's all doable.'

'I take it the Sea King would have been a better option?' asked the First Lieutenant.

'Oh yes, it's bigger and more stable but that said the Lynx is quite up to it.'

'Very well Jon, get the aircraft ranged as soon as you can. We'll conduct a very quick brief once you're ready to go. Also Paul, I would like you to get the Sea Boat prepared as a back up, in case the helo has problems.'

Only half an hour later, Jon, with Brian alongside him, launched off the heaving Flight Deck in the Lynx. The ship had slowed down in its dash towards the casualty, in order to give them reasonable deck movement. The Flight team had worked wonders to move the helicopter onto its spot and get it ready. They also had to get the ship's Doctor briefed and dressed for the trip but it had all come together remarkably quickly.

Once the aircraft was in the cruise, at maximum speed, heading towards the position of the Motor Yacht, Jon had time to talk to the two people in the back. 'OK guys, sorry it's so bumpy but the weather still isn't perfect and we're flying flat out. When we get there, I'll assess the situation. What we will probably do is a hi-line transfer. Tommo, as crewman you'll go down first with the stretcher, you know what to do. Then we'll send the Doc down next, OK?'

'Fine Sir, just like we practice.'

'Right Doc, are you happy to go down on the winch? You'll have Tommo on deck to help you in and Brian up here operating the winch so should be fine.'

'Actually I've done one of these before, so yes quite happy.'

'Good, now eyes out everyone, spotting even a seventy foot boat in this sea, isn't going to be easy.'

They flew on for another few minutes, then Brian who had been studying the radar intently, spoke up. 'I've got something Jon, in about the right position. Come left five degrees, it's about twelve miles away.'

It wasn't long before they could see the boat. 'Bloody hell,' remarked Brian. 'A rich man's toy if ever I saw one. It looks like there's a good clear area on the stern though. I'll give them a call. Daddy's Girl this is rescue helicopter Four Nine Nine, we have you in sight, we'll be with you in a few minutes, over.'

'Rescue helicopter, this is Daddy's Girl thank you, what do you want us to do, over.'

Brian looked at Jon. 'The usual mate?'

Jon nodded. 'Yes give her the brief, while I fly over and do an assessment.'

'Right, Daddy's Girl, can you turn onto a heading that gives a wind over you port bow, I suggest about due west for a start. Oh and what's your name?'

'Oh er, my name is Jacky, my brother is driving. I hope that's OK.'

'How old is he Jacky?'

'He's fourteen but don't worry he's very experienced.'

'That's fine, because we're going to need you down at the stern. What we will do is lower a light line down and then fly it close enough for you to get hold of. Once you have it, we'll back off a little and lower our crewman on the winch, alright so far?'

'Yes I understand.'

'Don't do anything until he has touched the sea, because he may need to be earthed to stop you getting a shock. Then we will get as close as we can and you can help get the crewman onto the deck by using the line. Once he's with you, we'll repeat the process and lower our Doctor to you. Is that all clear?'

'Yes I think so. I'll go to the back now.'

'Good girl, make sure your brother holds a steady course and remember to wear a life jacket. We don't want two casualties.'

'OK and I'm taking a portable radio with me.'

'That's fine but when we are close, the noise will probably be too loud to use it.'

As Brian finished his brief Jon turned the aircraft back downwind of the motor boat, which had now turned into wind. He brought the helicopter into a high hover.

'Should be fine Brian,' he said. 'That raised deck area at the back seems pretty clear of obstructions.'

'Right, I'm climbing out and I'll give you winch control if I need to.' So saying Brian unstrapped and carefully clambered out of his seat to get into the rear cabin, so he could give Jon hovering instructions and set up the rescue winch.

As this was happening, a door on the Motor Yacht opened and someone dressed in red foul weather gear and a lifejacket came out and waved to them. Jon couldn't see very much except for blonde hair, whipping away in the wind. She put something to her lips.

'Rescue helicopter, this is Jacky do you read?'

'Yes Jacky, this is Jon the pilot, I read you clearly, please standby for few minutes.'

Turning to look over his shoulder to see how they were getting on in the back, he commented, 'the girl's ready guys, looks quite cute even from this distance.'

Brian snorted. 'Even in a rescue situation, you just can't help your self can you?'

Jon laughed. 'Nothing wrong with looking, anyway you chaps ready?'

'Just about. Right I'm lowering the hi-line.' And he lowered the weighted line by hand, slowly out of the open cabin door until it had touched the sea. 'Right Jon come forward and right twenty yards.'

They slipped into their well practiced routine, with Brian providing instructions and Jon flying the helicopter as instructed. The line was slowly brought towards the stern of the vessel.

'Right Jacky, grab the line when you can.' Jon called on the radio.

She didn't answer but moved to the guardrails, reaching for the weighted bag as it swung towards her.

'That's one gutsy girl,' observed Jon, as she made a successful grab for the line. Brian paid it out, as he instructed Jon to move a little further away. Within minutes, Tommo was clipped onto the winch, with an empty stretcher and being lowered towards the sea. He touched a wave and then Jon brought the aircraft back to the stern of the yacht. In an amazingly well coordinated movement, the girl pulled the line, as the helicopter got as close as it could before Jon lost sight of it and then Tommo was on deck. They watched as he unclipped himself and the empty winch cable was pulled back up.

With the help of the crewman, they soon repeated the operation and the Doctor was on deck as well. There was a conference and then the crewman and Doctor disappeared into the ship.

'Jon, this is Jacky over.'

'Yes, I hear you loud and clear.'

'Your Doctor and crewman have gone down to look at my father. They say they shouldn't be long.'

'That's fine Jacky, now once we have your father on board we will probably take him back to our ship. But what about you? Do you want us to get someone to help you take your yacht back to Bermuda?'

The girl laughed. Even with the static of the radio, it sounded quite delightful. 'No thank you, I'm fully qualified to take her and it's not far to Hamilton.'

'As long as you're happy that's fine, our ship is going there as well, to Ireland Island to refuel so we can land your father there.'

They were interrupted by the door on the deck opening and the crewman re-appearing. The girl handed the portable radio to him.

'Four Nine Nine this is Tommo. The Doc says the casualty needs to be taken off. He has a back injury, as we suspected but the Doc can't assess the real damage until he has him back on Chester. I'm going below again to help get him on deck.'

'That's fine Tommo we'll be here.'

The girl came back on the radio. 'I think I should go and help. What should I do with this line?'

'Good question, just leave it on deck, don't for goodness sake tie it to anything. I should be able to hover close enough so it doesn't get pulled off.'

It took some time to get the casualty strapped into the stretcher and carefully manhandle it onto the deck but eventually it was done. They decided that the Doctor should come up with it, so that Tommo could stay on deck and control the lift. Brian lowered the winch wire as Tommo pulled it in and both the stretcher and the Doc were hooked on. With the crewman on deck to supervise, Jon was confident all would be well. So what happened next caught him by surprise.

'OK Jon,' called Brian. 'Move forward and right, standby, now, come up ten feet.'

Jon pulled up on the collective lever and the helicopter should have plucked the casualty and Doctor clear of the deck. Just as the winch wire took the load, the Motor Yacht lurched slightly. It wasn't much but as luck would have it the edge of the stretcher caught the top of the guardrail as it lifted clear of the deck holding it in place for just a second. When it flicked clear, it swung hard away and the tug on the light line almost pulled the crewman over the side. The line then snapped at the weak link, designed for just that eventuality and the crewman fell on his back. However, that wasn't the problem now.

'Shit Jon, we've got an awful swing on, come up before it swings back and hits something.'

Jon was completely unsighted now and had to rely totally on what Brian could see as he lay down and looked out of the cabin door. He pulled up further, until the radar altimeter showed forty feet.

'Good, well done mate, we're clear of everything now,' said Brian, not sounding at all sanguine. 'Shit, it's swinging all over the place. We're going to have to damp it down somehow.'

'Can't you do it by hand, on the winch wire.'

'I'm trying but the wind seems to have got it and I can't get enough leverage. Sorry we're going to have to give them a dunking, can you come down about twenty feet.'

Jon slowly brought the aircraft back down. Luckily, he could use the Motor Yacht as a visual reference, although God knows what they were thinking, as they watched the drama in front of them.

As soon as Jon had the helicopter in the lower hover, Brian slowly lowered the winch. 'I'm going to try just to get the docs legs to hit a wave. That should steady things up.'

The Doctor, who was staring up at the helicopter, seemed to understand what they were up to and pushed his legs down as Brian lowered the winch. His feet and then is knees caught a wave with a violent splash and suddenly the swing was under control. Brian swiftly bought the winch up and they were quickly at the door of the helicopter and then being brought into the cabin.

Jon got straight on the radio as soon as he saw that the Doc and casualty were secure.

'Daddy's Girl, sorry about that but we have your father on board safe and secure now.'

The girl answered. 'Thank goodness, what do we do now?'

'Can I talk to my crewman please?'

'Yes hold on.'

'Hello Sir, are going to try to get me off?'

'No, I don't think so, Tommo. We haven't got a spare hi-line and anyway you could be of help taking the yacht back to Bermuda. So you lucky bastard, have a good trip and we'll see you later today. Chester should be docking in a few hours, at the naval base so get yourself there as soon as you can.'

'Righty ho Sir, seems I've got the bums rush again.'

'Why do I think you don't mean that?'

There was a chuckle over the radio before Tommo responded. 'Yes, well Sir you haven't seen how good looking the company down here is I suspect I'll manage.'

## Chapter 4

The two boys were running along the cliff. Below them the surf generated by the last tropical storm, crashed against the rocks, occasionally throwing spray right up over their heads, even though the cliffs were quite high. The path was narrow, with the scrub of the forest, starting only yards from the edge. The weather now was hot, clear and blue. The large swell was the only testament to the wind and rain of the last few days. Cooped up in their small house while the tempest raged, the boys were now like freed wild animals, revelling in their release.

'Come on,' yelled Felipe the older boy, to his brother Flavio. 'Let's see what the storm has done to the spire.'

Flavio was only a year younger and almost as tall as his brother. Nevertheless, he had trouble keeping up. He wasn't going to let his brother get away though. He knew he would be teased mercilessly if he did. The spire, was a spike of rock, standing on its own just off the main cliffs and their father was always predicting that one day it would be destroyed by one of the regular summer storms. The two boys crested the little rise that blocked their view and stopped, catching their breath and looked disappointedly at the scene. It was still standing, as serene as ever, with white waves breaking around its base.

'I can't see any damage,' said Felipe. 'I was sure that something would have happened.'

'Yes, well look further on, something's definitely happened there,' responded Flavio pointing further along the coast. 'It looks like a whole part of the cliff has gone.'

The older boy followed his gaze and without a word set off at the run again. His brother followed, grimly determined to keep up. In the end he couldn't and it probably saved his life.

Suddenly up ahead, his bigger brother simply disappeared. One moment he was running hard, whooping and jumping the small bushes that dotted the path. Then he was gone. There had been no noise, nothing.

Flavio skidded to a halt, assuming his brother was playing a trick on him. It wouldn't be the first time. He looked ahead carefully, to where his brother had vanished but still couldn't see how he had pulled off the trick. He started running again but more cautiously this time, expecting Felipe to jump out at him at any moment. He was just able to stop in time. Suddenly, ahead of him, past a small lip of the path, the ground simply disappeared. A crevasse had appeared out of nowhere, his eyes followed it towards the damage to the cliffs further on.

'Felipe,' he yelled desperately, although he already felt the dread in his heart that his brother was down in that awful gash in the ground. Part of him was praying that Felipe would still jump out on him and laugh at his shock. Approaching the edge carefully, he got down on his knees and looked down into the darkness. Despite the brilliant sunshine, he couldn't see that far, the gap narrowed considerably as it descended.

'Felipe,' he yelled down the chasm. 'Are you there? Can you hear me?'

He thought he might have heard something but it could also just have been the wind funnelling up from the sea. Looking around again, he was now certain that his brother couldn't still be hiding somewhere. What should he do? Realising that there was only one option left to him, he started running again. But this time he ran like the wind, back to his house, back to his father.

Phil Masters was slightly out of breath by the time he arrived at the big white stucco house on the top of the hill. '*I really need to get more exercise*,' he thought, not for the first time. '*I wonder what Paulo wants this time? Hopefully something interesting, it's been quiet for too long.*'

Nodding at the guards at the gate to the short drive, he made his way into the cool of the hall. Maria the housekeeper was there.

'Morning Maria, is the Boss man around? Apparently he wants to see me.'

'Oh, good morning Phil, yes he's in his study.'

Phil smiled at the middle aged but still remarkably attractive woman, mentally reminding himself, he really ought to make a play for her some time. The way she looked at him, convinced him that it might be well worthwhile, even with the danger of that bruiser of a husband finding out. What was life without a few risks?

Smiling inwardly, he took himself up the marble stairs two at a time and knocked on Paulo's study door.

'Come in Phil,' came the Boss's voice and Phil went in to the wide spacious room with the open balcony looking out to sea. Paulo was seated at his desk, facing the view with his back to Phil. He looked around as he heard him approach.

'Take a seat Englishman, we need to talk,' and he indicated a cane seat to one side if the desk.

Phil sat and crossed his legs, looking at Paulo with an inquisitive stare. 'Something up Boss?'

'Yes Phil, I need a change, frankly things around here are too dull. I've decided to expand the empire. We're going to take on the Marcello brothers.' He looked at Phil clearly waiting for a response.

Phil wasn't surprised, although he had been hoping things weren't going to move in this particular direction. 'Are we doing this because it makes good business sense or merely because you need the excitement Paulo?'

'Does it matter?'

Phil shrugged. 'I guess it does, because as there will be some considerable personal risk to me, then I would like to know why I am being asked to get involved.'

Before Paulo could respond the door flew open and Manuel came in. 'Boss, sorry to interrupt but we have a problem down in the village.'

Paulo frowned at the interruption but motioned to Manuel to continue.

'It seems the head overseer's sons were out on the cliffs this morning and one of them has fallen down some sort of ravine.'

'Don't you mean over the cliffs? There are no ravines around here.'

'Apparently there are now. A part of the cliff has fallen, probably due to that last storm and a crack has opened up. The oldest son has fallen into it.'

Paulo sighed. 'Sorry Phil, we'll have to continue this later. I can't be seen to ignore my people. It's all part of the way we live here. I'd better go.'

'That's alright Paulo, I've got some climbing experience. Maybe I can help.'

'You don't have to you know.'

'Yes I do, I consider myself part of the family now as well.'

Paulo clapped his hand on Phil's shoulder. 'Yes, maybe you are,' he smiled.

Half an hour later, ten men stood at the edge of the new ravine. Paulo, Phil and Manuel were being helped by the boy's father and other men from the village. Little Flavio had indicated where it had all happened and had been taken away by his mother. Everyone feared the worst and it wasn't felt to be a good idea for him to see the broken body of his brother when they found it, because that was what everyone feared. Even with the brightest torches they had with them, the only thing that could be seen was the sloping earth and rock sides of the new cleft.

'He must be below that overhang,' observed Phil. 'We don't know how far down it goes because we can't see beyond it. Has anyone here done any climbing?' he asked, looking around at the worried faces of the men. No one said anything.

'Right Paulo, I suggest then that I go down there because I used to do a bit as a hobby a million years ago. Does anyone object?' He took the relieved silence as assent. 'OK, this is what we'll do. First, we throw down two lines one for me and one to bring anyone else up. Someone go down to Maria II in the Land Cruiser and tell the crew we want two of the longest Spectra lines on board, the rigging box and the man overboard sling. They'll know what I mean.' When everyone hesitated Phil continued. 'Manuel take charge, you know the guys on the boat.'

Manuel gestured to two other men and they set off running back to where the cars were parked, a quarter of a mile away.

Meanwhile, Paulo had been looking hard at the situation.

'What I don't understand Phil, is why the crack has appeared in the first place. Look, the cliff has fallen in over there but that happens quite often along this coast. There's never been anything like this before.'

Phil looked at where Paulo was pointing. 'Would you believe I have a degree in Geology Paulo? Not what you would expect for an ex British naval officer I know but there it is. Now, look at the rock over there. It's a different colour. What you have here is a natural fault line between two layers of igneous rock.

The whole Caribbean was formed as the result of volcanoes. There were probably two here at one time and this is where the lava flows met. I guess when the cliff slipped, it started a small chain reaction, to relieve the stresses along the join. Mind you, even so it does look a little odd. Still, I don't suppose the reason really matters.'

It took another fifteen minutes before the sweating men reappeared, loaded up with two large coils of rope and two boxes.

'Right, tie the ropes to those two trees and pass me one of them.' Phil went to inspect the knots the men used and then threw one rope down into the cleft. He then took out some webbing and caribena clips from the yachts rigging box and got ready to use them as an improvised abseiling system. He then carefully tied the harness used to haul unconscious bodies back on board the yacht to the end of the other rope. 'I'll go down and investigate. If I need the rescue strop I'll call for it. You'll have to man haul them both up. Does everyone understand?'

Paulo answered for them all. 'Yes Phil and we won't forget this, whatever the outcome.'

Phil shrugged, 'I'm just the best qualified for the job. Right here we go.'

Standing on the edge of the cleft, he let the rope take his weight and carefully stepped backwards. In small slipping steps, he made his way down the almost vertical rock face. Within a minute, he was past the blocking overhang and was able to shine his torch all the way down and immediately saw the body of the young child caught on a ledge. He was ominously still. Looking further down, he could see that the cleft narrowed even further and there was a glint of sea water right at the bottom. The child might have survived but had he missed the ledge, he would certainly have died.

He managed to get level with the body but then had to swing across by pushing against the opposite wall. It took several attempts but eventually he managed a precarious stance on the remaining part of the ledge. The boy was breathing but there was a horrible gash on his head. A pool of congealed blood surrounded him. Phil looked up and couldn't work out how he had managed to actually land on the ledge in the first place. He then saw a scrap of clothing on the opposite wall and realised the lad must have hit that side first and literally bounced as he fell down further. Carefully Phil investigated and found that the boy's right hand trouser leg was ripped and a further gash was evident.

*'If we get you out of this we're going to have to rename you rubber boy,'* he thought. Then looking up towards the daylight, he called for the rescue sling to be lowered to him. It was soon in sight and dangling tantalisingly close but just out of reach. He was forced to swing off his perch to grab it and then repeat his swinging to get back on the ledge. The sling was designed for an adult dressed in bulky foul weather clothing, so there was plenty of room for the little boy, who couldn't have been more than twelve years old. Soon he had him safely secured but then the next problem reared its head. He couldn't just launch the sling off the ledge, as the boy would probably swing across and hit the other wall. Calling for the men above to take up the slack he carefully cradled the lad and they both swung off the ledge together. Unable to fend for himself he slammed hard into the opposite wall and felt his own head take a knock. For a second, he literally saw stars but mercifully stayed conscious. He was then able to instruct those at the top to haul up the casualty.

While he waited to hear that the boy was safe and get himself hauled out as well, he had the time to look around. It seemed that his theory about the cleft was probably correct, except for one thing. His investigations were cut short when he found himself being hauled vertically upwards towards the light. It only seemed like moments and friendly hands were pulling him over the edge and onto solid ground again. Still a little dazed from the knock on his head, he was amazed by the reaction of the men. The little boy was already on his way to the vehicles but everyone was certain that he would survive and they all wanted to thank him at once.

When the euphoria had died down a little, Paulo approached him. 'That was very brave my friend. The men and I will never forget it. We are in your debt but we had better get you to the Doctor as well. You seem to have lost your fair share of blood from that head wound.'

Phil reached behind and felt the warm traces all over his neck. 'Oh well, head wounds always bleed a lot, I'll be alright.

But look, maybe you should put your plans about taking on the Marcello clan on ice for the moment.'

'Oh, why do you say that?'

'Well, I think I was only partly right about why that crack opened up. You see the ledge I found the boy on, was made of concrete.'

## Chapter 5

Bermuda is shaped like a giant fishhook resting in the Atlantic Ocean and has the tiny naval base at Ireland Island at its tip. HMS Chester was tied alongside the sole jetty. Fuel hoses snaked across her decks. The Lynx helicopter was ranged on deck and the Flight engineering staff were frantically jacking up Nellie the Sea King, to fit a new undercarriage sponson strut before the ship sailed.

Jon and Paul Tarrant were walking on the Flight Deck, carefully keeping clear of all the activity around them.

'I know I'm going to regret asking this Jon. I know why the Lynx is called Eric, sort of that is, as it's the same machine you had during the Falklands but why Nellie?' asked the First Lieutenant, as he peered in at all the bustle in the hangar.

Jon laughed, 'Oh that's easy, there's no trick. She's big, grey, a little wrinkled in places and has a massive trunk, well cabin at least.'

Paul looked disappointed. 'Damn, I had a bet on with myself that it was one of your ex-girlfriends.'

'Sorry to disappoint you then. Anyway, I would never go out with a girl called Nellie. I do have standards you know.'

Just then a taxi pulled up and Leading Aircrewman Thomson got out and started up the gangway with a grin on his face that only got wider when he saw Jon standing watching him.

'Seems like your chap has enjoyed himself,' observed Paul.

'Hm, let's see how he got on. Afternoon Thomson, how did it all go?'

Thomson paused at the top of the gangway, to salute the Ensign and then went over to the two officers. 'Pretty well Sir, the girl certainly knows how to handle a boat and we got into Hamilton with no problems.'

'Did you ask her what on earth they were doing out there in those conditions?'

'She said the forecast was a pack of lies and once they realised how bad things were, they decided to turn around. That was when her dad slipped down the ladder. How is he by the way?'

'Ah,' said Jon thoughtfully. 'Physically he's alright, just a very bruised coccyx apparently and he should make a full recovery in a couple of weeks.'

'There's something more isn't there Sir?' asked Thomson shrewdly.

'Yes well, the good Senator, because that is what he is, is also convinced that God conducted the rescue and has being trying to convert anyone in his vicinity to his cause. Luckily, the Ambulance took him off as soon as we got in otherwise he would have had us all praising the Lord and shouting Hallelujah by now.'

Thomson didn't look surprised. 'Er, yes Sir, Jacky did warn me.'

'So, how was the young lady, Thomson? What's she intending to do?'

'She said she would be over as soon as she's been to the hospital, to thank you all. Mind you, that might take a while. Have you seen how slowly they drive around here? The speed limit is twenty and they all stick to it.'

The First Lieutenant nodded. 'I know, I was here a few years back. It's enough to drive you mad but you really have to be careful because they enforce it very heavily.'

'Anything else Thomson? Otherwise I suggest you get below and get out of that rubber bag,' asked Jon.

'No Sir, although I suspect you'll be quite pleased to meet the young lady. I certainly was,' he replied with a cheeky grin.

'That's quite enough Leading Aircrewman. When I need your help with women I'll ask for it.' Jon replied with mock asperity.

'Sorry Sir, yes I'll go and get out of my flying gear.' He didn't look admonished at all as he made his way past the two officers and through a screen door.

'Cheeky bugger,' observed Paul.

'I guess so but a damned good crewie all the same. So what's the plan now Number One?'

'Well, we stay here tonight and set off at first light heading south for the Bahamas. We need to be on range in a week, so we stick to plan A and head to Nassau next weekend for briefings and then go play with the submarine on the AUTEC range, starting on the Monday.'

'Good, we need to get the two aircraft working together as soon as we can. Bloody hell what's going on over there?'

The two officers as well as all the others on the Flight Deck stopped work to look at the large truck that had pulled up moments before. A pretty young girl with a microphone and a cameraman were ignoring Chester and making their way over to the beach, the other side of the jetty, where a number of Chester's crew were taking a few hours off to lie on the sand in the sun.

'I suppose I'd better go and find out,' said Paul and he made his way down the gangway in pursuit of the TV crew and to the amusement of the rest of the ship's company who were watching.

In a few minutes he had returned and went over to Jon. 'Quite amazing, they see warships all the time but they've never seen anyone sunbathing in January before and decided to put a bit on the local news. Notice they're all wearing jumpers. I left them to it as the sailors were giving them some amazing accounts of the storm and I would hate to stand in the way of Jack and a good story.'

Jon laughed. 'Yeah, I just hope they have the sense to realise when they are being spun a yarn.'

They were interrupted by Brian coming up with a signal in his hand. 'Hi guys, just come up from the Signals office. Sorry but Zorbin again.'

'Eh?' queried Jon.

'Zorbin changed old mate,' replied Brian. 'Hey great! I've found some Jackspeak you didn't know. That's a beer you owe me. Anyway, we're not waiting until tomorrow we're sailing as soon as we're refuelled. Apparently, a real Ruskie sub has been detected by our dear old US cousins south of here and Fleet think it's a great opportunity to try out our new kit against an actual Soviet. Never mind that we haven't even practiced the basics yet.'

Paul sighed, 'I guess I'd better pull those sailors away from the TV people and get the ship ready. Sorry Jon but it looks like you'll never get to meet the Senator's glamorous daughter. Mind you, if she's anything like her father you're probably better off for it.'

Two days later, Jon was flying back to the ship in a repaired Nellie. He wanted some hours in the Sea King and the hunt for the mysterious submarine was the perfect opportunity. Seated in the co-pilot's seat was Peter Jenkins one of his other Sea King pilots and in the back were Brian operating the radar and Thomson, whose job it was to operate the dunking and passive sonar systems. Something he had done a lot of, to no result.

'Bloody Yanks, it must have been a farting whale again, because there sure as hell is nothing out there,' remarked Brian. 'I got suspicious when the ship's towed array couldn't pick anything up. If it had been a Victor Three, we would have heard it miles off.'

'Maybe,' responded Jon. 'But remember we're hearing stories that the Soviets have twigged to how noisy their subs can be at last. Our little trip north last year may have had something to do with that.'

'Er Sir, what was that all about?' asked Peter. 'We've all heard rumours but no one seems to know anything.'

'And I'm sorry but that's how it stays. I shouldn't have mentioned it just then. But even so, a quiet Soviet sub is going to much harder to find.'

'Well, I don't think there was anything there in the first place,' replied Brian. 'We've dropped loads of sonobuoys and pinged all over the place and there's no sign of anything. I reckon those American P3 Orion patrol aircraft lot were just making things up to pass the time.'

'Well, look on the bright side everyone,' said Jon. 'No submarine means we get into Nassau in time for the Cocktail Party, so some good's come of it.'

## Chapter 6

'Can you see anything Englishman?' Phil could just hear Paulo's voice from way behind him.

'Yes another door, I'm coming back up,' and he started wriggling and climbing the rope he had tied to a tree above, up the narrow tunnel he had excavated through the rubble. On reaching daylight, he heaved a sigh of relief and took a breath of clean air.

'It's exactly as I expected,' he said with a note of excitement in his voice. 'Once we found the outside door with the metal detector, then I was pretty certain there would be another one further down. It seems someone put a small demolition charge between them to seal the whole thing up.'

Paulo looked at Phil with a frustrated air. 'Right, are you going to finally tell me what this is all about? Ever since yesterday when you rescued the boy, you've been like kid on a treasure hunt.'

Phil's face was covered in dust and sweat and his muscles ached from digging but he had never felt more invigorated in his life. He realised he owed his Boss a bit more of an explanation, not the least because he knew the man could have a very short fuse.

'Look, you know that when I was in the navy, I was a submariner, right?'

Paulo nodded.

'Well, I've been in love with the sea and submarines ever since I was a kid and their history has become a bit of an obsession with me, particularly the last war.'

'What the hell does that have to do with this hole in the ground?'

'I'm coming to that. The Germans were incredibly innovative. We all get to hear about the War of the Atlantic, with their submarines against our convoys but one thing has always puzzled historians and me for that matter. They seemed to be able to deploy their submarines in places they shouldn't have been able to get to. Or rather had they got that far they would never have been able to get home again.'

Light started to dawn in Paulo's eyes. 'So they had some sort of resupply base on this side of the Atlantic.'

'Got it in one but no one has been able to find it, or even prove its existence for that matter. There was nothing in the records of the Reich that showed it ever existed. But just think, if this is actually it, what a fantastic base for your business it would be. If the Allies could never find it during the war, then no drug enforcement agency stands a chance.'

Paulo was starting to get caught up in Phil's infectious attitude but could see one glaring problem right away. He walked over to the cliff face, which was about fifty feet high. About two hundred yards further on was the rock fall that had caused all the problems in the first place.

'Come here Phil. Look down there, there's no jetty, nothing to allow boats to tie up to, so if there is something there, how on earth did they get in and out?'

'Actually, I think I've already worked that out. Look at the colour of the water just below our feet. See how much darker it is? There's obviously quite a deep channel going out to sea quite a way and it comes right up to the cliff edge. I think there is a bloody great cave under our feet and they got in and out underwater.'

'Oh great, so even if it's there we will need a submarine?'

'Not necessarily, we can use SCUBA gear and yes, even a small submarine, they are around you know. The only reason I haven't suggested we get some divers to go down and look for an underwater entrance, is that the swell is just too big at the moment. If we can't get in from on top, we may have to do that eventually anyway.'

'Alright Phil, we all owe you one for what you did yesterday and I'm willing to go so far on this but you'll have to convince me a lot more. I get the feeling that this is really about your submarine hobby more than anything else.'

'Thanks Paulo, it may seem a little farfetched but I truly believe that if what I think is there is still in a useable condition, then it could give your business something totally unique.'

The next morning with the help of some of the men from the village, Phil had fully excavated the tunnel leading down to the lower steel door. The upper one had been flat with the ground but the inner one was vertical in the face of the large shaft. Only the top part of the shaft had been damaged and only a few feet further down the concretes sides were surprisingly intact, with metal rungs concreted in. From the design of the door's hinges he could see it opened inwards and there was a large locking ring in the centre, rather like that of a warship. It was clearly of military design. Unfortunately the explosion above it and the weight of rock that had been sitting on it for so many years had bent and warped the locking mechanism. One of the men from the village had brought up some oxyacetylene cutting gear and was busy cutting through all the locking spigots around the edge. When the last one was clear, he called Phil, who moved closer to look. Once the metal had cooled, the two of them pushed hard but the door remained solidly stuck.

Paulo came down to inspect the situation.

'Why on earth are there two doors anyway Phil? Surely one would have been enough?'

'That's a very good point and looking at the way this has been designed, I would say this is an air lock of some sort. Maybe they wanted to keep pressure up inside for some reason. Anyway we'll soon know.' He stood back as the man with the cutting gear returned with a sledgehammer and got ready to swing at the door. Phil and Paulo stood well back as he took his first mighty swing. The noise was deafening and rust flakes flew everywhere but the door remained stubbornly closed. It took a dozen reverberating blows, when suddenly the door flew open, to a blast of dry and musty air.

With mounting excitement, Phil called for the powerful torches they had brought. He looked at Paulo with a questioning grin.

'No my friend, this was your discovery, you may have the honour.'

Without saying anything, Phil turned on his torch and entered. He was in another short tunnel. When he got to the end, it split into two directions. To the right were several doors spaced along about a hundred yards of corridor but if his above ground indications were correct, then the left tunnel was the one he needed. All he could see was a black opening. He went to the end and looked out into an echoing black space. Some metal stairs led down in front of him. He shone his torch down and almost dropped it when he saw the gaunt grinning face looking up at him. Teeth were stretched over a cadaver like face and lifeless eyes stared at him from below a black cap.

'Jesus, what the fuck is that?' Holding a primal terror back, he forced himself to look closer. The mummified body was dressed in some sort of black uniform.

'Paulo come here and bring more light, some of the previous residents are still around.' He hoped Paulo couldn't hear the tremor in his voice.

He was soon joined by Paulo and two other men, all holding powerful torches. Their reaction was similar to his, especially when they saw another body further down the stairs. Phil bent down to examine the first one.

'These aren't sailors. This is an SS uniform, what the hell were they doing here? And look, someone shot them.' He could clearly see bullet holes across the torso. 'What on earth happened?'

He started down the stairs carefully keeping clear of the second corpse and shone his torch further on. He gasped. 'Oh wow, Paulo come here, look at that.'

Visible now in the combined light of the torches was a massive black bulk sitting between two concrete wharves. The conning tower and gun just ahead of it immediately identified it as a submarine.

'Paulo, do you know what you are looking at? That my friend, is a German Mark Twenty submarine. None are meant to have been built. The whole programme was meant to have been cancelled. Clearly all the experts were wrong. My God, this is fantastic.'

Paulo wasn't so sure. 'Phil look, it's covered in more bodies. Come on, something terrible happened here, who cares about a bloody relic of a submarine.'

Phil was having none of it. He walked carefully across the gangplank that still bridged the gap between the dock and the casing. The first body he came to was clearly that of an officer. 'This must have been the Captain, look at his rank insignia. But goodness, look at the condition of the submarine, it looks brand new.' He shone his torch over the casing and onto the gun. The metal looked untouched by time. There was no sign of rust or corrosion of any sort. He shone his torch over the side and realised there was no seawater.

'Paulo look, how on earth did they get it in here?' He walked down the casing to the stern and shone his torch into the darkness. A massive slab of concrete blocked his view. Looking up, he could see what looked like giant steel screws disappearing into the rock overhead.

'Yes of course, that's a door. They could crank it up and flood the whole cave for the sub to enter and close it and pump the whole place out again. No wonder everything in here is so well preserved and no wonder this place was never discovered.'

Paulo joined him. 'Well Phil you were right and I apologise for doubting you but I still fail to see how we can utilise this place. The equipment in here must be almost forty years old. How do you expect to make use of any of it?'

But Phil wasn't to be put off. 'Look Paulo, look at the condition of that door and its lifting mechanism. It all looks perfect and yes of course, much of the equipment here may be useless but modern pumps are easily acquired and generators and lighting. Come on, this is the just the place to store and then despatch your stuff. Surely you see that?'

Paulo grudgingly had to admit that Phil had a point. 'OK, well we'll have to get all these bodies out of here and buried somewhere. I'll get the men working on that right away.'

'Fine and then I suggest that I do a complete survey of the place and see what looks serviceable. Do you think we can get a generator and some portable lighting up here soon?'

'I don't see why not but Phil there's one serious problem you haven't considered.'

'Oh yes, what's that?'

'How do we get rid of this useless great thing we're standing on? It's blocking the exit and is taking up almost all the room down here.'

Phil looked at his Boss with a strange expression. 'Why do we want to get rid of it, when we can use it?'

## Chapter 7

Brian stuck his head around the wardroom door. 'Anyone seen our illustrious Flight Commander?'

His query was met with negative remarks, some of which weren't that polite.

He made his way up to Jon's cabin. It would be unusual to find him there at this time of day but he hadn't been able to track him down anywhere else. Knocking on his door, he heard a muffled voice telling him to come in.

He opened the door and peered around. 'Wotcha mate, I've been looking for you everywhere. You know mail has been piped? Hey are you alright?'

Jon looked up with an odd expression on his face. 'Already got my mail, that's why I'm here,' and he held up the letter he was reading. 'You know the real problem with having my Christian name, is that letters from your girlfriend can start the same way but have several meanings.'

'No sorry, lost me there.'

'Well, this one starts with 'Dear Jon.''

The penny dropped. 'Inga?' Brian queried.

'Here, look for yourself,' and he handed the letter to his friend.

Brian declined the invitation. 'Sorry, don't really want to see your personal stuff, if you don't mind.'

Jon shrugged and took it back. 'Well I can't say I'm surprised. You know, even though she was in Norway for some time, it was up in the boondocks and she was really surprised by the reality of life outside the Soviet Union. Mind you, I thought she might have waited a little longer before finding someone further up the ladder than some scruffy naval officer.'

'Is that what she says?'

'I can read between the lines. That's one ambitious young girl and she's pretty bright too. She'll be married to a millionaire in a year two, you just wait. I'd like to know who helped her write it though. Ending with 'I hope we can remain friends' is just too corny for fucking words.'

Brian could see that his old friend was taking it quite hard. 'Right, well we've got the Cocktail Party tonight, so we can drown your sorrows then but you need to get your mind on other things. The reason I was looking for you was that our local military guy is here and there will be a briefing in the wardroom in ten minutes.'

'Fine, I'll be there.'

As he left Jon in his cabin, Brian was worried. Knowing Jon as he did, he would need a careful eye kept on him. Two weeks off the booze and being dumped by Inga was going to be a lethal combination if not carefully managed. He would have a quiet word with the other aircrew. The Flight Commander would need management tonight.

Fifteen minutes later and all the ship's officers were seated in the wardroom to listen to the local resident naval liaison officer. Lieutenant Commander Cliff Watkins had been in the Bahamas for several years and it was his job to brief all ships on the local situation when they arrived. In addition, there was an officer in a strange uniform, who he introduced as Lieutenant Glen Thomas from the US Coast Guard.

'Good Morning gentlemen, I see a few familiar faces in the audience,' he said looking at Jon and Brian. 'I seem to remember you two from HMS Prometheus, when she visited a couple of years back.'

Jon nodded.

'Right, well some things have changed, which is why I have my Coast Guard colleague here today and he will discuss certain developments regarding the drug smuggling situation. However, first I'll just talk about procedures on the range and general administration. As you know the AUTEC range is managed from Andros Island, just to the south of here and the underwater section called the Tongue of the Ocean is deep enough for submarines to operate and give you all the practice you require.' For the next fifteen minutes he went through the basic procedures and range safety requirements before finishing off.

'Now Jon, I know you will remember my warning from last time but it still stands. Do not fly over the western coast of Andros. We know it's an area where the druggies transfer their loads into cigarette boats to get them into the US and so there is still a danger that they may take a pot shot at you. However, as I said at the start, there have been a couple of developments since you were last here, so I'm going to hand over to Glen from the Coast Guard to bring you all up to date.' He stepped back to allow the American officer to take front stage.

The Coast Guard officer, a slim tanned man with a very close crew cut and very hard expression, cleared his throat as he looked at the assembled officers. 'As you know gentlemen, the US has no direct jurisdiction in the Bahamas, until we are in international waters but as you will be staying for several months after your trials period and working with us, it was felt useful for me to come and brief you right at the start. As some of you know, we have a real drug problem in these waters. Cocaine in particular, is bought up from South America and taken into the Gulf of Mexico or Florida. It is very hard to stop it all but we do our best. You may not know it but the US Coast Guard is a fully paid up member of the US military forces and just like you we carry arms. But we're stretched very thin and the coastlines are very long. I hope you will be able to visit us when you dock in Port Everglades some time and we can show you some of the tricks these guys get up to.'

'Yes, we were shown some of them last time,' said Jon. 'They were quite staggeringly clever.'

'You're right Sir,' replied Glen. 'But there's a difference now. For some reason our success rate has been falling dramatically. We know the stuff is still getting in, from the reports we get back from the local Police forces but the number of intercepts we are managing are down by over thirty per cent and we don't know why.'

'So, they've come up with some new wheeze?' a voice from the crowd asked.

'That's about it and we have no idea what it is. I hate to admit it but if this were a shooting war we would be losing very badly now.'

'Have you no idea what they are up to?' asked Brian. 'Surely, there must be some intelligence.'

'We know there are several large cartels or families responsible for the majority of the trade and so we think one of them must have come up with something original but who it is and how they are doing it has got us beat.'

Captain Peterson stood up. 'Thank you Glen and Cliff. Right gentlemen, there's a lot to think about here. Our initial focus has to be on the aircraft and submarine trials but then we can go smuggler hunting. If anyone sees or hears anything let me know. After the trials, we'll be visiting Florida and we will be able to continue these discussions then. Any further questions?'

There weren't and the meeting broke up for lunch.

Later that day, all the ships officers were back in the wardroom for yet another briefing. However, this time the reason was social.

'Shit, don't we look like a lot of ice cream salesmen,' muttered Brian as he surveyed the room. Everyone was in 'tropical' clothing, which for formal occasions meant a long white jacket and trousers, known in the navy as an Ice Cream Suit.

'Better than our day rig, I'm fed up with remarks from the shore, about white knees sticking out of shorts,' replied Jon. 'Still they may laugh but at least it keeps us cool. Its been bloody hot today.'

'Right, pipe down all of you,' called the First Lieutenant cheerily as he entered. 'Sorry to have to drag you all in here but this is Chester's first official Cocktail Party and I just wanted to make sure we all know how I want it to run. And before any of you lot argue, I know this is a democracy, one man one vote and all that. The problem for you lot is that I am that man and it's my vote, got it?'

A ripple of laughter went around the assembled officers.

'I'll keep it simple. Mingle and be polite. Do not spend all your time chatting up the totty and ignoring the big wigs.'

'Why are you looking at me?' asked Jon.

'Because I know you aircrew types. I spent my last two years in a Carrier remember?'

'Drat, foiled again.'

'Yup, but that doesn't mean you can't hoover them all down here for a party afterwards. I shall of course be monitoring all officers' performance on their success rate in this regard. Now keep everyone's glasses filled. The more VIPs that have trouble getting down the gangway the better, especially if their daughters have been left behind. But I want everyone to leave feeling that they have had a great time and that Chester has done them proud. However, I don't want any of you lot staggering, until the last one has gone. Everyone on the same hymn sheet?'

Nods all round.

'So, muster on the Cocktail Party deck in thirty minutes. That's your Flight Deck Jon, if you don't know where to go.'

'I think I might possibly find it Number One.'

As the officers all filed out, Brian surreptitiously signalled to the other Flight officers to stay behind. Soon, the room was empty except for them.

'Right, you lot listen up,' said Brian as he looked at the other four officers. There were the 'twins' Pete and Peter who were the other Sea King pilots and called the twins because they had almost the same name and looked strikingly similar, even though they weren't related. Both were blonde, with tall lanky figures, although Pete was several years older. Mike Hazlewood, a rather tubby Yorkshireman, was the other Observer and Steve Makepeace, a red headed Scot, was the second Lynx pilot. All were Lieutenants and had already formed into quite a close knit team under Jon's leadership.

'Now, some of you may know that Jon and I got up to no good last year and that's all I'm going to say about it, so please don't ask. However, one thing he did bring back with him was this rather gorgeous girlfriend, called Inga.'

'Yeah, I've met her,' said Steve. 'He brought her down to a Ladies Night at Portland before we left, what a cracker.'

'Yes, well for goodness sake don't let him know that I've told you this but she dumped him by mail today and he's taking it quite badly.'

'Shit, so would I if crumpet like that had slipped through my fingers,' observed Steve.

'OK but look, I've known Jon for quite a time and I suspect he will be planning to tie one on tonight as a consequence. So, it's our job to keep him roughly on the straight and narrow.'

'What, you mean keep the booze out of his way? How the hell do we do that?' asked one of the twins.

'No, that won't work. Look, keep him busy. Make sure he doesn't get the time to stand alone and get pissed. Feed him guests and the like. Bloody hell, even talk to him yourselves if you have to!'

That got a laugh.

'Once the official bit is over, we can let the reigns loose a bit, alright? I just don't want him making a dick of himself on board. We can make sure he does that at some night club later on. I know him, he'll get bouncy, that's the dangerous phase and it comes just before he falls asleep, then we bring him home. Everyone alright with that?'

There was grinning agreement from all of them.

'Time to party.'

Half an hour later and the first guests started arriving. The ship's officers were all standing casually around on the Flight Deck, which had been transformed for the occasion. Blue and white striped awnings had been erected all round, then roofed over like a giant marquee. Both aircraft had been turned around, so that their nose's stuck out of the open hangar doors. Tables, covered in white cloths and large quantities of food and drink were set along the wall opposite the gangway. Even the Lynx landing grid, in the centre of the deck had been transformed, with the insertion of some small shrubs and a garden fountain.

'Jesus, it looks like a sodding whore house,' said Jon as he arrived with Brian and the rest of the team. 'Look what they've done to my grid. Right, where's the booze?' and he made a bee line for one of the tables.

The rest of the team joined him and grabbed a 'Horses Neck' each; a Brandy and Ginger which was the drink of choice for all of them. Turning towards the gangway they all waited for the opportunity to meet a guest.

It seemed like only minutes before the party was in full swing. Brian's plan seemed to be working. Someone had skilfully got a local vicar latched on to Jon, who seemed to want to monopolise his time. Oddly, every time Jon made a pleading look for rescue to one of his colleagues, it was ignored. He even seemed to be having trouble catching the eye of any of the passing stewards to replenish his glass.

Suddenly, there was a booming voice to his right. He recognised it instantly.

'Where's that helicopter pilot who plucked me from the sea the other day?' The voice could be heard over the hubbub of noise with ease.

Jon was surprised to find he was relieved to hear it, as it at last gave him an excuse to prise himself away from the vicar.

'Senator, how good to see you. I thought you would be laid out for some time?'

Last time Jon had seen the man, he had been horizontal in the ship's sick bay. Now he realised just how tall he really was. Wearing a Stetson, with a gut hanging over his waistband and a red florid face, Jon thought he looked like a caricature. Everyone's expectation of a loud, southern states American.

'Take more than a bruised tail bone, to keep a good American down, praise the Lord. I just had to come to thank you properly in person. Hey and I hear you are going to be doing some anti-drug smuggling work. Now that is one of my crusades son, I work in the Senate on a committee that looks into that, so we must talk some more.'

Before Jon could respond, a girl pushed the bulk of the Senator to one side. With an exasperated sigh she held out her hand. 'And I'm Jacky his daughter and as usual he forgets I'm even here. I wanted to thank you as well.'

Jon took her hand, it was petite and cool, just like the girl herself. Surely this princess couldn't be the offspring of such an oaf? But the family resemblance was there. However, in her case, it translated into an impish grin below a tumble of honey blonde hair. Her smile was stunning and infectious. He found himself grinning inanely back at this vision of loveliness, completely at a loss for words.

## **Chapter 8**

Paulo Mandero realised he was actually starting to get excited about his mad Englishman's plan. When they had first discovered the old German base with its massive occupant, he thought it was just a curiosity. He liked Phil enough to indulge him for a while and he admired the courage he had shown rescuing the little boy. However, he was now beginning to realise that there really could be a lot more to the discovery than he had first thought.

'Tell me again what you've discovered Phil, to be honest it still all sounds a bit hard to accept.'

Phil who was seated in the Paulo's study once again, consulted his notes. 'Firstly, we've taken all the bodies out and buried them. From what we can work out, the SS guards shot the base staff and crew and then they were shot themselves by whoever put the explosive charge in the entrance. Whatever happened, it's long in the past. We've got power to the base, we hooked up a generator. We've had to run new lighting circuits. All the original stuff is completely shot but now we can we can see what we're doing. We're working on getting a proper feed from your house and that should only take a week or two then we can ditch the generator. As we expected, most of the other equipment is junk although some of the machine tools can be used, like lathes and drills. They had several workshops and a large stores area. The majority should be chucked out but it will provide a great deal of storage space for our product if we need it.'

'What about that massive sea door?'

'Ah yes, that's going to a problem. The lifting mechanism, those screws we could see, seem to be intact but the electric motors that they're connected to are useless. However, I'm pretty sure we can get a modern alternative. We've dived outside and there doesn't seem to be any issues there. We even found the remains of some underwater lighting they must have used to guide the submarines in. It's completely destroyed now but again we should easily be able to replace it with a modern alternative.'

Paulo was impressed but this was all secondary. Unless they could come up with something to do with the submarine all this was a waste of time.

'And that big metal monster Phil, what are we going to do with that?'

'Look, I know you're sceptical but that's where I've spent most of my time. When they left her, they shut all the hatches, so the inside is pristine, literally. Even the bedding could be used again. We've even managed to crank over the diesel engines by hand, so they haven't seized up, which would have been a show stopper.'

'So, what are you saying? We could just start it up and drive it out of there?'

'No, that would be expecting too much as you well know. But we should be able to flood the dock and get her out if we need to. So as a minimum the base should be useable.'

'Come on, I can see that look in your eye.'

Phil took a breath. 'Right here it is. I believe there is no reason why we can't make that submarine work again,' and then seeing the look on Paulo's face he quickly continued. 'Look, give me some credit, submarines were my profession for twelve years. I do know what I'm talking about. That machine was brand new when it arrived after only a few weeks at sea and it's been effectively hermetically sealed ever since. What's more, it was converted from its original role so that the large fuel tanks were able to carry stores. We could easily get several tons of our stuff in her with room to spare.'

'Phil, let's just say we could get it to work. Where would we find a crew and how would we train them?'

Phil knew he had to be realistic with this man. 'Actually, in some ways the problem's worse than that. Firstly, we need to get hold of a German speaker to translate the manuals. That shouldn't be an issue of course but we need to maintain security, as I am sure you will want. Secondly we are going to need batteries and I mean a lot of batteries. The ones in the sub will be totally useless.'

'Oh why? Have you checked them?'

'I don't need to. Lead acid batteries, if left for anytime, deposit sulphur out of the acid, on their plates and they can't be recovered. Being left uncharged for forty years will have totally trashed them.'

'So what would we need?'

'The largest truck batteries we can get our hands on, maybe hundreds of them depending on the size. The sub has a snorkel, so we can have propulsion and recharge using the diesels at sea, while staying underwater but we will need to be under battery power as much as possible. The US Coast Guard doesn't have any anti-submarine capability but we will still have the need to remain silent on occasions.'

'And crew?'

'Well, firstly, we are definitely not going to fight it like a wartime sub and we will not need to be at sea for long, so the crew could be fairly small. I'm estimating as little as twenty. Also, we won't need to go deep or anything like that, so operating should be fairly safe. Look, why don't you come down this afternoon and see for yourself?'

Paulo sighed and leant back in his chair with his hands behind his head. 'Alright, I'll be down at about two. You know, I must be mad but I actually believe we might make this work. I'll see you then.'

Taking the hint Phil got up and left.

When the door had closed Paulo turned to look out over the sea from the study window and reflect on recent events. His boredom of recent weeks had certainly vanished and not only because of the discovery of the Nazi relics. Before Phil arrived that morning he had been reading a letter from his contact in Washington. It seemed that the American government were starting to view the activities of himself and his other Columbian producers with enough concern that they might actually get off their backsides and do something serious. A new Senate committee, headed by a real redneck called George Musgrove the Third of all things, was starting to throw its weight about. The word on the streets was that he might just get sufficient funding to make life difficult. The discovery of the base and submarine could not have come at a better time. Assuming it all came good of course. Even so, he would send a reply to his mole and ask for any information about what was really going on and what progress they were making. His mole was very well placed to find out.

His thoughts moved on to more domestic issues. He was almost regretting getting rid the last girl, even if she was tediously unimaginative. He would send Manuel into town and get one of the local girls up here in the meantime. However, he would need a longer term solution as well, someone who would stand up to him. Now that would make a change.

At two o'clock, Paulo arrived at the submarine base entrance. A rough track had been cut through the jungle to allow vehicles to approach and park out of sight. It was another of the Englishman's ideas and once again Paulo was impressed by his foresight and planning. He made his way down the now well lit entrance and into the massive dock area. There was no one in sight, so he made his way over to the submarine and called down the open hatch near the bow. Looking down he could see into the submarine and suddenly had no desire to go any further.

'Anyone there?' he shouted again.

A few seconds later Phil appeared at the bottom of the ladder. 'Come on down Paulo, let me show you around.'

Swallowing hard and because he didn't want to appear weak, he started climbing down the metal ladder. There was a strange smell. A combination of musty age and diesel, it wasn't pleasant and added to his sense of panic. Reaching the bottom of the ladder, he forced himself to look around. Ahead of him were some strange long empty racks. Breathing hard to stay calm, he looked at Phil questioningly.

'Torpedo racks, it seems the only ones they were carrying were loaded in the tubes. We've checked and they're still there, four of them. At the moment we have no way of removing them so it's probably best just to leave them alone. They should be safe even after all this time, although they are almost certainly battery powered, so they will be useless as the batteries will be trashed.' And he noticed the sheen of sweat on Paulo's face. 'Are you alright Boss?'

'Yes fine, it's just that I get claustrophobic on occasions and this is one of them, I'll be alright in a minute.'

'Sure you don't want to continue up in the base? There's not too much to see here, unless you want to come to sea with us.'

Grateful for the offer, Paulo nodded and climbed back up into the more open space above.

'Right, let me show you around,' said Phil and he gave Paulo the guided tour of the workshops and offices, all now mercifully empty of mummified corpses. They finished off in what had been the main control room. Manuel and two of his staff were removing a couple of crates.

'Where are you taking all that stuff?' asked Paulo.

Manuel answered. 'We got a digger from the town Boss and we've dug a pit. The bodies and all the useless stuff is going into it. This is the last and we will fill it in this afternoon.'

'Yes,' said Phil. 'That takes care of all the rubbish but much of what is left needs translating. As I said before we need a German speaker.'

One of the men spoke up. 'Sir, there's that old guy in the next village, the old drunk. He's always claiming to be German and that he fought in the War. Shall I go and dig him out? I know where he lives.'

Paulo looked at Phil who nodded back. 'Do that, don't bring him here though, take him up to the house. We'll talk to him this evening.'

Later that evening Paulo and Phil were on the veranda when Manuel ushered in an old man. His face was lined and he was very thin. It was almost impossible to assess his age. He could have been anything from fifty to seventy. Dressed in rough clothes and in need of a good wash, he looked terrified when he saw Paulo. Being summoned to the house of the most powerful drug lord in the area, late at night can't have been easy. His fear didn't seem to subside even when he had downed several drinks in quick succession. However, the alcohol did seem to have the effect of loosening his tongue a little.

'Now, what's your name?' asked Phil, in what he hoped was a reassuring tone.

The man mumbled something and Phil had to ask again. Eventually he managed to make out the name of Manfred.

'And you are originally from Germany?' That seemed to make him even more nervous.

'This getting us nowhere,' said Paulo in frustration. 'I think we'd better get Manuel to take him back.'

'Hang on, let me try something else,' responded Phil. He turned back to the German and handed him a log book which he had brought up from the base.

Manfred looked at it for a second and started shaking. However, when he spoke his voice was remarkably clear. 'You've found it, haven't you? After all these years,' and he looked at both of them with a strange expression. 'Were they all dead?'

'Yes, all of them my friend,' replied Phil and then he realised something. 'You were one of the base staff weren't you?'

Manfred nodded.

'So why weren't you in there with them?'

Tears were welling in the German's eyes. 'I had been given leave. You see, I had made a local girl pregnant and managed to talk the Commandant into allowing me time to get married. Her parents were very insistent. He was a good man, he shouldn't have allowed it and so there was no record of my absence. We all knew the war was finishing, so the rules meant less and less. We were all making homes here if we could, because no one wanted to return to Germany. When I got back, I found that the entrance had been blown up. There was no way in.'

'What was your job on the staff Manfred?'

'I was an engineer. I had served on U-boats before you see, so I was one of the staff who carried out repairs on boats when they came in. How did you find the base?'

'That last storm, there was a landslip and we spotted part of the concrete wall. We've opened it up now and we need your help.'

'What happened to them all, do you know?'

'Was there a submarine docked when you left?'

'No, we were expecting one but weren't sure when it was going to arrive.'

'Well it seems someone didn't want anyone to know about it, because the crew of the submarine and all the base staff were in there. They had all been shot.'

Manfred closed his eyes for a second. All his fear seemed to have vanished. 'What do you want me to do?'

## Chapter 9

Nellie was trundling her way across the dark blue seas of the Tongue of the Ocean, towards the main range site on Andros Island. The twins were up front in the driving seats and Brian and Tommo were in the rear. The day's trials were complete and they were heading to the island to collect the ship's staff who had been viewing the results in the main operations room ashore.

'Jesus, just look at that,' said Pete who was flying Nellie and he lowered the collective, banked the aircraft and dropped down closer to the sea surface. 'Christ it looks almost as big as us.'

Below them the giant Manta Ray ignored the big helicopter now circling it and slowly flapped its massive wings as it made its way to wherever it was going.

'That's the biggest I've ever seen,' commented Brian who could see it now out of his side window. 'If we head away from the range site, so we can approach it from up the coast, then we can follow the reef. When Jon and I were here the other year you could see an amazing amount of wildlife, everything from Hammerhead Sharks and Dolphins to giant Turtles.'

'Talked me into it,' responded Pete, who turned the aircraft towards the distant low lying island. 'And anyway, changing the subject, is it right we're off to Fort Lauderdale this weekend, rather than Nassau again?'

'I believe so,' responded Brian. 'And that's another good run ashore believe me. There are more night clubs and bars in a small area than I've seen anywhere else.'

There was a chuckle from up front. 'I wonder if our illustrious Boss will bother with them. Seems to us he might have other things on his mind.'

'Hmm yes, he did seem a bit smitten at the party the other weekend.'

'Smitten, you couldn't prise him off that girl with a jemmy. There we were worrying he was going to drown his sorrows and make a dick of himself because his girlfriend had chucked him and he went and got another one the same day. Did anyone see where he went after the wardroom party?'

'Nope, although he didn't get back on board until just before colours and he did have a big grin on his face. Anyway you two reprobates up front, leave him alone, he's had a hard time for many reasons recently, maybe this will be good for him.'

'Yeah, we understand,' came a chorus from the cockpit.

Then Peter continued, 'mind you it would be nice one day to find out what you two really got up to. Hey I've just had a thought.'

'Go on.'

'Does anyone know whether she has any sisters?'

An hour later and the ship's Operation's staff and aircrew were gathered together in the dark air conditioned operations room, to look at the trial results.

'Right gentlemen,' said Captain Peterson summing up the briefing. 'That's the last run we'll be doing on the range here. It all seemed to go well, so now we need more sea room to give the submarine more evasive capability. We'll go into Port Everglades at Fort Lauderdale on Saturday for a week, so that the ship can do some maintenance and then we will head off into the Caribbean Sea to play for real. Any questions?'

Jon who was seated in the front row knew he should be paying more attention but a certain face kept appearing in his vision and ruining his concentration. The night of the Cocktail Party had been amazing. At one point he thought he should be feeling guilty about finding a new girl so soon after Inga but he had to remind himself that she chucked him, not the other way round. And anyway, Jacky was different. In some ways, she reminded him of Inga; she had blonde hair and a slim figure but in actuality they were poles apart. Jacky was vivacious, outgoing and clearly had one hell of a brain, although sometimes she seemed almost manic. Her honours degree in engineering from an Ivy League American University clearly demonstrated that. She seemed to be extremely well informed. Of course, having a father in the American government helped just a bit. Inga, on the other hand had always been rather introverted and self centred. When the Cocktail Party had finished, he didn't even have to make any attempt to spirit her away ashore, as she made the first move and suggested dinner at a fantastic seafood restaurant that she knew from previous visits to Nassau. Now, that was a girl who knew her own mind.

She and her father were staying in the same hotel but that hadn't seemed to matter when they sneaked back to her room at two o'clock in the morning after some vigorous exercise in a night club that she also knew. However, what was frustrating and intriguing at the same time was that he ended up sleeping on the couch. Yes, they had kissed a little but she suddenly made it clear that anything more was not on the agenda. In the end, they had started talking and it had lasted for most of the night. Her father had clearly been a major factor in her life and it was also clear to Jon that although Jacky seemed to respect the man, she hated his evangelical fervour. He did wonder whether there was something more to the relationship. He couldn't put his finger on it but there almost seemed to be something slightly incestuous in her manner but no matter how he probed, he wasn't able to get under her guard enough to dig it out.

So when he made it back on board in time the next morning, he was tired but also extremely frustrated. However, he wasn't going to let on to his buddies back in the wardroom that the evening hadn't been quite as they all believed. After all he had a reputation to live up to. Anyway, the news about going to Fort Lauderdale was perfect as Jacky lived just down the coast and the boat 'Daddy's Girl' was berthed in the marina in Port Everglades, only a stone's throw away from where Chester was due to berth. The thrill of the chase was half the fun after all.

'Flight Commander, are you there?' asked the Operations Officer who had been speaking.

Jon realised he hadn't heard a word the man had said and decided that honesty was the best option. 'Sorry Ops, I was miles away, what did you say?'

'Do we need to do any significant work on the aircraft while we are alongside?'

'Er no, they're all up to date as far as I know.'

'Good, because the Coast Guard have requested that you take Eric the Lynx over to Opa Locka, their air station next week, so they can have a look at him. Will that be feasible?'

'Yes of course, as long as the port authority don't mind us flying from alongside.'

'I don't see why they would but I'll make sure it's all sorted.'

Four days later, Jon and Brian were in Eric flying up the coast of Florida.

'So how's it going with the lovely Jacky then mate? You seem to have been spending quite a bit of time ashore with her these last few days.'

'I'll take that as a reprimand, sorry but I'm sort of infatuated a bit. I hope the guys don't mind?'

Brian snorted. 'Of course not, anyway, it's none of their bloody business, is it?'

'But I am the Boss, I suppose I should be around.'

'Listen mate, it's our spare time, we can do what we want and anyway don't worry they've all been enjoying themselves, probably haven't even noticed you're not around. Anyway, is everything alright?'

'Er, actually things are a bit odd. That girl is what they call highly strung. One minute she's on a high and I can barely keep up, the next I'm having to coax her out of the blues. It can be bloody hard work at times.' He didn't add that even though he had managed to get her into bed, even that had been weird at first. It was almost as though she was scared of men, although once he broken through her reserve, things had become rather fantastic to say the least. He couldn't wait to see her again tonight.

'That's enough about my sex life, where's this bloody airfield?'

'Over there, see it just inland a bit?'

'OK, got it. I'll give them a call. Opa Locka this is Navy Four Nine Nine, we are inbound for the Coast Guard facility and are currently two miles south of you, at one thousand feet, airfield is in sight, is the circuit clear over?'

The airfield responded immediately. 'Navy Four Nine Nine good afternoon, yes you are expected and I have no traffic at this time, you are cleared to the ramp on the south side of the main runway.'

'Er Tower, this is Four Nine Nine, would you object to me doing a couple of fly passts while the circuit is clear?'

'No problem, we would be happy to see what you can do, over.'

'Now there's blatant encouragement if ever I heard it,' said Brian tightening his straps in anticipation of what he knew was about to happen.

Jon ginned gleefully. 'Well they did say we could, so here we go. Time for some more of that good old pilot shit.'

He lowered the collective lever and dived the aircraft towards the large concrete apron in front of the Coast Guard building, where several old fashioned, red and white helicopters were parked. He could see people standing and watching and more coming out of the building, as they heard the menacing growl of the approaching Lynx. The helicopter was vibrating hard at its maximum speed of one hundred and fifty knots, as he levelled out only a few feet above the ground.

'Jesus Christ,' muttered Brian as they shot past the crowd, only a few feet away and Jon pulled back on the cyclic. The aircraft shot up vertically and slowed down. When he judged the speed right, he banked over hard and the little machine almost inverted as it turned and started to hurtle back towards the ground. He didn't let it go right down however and levelled off when the speed was at one hundred and twenty knots. He then slammed the cyclic hard over to the right and held it there as they rotated over in a perfect roll. He then dropped down to the ground and pulled the nose up hard. Instead of coming to a hover, he held the nose up and the aircraft was soon accelerating backwards until it reached fifty knots when he lowered the nose hard and they shot back upwards vertically but this time tail first. At about four hundred feet, they stopped before diving down again. This time, Jon brought Eric back into the hover and landed in front of the crowd who started clapping spontaneously as he shut down the engines and rotors.

'Four Nine Nine is that a helicopter or a jet fighter?' came the call on the radio.

'Glad you enjoyed it Tower, maybe we should get the Coast Guard to buy some.'

'Hey, have a good day.'

Jon grinned over at Brian. 'Well that blew a few cobwebs away. What say you we go and talk to our new Coast Guard chums?'

It took quite a time to show the astonished Americans around Eric. The general consensus was that they had never realised a helicopter could be so manoeuvrable. Glen Thomas, the officer who had briefed them in Nassau, was there to greet them and when he showed Jon the single engine CH Fifty Two relic from the fifties that they had to rely on, he wasn't surprised.

'Bloody hell Glen,' exclaimed Jon. 'That thing should be in a museum.'

'Tell me about it but there is a move to buy something new now and I think your little demonstration may have inspired a few of us to apply more pressure. By the way, why are there two crossed out aircraft painted below your door?'

Jon was looking a bit embarrassed by the question, when Brian who had overheard chipped in. 'This is the same machine that Jon and I flew during the Falklands War, Glen. One of those planes, the one with the brown line through it, is a Mirage that tried to shoot us down. We gave him a brown line to match the colour his trousers when he found out we could shoot back. But the other one with a red cross is an Argentinian Pucara and Jon did shoot that bastard down because he was trying to do the same to us.'

'Jesus, what did you shoot him with?'

'Oh, we had a small cannon fitted on the starboard side, they've been withdrawn since the war, something to do with not being safe enough for peacetime use.'

'Well guys, you've got my admiration but come on in and we'll talk about the new enemy, the ones we're fighting out here.'

Glen led them into their flight briefing room, where several other officers joined them. Coffee and enormous quantities of donuts appeared from nowhere and they settled down while Glen fired up a slide projector.

'Guys, I could talk all day about how our drug smuggling friends operate but here are just a few examples. The crashed aircraft in this picture is just one of many, you'll see them everywhere. They just crash land them in the Everglades at night.'

'Hang on, aren't there alligators out there?' asked Jon.

'Sure are, or 'snapping logs' as we call them but these guys get paid a lot of money and seem to be prepared to take the risk. Or here, we have an innocent looking Motor Yacht.' And he changed the slide to show a very sleek modern looking powerboat. 'The guys on this got arrested for smuggling dope and went to prison for five years. The boat was put up for public auction and it was only later that we discovered that the guys who bought it back took out millions of dollars of coke that had been fibre glassed right into the keel. So you can see people are even prepared to go to prison as a way of blind-siding us.'

'Do these guys get paid or what?' asked Brian.

'Well in some cases we think so or maybe their families are taken hostage, we don't know. What we do know, is there are some seriously nasty bastards in this trade.'

'Didn't you say that your arrest rate had dropped?' asked Brian. 'So these examples must be reducing.'

'Yes, you've got it. We've no idea what their new tactic is. Anyone would think they were using submarines.'

## Chapter 10

Phil Masters tried to settle his pulse rate. The last six months, with all the pressure and problems had been worth it. At last he was at sea, ten metres under the water in a fully functional, German, war time submarine. Who would ever have believed it? He still felt like pinching himself to make sure he wasn't in a dream.

There were so many occasions when he didn't think they would make it. The biggest problems had been in getting the hydraulic and compressed air systems to work. All the seals had dried out and perished. It wasn't as if you could just go to an engineering catalogue and order new ones. It was weird, the things he worried about at first like the diesel engines and the batteries had been easy to sort out. But he had lost count of the number of times he had been alerted to yet another spurt of high pressure hydraulic fluid or blast of compressed air from a seal they didn't know was there.

Manfred the engineer had really made the whole thing possible. Without his detailed knowledge, they would probably never have managed to get the essential systems on line. Once Paulo had thrown himself into the project as well, other issues like a willing crew had been solved. It was amazing how many ex servicemen could be recruited, if the money was right. He only had a minimum crew but they were all sufficiently experienced that training had been relatively straightforward. Phil knew that Paulo had committed a lot of his money to the project, without any guarantee that it would work and was grateful but also apprehensive. If it all went wrong, he knew Paulo could be unforgiving in the extreme. But he had become so caught up in the project he knew he would take any risk to see it through.

The most worrying day for Phil had been when they finally flooded the cavern. The water was let in by small sluices, to one side of the main door, allowing the sea to rush in but under a degree of control. The main door could not be opened before the levels had equalised, which in the case of the cave, was when the water was almost to the top of the entrance staircase. Because the submarine was so big they couldn't let it float up with the water level, as it would hit the ceiling of the cave. Consequently, they had to open all the ballast tanks and let them fill up as the water came in and remain submerged. In a modern British submarine, there would have been an escape compartment and emergency breathing apparatus to allow the crew to muster in one place and get out should the need arise. In this machine, there was no such facility and even though they would only end up a few feet underwater, Phil knew there was much that could go wrong. In the end it had been an anticlimax. They had barely been aware of what was going on outside and the sub stayed firmly on the bottom, dry and snug.

From then on, they had tested out all the systems one by one. The only things they had left alone were the gun on the casing, although all the ammunition had been removed and the torpedoes, which stayed where they were as they had no realistic way of removing them.

This morning, they had finally left the cave. Reversing out hadn't been easy. The dive planes were of no use when going backwards. It was a problem that Phil had been worrying about. Clearly it could be done, he had a few theories but in the end Manfred confirmed what he had been thinking. When they had SCUBA dived the sea bottom outside the entrance, they had found remains of wooden sleepers everywhere. Manfred explained that these were there to allow the submarine to reverse out while still negatively buoyant and slide along the bottom on the wooden path. It was a simple matter to lay new sleepers and the problem was solved. As soon as they were clear, they were able to surface and engage the propulsion forwards and get proper control. They timed it for just before dawn, so that they would be unobserved and it had all gone surprisingly well.

'Listen up everyone, systems checks please.' Phil called over the intercom. 'Engine room?'

Manfred's voice came out of the speaker above Phil's head. 'All good, electric motors are running smoothly and battery levels are good.'

'Helmsman?'

The three men sitting next to Phil responded one by one.

'Rudder functioning. Forward planes functioning. Aft planes good.'

The various compartments then checked in confirming that they remained watertight. He even had a report that the hydrophones were working, although by any modern standard, as a sonar detection system, they were primitive in the extreme.

'Right, up periscope,' called Phil and with a hiss of hydraulics the main scope lifted up out of its well. He looked through the binocular eyepiece, marvelling at the quality of the German optics. They were as good, if not better than anything he had used in the British navy. The coastline was clear behind him and the two transit markers, they had placed on the cliffs, could easily be seen. Returning to the cave would be a lot easier now they were there.

There were two final things he needed to do now before he was fully confident in his new command.

'Right everyone, as you know, this submarine was designed to dive down several hundred metres. We have no intention of going anything like that deep but we do need to confirm we can at least get down far enough to dodge anything on the surface. All compartments standby and report any issues, we will be diving to fifty metres shortly.'

He then turned to his planesmen. 'Make depth fifty metres.'

The two men had been recruited by Paulo some months ago. Both were American and had served in the US navy on conventional subs. They had little difficulty in controlling a gentle descent, by angling the forward planes down slightly.

Phil watched the depth gauge, as it crept slowly downwards. At fifty it stopped and no reports came in. He grunted in satisfaction. 'Well done everyone, that's quite deep enough. Right, back to periscope depth please.'

Once they were cruising at ten metres again Phil called the engine room. 'Manfred, are you ready with the diesels?'

'All ready,' came the prompt reply.

Looking at the crewman by the snorkel control panel, Phil gave the order. 'Raise snorkel.' There was a hiss of hydraulics followed by a gentle thump.

'I'm having to compensate quite a lot,' called one of the planesmen. 'But I have it under control.'

'Good,' responded Phil, knowing that the drag of the snorkel mast now sticking just out of the water was affecting the trim of the submarine. It had also taken two knots off their speed. 'We did expect it. Right open the snorkel master valve.'

There was a sudden hiss of hydraulics, followed by a frantic cry from the engine room. 'FLOOD, flood, major water ingress in the engine room.'

'*Shit*,' thought Phil. '*It had all been going too well.*' Clearly the snorkel had a major leak probably where it mated with the hull.

'Blow main ballast,' he ordered in a calm voice that belied his concern. 'Standby to surface.'

There was the comforting hiss of compressed air forcing water out of their ballast tanks and the submarine started to rise.

'Leak has stopped,' Manfred reported.

'Get yourself up here Manfred,' ordered Phil. 'We need to find where that water is coming from and get back underwater as soon as we can.'

The old engineer was in the control room in seconds. 'Let's close the snorkel valve and lower the whole thing back down that should stop the leak,' he suggested.

Phil felt a fool for a second. '*Why hadn't he thought of that?*' However, he gave the orders and the submarine slipped back underwater. They had probably only been on the surface for a few seconds. Nevertheless, he scanned the horizon carefully through the periscope as soon as he could, while Manfred went back to the engine room and reported that the leak had stopped.

'Right, that's enough for one day, Phil announced to the control room staff. 'Let's take her home.'

That evening Paulo threw a party. A bus load of girls from the city had been supplied, along with enough food and booze to feed an army. The crew were delighted and gathered around the massive swimming pool to settle in to a night of relieved, drunken, debauchery. Phil was standing talking to Manfred as they shared a drink and looked at the crew who were starting to remove their clothes and inhibitions in equal amount.

'Manfred, you seemed to have been rejuvenated by our little project,' observed Phil. 'My God, is that just orange juice you're drinking.'

Manfred raised a sardonic toast back. 'I haven't touched a drop since you took me back into the base all those months ago. It may seem odd to you but my life seems to have been on hold ever since I left there forty years ago and now I have it back. I never believed in the Third Reich but I did believe in my submarines. I have you to thank for giving them back.'

Surprised by the intensity of the reply, Phil couldn't help but feel a glimmer of a sympathetic response. 'You know, strange as it may seem, I really understand that. When I was in the navy, I loved submarines. Losing them was a sort of living death. But now we both have it back. She may be an old wartime relic but she's totally unique and what an opportunity.'

'So you have no qualms about the way we're going to use her?'

'A couple of years ago I had to make that decision when I discovered who Paulo actually was and what he did. When he took me on, I thought he was just some rich yacht owner. Then I found out how he got his money and was forced to confront my feelings. I look at it this way, people choose to use drugs, hell we're all doing that here and now with this booze, it's just another drug after all. If society decides to impose a set of almost arbitrary rules on what is allowed or not then that's not my problem.' Then with a wide grin, 'and there's a shit load of money to be made.'

Manfred looked at Phil shrewdly. 'It seems we have similar views. I would like to make this work and make enough money to retire somewhere comfortable. But don't underestimate Paulo, his reputation is dreadful. You may be his golden boy for the moment but he will strike like a snake if anything goes wrong.'

'Don't worry, I'm well aware of what sort of man he is.'

'I wonder. People live by very different standards out here. You've only been working for him for a couple of years. I've been here for most of my life. Just be very careful my friend. By the way, I have some news for you. The leak on the snorkel was easily fixed, so we should be ready for our first run whenever Paulo wants.'

'Excellent, I'll tell him. I'm going to talk to him in a minute anyway. But there's something else isn't there?'

'Yes, the torpedoes.'

'What about them? Is there a problem?'

'Quite the opposite, we opened up the tubes up the other day to check and they all seem in excellent condition. The only odd thing was that they were the older G Seven A type that was rarely used in the war. The normal ones must have been in short supply by that stage of the fight.'

'If I remember correctly those were compressed air and kerosene powered, no batteries to become useless over time.'

'Correct and although they leave a trail of bubbles they are still fully charged and ready to go.'

Phil thought for a moment. 'Let's just keep that to ourselves Manfred. It might be a useful thing to have up our sleeves.

Manfred nodded. *'Maybe this man wasn't quite as naive as he'd first thought.'*

## Chapter 11

The sleek, newly painted, grey, relic of the Second World War, slipped slowly under the water as she was designed to do and headed north. It was the middle of the night and the moon had set. No one saw her go and hopefully no one would see her until she returned home to her base in about two week's time.

In the control room, Phil gave a mental sigh of relief. All seemed to be working well and they would stay submerged now until reaching their destination for the offload.

He called Mike Spencer, his second in command, over to the chart table. Mike was another of Paulo's recruits. Phil still hadn't worked out how Paulo was able to get hold of these people but had decided not to ask. As long as they did their job who cared? Mike was a late middle aged, burly, slightly overweight American who had served on US conventional submarines just after the war had ended. Phil suspected that like many of the crew, they were using this job as a precursor to a very comfortable retirement. And why not? It was exactly what Phil had in mind for the longer term as well.

'Right Mike, sorry about the secrecy but Paulo and I wanted to keep our operational plan under wraps until we'd sailed. I'll go over it with you now but please, if you have a better idea, then it isn't set in stone, we can always modify it. The only thing that we must keep to is the rendezvous of course.'

Mike looked at Phil and thought for a second. He had been annoyed when it was clear he wasn't going to be trusted with the plan before they sailed. However the Limey at least appeared to be flexible which might just be a good sign. 'Fine by me Boss, what've you got?'

'We need to get here,' said Phil pointing to a chart and indicating a point near the tip of Florida on the west coast. It's a National Park and therefore unpopulated. We can get quite close to the coast as its remains deep right up to the beach.

'Whoah,' Mike exclaimed. 'It's unpopulated because it's a bloody swamp full of fucking alligators and who knows what else, that's why.'

'Hey, don't worry. We're only going as far as the beach. The people we're meeting are quite expert at getting around their own backyard. They use these airboat things amongst other forms of transport. They know what they're doing. Now, we surface and take the stuff ashore by boat. There will be a storage facility on this beach. It's only temporary. We dump the stuff there and then it's up to them. We don't see them and they don't see us. No one gets to know about this submarine, that's really important.'

'Fine by me. So how do we get there?'

'We have two options and I would really value your input. The most direct route and the one I favour, is to head over to the western tip of Cuba and transit the gap between it and Mexico. We then route up past the Florida Keys. The alternative is to head for the other end of Cuba and make our way up the north Cuban coast, south of the Bahamas.'

'There is a third option. We could slip between one of the Windwards and go north about the Bahamas and down the coast of Florida. It's an area I know quite well.'

'Yes but the reason you know it, is that it's regularly used by the US navy isn't it? And don't forget the massive US base on Puerto Rico at Roosevelt Roads.'

'Good points all of them, yeah we need to keep clear of as much of all that as possible. No, I reckon that the direct route is the best and it keeps us in deep water as well.'

'Mike, if we need deep water we're in serious trouble. Don't forget we've only tested her to fifty metres.'

'I'm going to have to stop thinking like a regular submariner,' Mike observed with a wry smile. 'Do we know what this boat was actually designed to achieve?'

'Good question, there was nothing in the paperwork we managed to salvage but the standard German requirement for U-boats was about 150 metres as a design depth and a crush depth of about two hundred and fifty. There were several reports of boats going much deeper than that and surviving but I have no intention of finding out.'

'Good, let's just keep out everyone's way and do the job.'

'Right, so if you take over here, I'm going astern to talk to our erstwhile engineer.' So saying Phil went through to the rear of the boat where he found Manfred sipping tea from an enormous tin mug.

'All well Manfred? It will be a good twelve hours before its dark and we can risk the snorkel. How are the batteries holding up?'

Manfred turned and looked at the electrical board behind him. 'As well as we expected, they should be fine for this trip but modern vehicle batteries are not really designed for this sort of charging cycle. If we discharge them too far and then blast them back up to full with the diesels, it won't be long until the plates start to buckle. I reckon we'll have to replace them just about every trip.'

'Well, I guess we'll be able to afford it. Do you realise the value of the cargo we're carrying?'

'I saw how much is stowed in the tanks and can do the sums.' He smiled as he said it. 'I've had an idea though. We should try to get golf cart batteries; they're far more suited to this sort of deep cycle operation. Or even some of the modern gel ones.'

Phil clapped him on the shoulder. 'Forever the engineer my friend, we'll see what we can do when we get back. If this trip is a success I can't see Paulo refusing any request can you?'

Five days later, the submarine gently surfaced. They were five hundred yards off the deserted Florida beach. As anticipated, the night was pitch black with no shore lights, only the pale illumination from the stars above. Phil and Mike were the only two people on top of the fin. Mike was using his binoculars to sweep all around, as Phil ordered the electric motors to move them towards the beach. They slowly crept towards the gentle surf line, which could be seen as a series of white lines, ahead of the sloping shingle and sand. The submarine was as low in the water as they could safely make her, so that when the bow grounded on the sand, they were still a hundred yards from the shore. They knew their position was correct because just visible behind the fringe of trees at the water's edge, they could make out the outline of an old derrick structure. It was the legacy of an oil drilling attempt many years earlier that had ended in failure but hadn't been deemed worthwhile to salvage. It now acted as their beacon for what they needed to do next.

Phil called down the voice tube to the control room and a minute later the forward hatch opened and several men came out. There was a hissing sound and a large inflatable dinghy was soon tied alongside the bow. Mike disappeared down the ladder and quickly appeared on the foredeck and clambered into the dinghy. Within minutes, their precious cargo was being ferried ashore. It took half an hour and five boat trips. All the time his men were doing their work, Phil was anxiously scanning the surroundings. He needn't have worried, the place had been well selected. It was well away from habitation and even night fishermen shunned the area, as it was too far away for easy access. Even so, it was with enormous relief that he saw the partially deflated dinghy being pushed down the hatch, which then shut with a muffled clang. As soon as he had the report that the boat was secure, he ordered a small blowing of the ballast tanks and the submarine floated off the beach. He was then able to order the engines astern and the submarine slipped away into the night.

Seven days later and once again, Phil was in Paulo's study.

'What can I say my friend? All those months ago, when you suggested using that German relic, frankly I thought you were mad. At first, I only let you go ahead to humour you after you rescued that young boy. But it soon became clear that you might just be on to something. Frankly, I never really expected such spectacular success. Your cargo was fairly small this time but I think we can be more ambitious in the future, do you agree?'

Phil nodded. 'We've got more than enough storage space but we're going to have to do something about the batteries. By the time we got back they were just about shot, it's why we were late.'

Paulo frowned, 'I had to scour the local county for miles around to get the ones we used. What are you suggesting?'

'Well our tame engineer suggests gel batteries but such a large order could raise eyebrows. They're quite specialist and in limited supply. The alternative apparently, are those used in golf carts. Don't you own a golf course somewhere?'

'Not quite, I have a share in one. How many of these batteries do you think you'll need?'

'Absolutely no idea but I'll get Manfred to work it out and let you know.'

'Fine, now I suggest you go and get some sleep, it looks like you could do with some.'

Gratefully Phil took his leave and headed off to his little cottage down by the boat dock.

Paulo let out a sigh as Phil left the room, partly relief and partly excitement. When the submarine became overdue, he imagined all sorts of things that could have happened. There was a long range radio in her but it had been agreed that it would only be used in an emergency. That he had not heard anything, was still no reassurance that something hadn't happened. He hadn't committed that much of his stock as cargo for the trip and should have been quite sanguine about losing her, if that had been the case. However, he found that he was strangely caught up in the whole gamble. So, when he got the call from the base, that the sub had arrived, he even surprised himself at how elated he had felt. And that led on to the real excitement. He now had a unique smuggling operation that had proved to be viable in the extreme. He would effectively be able to control the American market. Until this opportunity arose he had to allow for quite a lot of wastage due to the efforts of the US Customs. He could disregard that now but his competitors couldn't. He smiled avariciously at the thought. Nothing lasted forever, he knew that but in the meantime he was going to make a great deal more money and hopefully drive most of his competitors into the ground.

## Chapter 12

In Washington, the meeting of the Senate Committee for the War on Drugs was winding up. Senator George Musgrove the Third wiped his sweating forehead with a large handkerchief. It was over forty degrees outside and the air conditioning was having trouble keeping up. *'Penny pinching civil servants couldn't even afford to get decent air conditioning, even here in the seat of government of the greatest country in the world,'* he thought sourly. Even so, his mood was upbeat. They were about to take a vote and if his behind the scenes efforts were effective, he would soon have his way.

'Right Gentlemen, a summary before we vote. The motion is that the committee recommends the actions laid down in our plans to take serious action against the flood of drugs coming into the country. This includes firstly, an increase in funding for the Coast Guard in general, for new aircraft and in particular for reinforcement of the units in Florida and Texas.' There were general nods all round the table. No one could possibly argue that logic.

'Secondly, that units of the US Marines are seconded to the Coast Guard in Florida, as a special task force, to reinforce their overall manpower.'

He could see the frowns already appearing on some faces as he said the words. He continued, in order to override any objections before they could be voiced. 'And that they be given special powers of arrest and incarceration. Including clandestine operations outside our own borders.'

He stopped and looked at his colleagues again. A quick count of expressions made him sure that he was going to carry the day. All that behind the scenes arm twisting was going to pay off, he was sure of it.

Before he could speak further, a voice interrupted him from down the table. 'This is crazy, the Marines are not policemen, they're needed elsewhere. Have you forgotten the threat from the Soviets? Why have we got a Drugs Enforcement Agency if we also need the Marines.'

'Hiram, we've debated this endlessly. The President gave us the authority to make these decisions. How much longer do you want to prevaricate? I'm sorry, we've done the studies and assessed the costs. We've consulted everyone we can think of. The DEA does not have a mandate to take the sort of action we are contemplating and are definitely not equipped or trained to do so. So, as chairman, it's my right to call a vote. A simple show of hands will suffice.' He pre-empted any further dissent, 'those in favour please raise their hands.'

He looked around the table, as several hands immediately shot up. Only five at first, which meant the vote would be tied. He stared intently at one member at the end of the table and the final hand he needed was slowly raised.

'Carried, thank you gentlemen. The report and its findings will be with the President and the Joint Chiefs this afternoon. Maybe at last, we'll be able to start making serious progress dealing with the scum trying to subvert our children. It won't happen overnight but at least we've taken the first step.'

A few minutes later, he left the building with a spring in his step. It had been a hard fight but he'd won. He knew his opponents were against the plans, not because they disagreed with them particularly. It was more because his victory represented a clear increase in his political power base. The Machiavellian politics of Washington, often meant that this was more important than any real outcome. Well let them all stew, he hadn't done this for personal gain, he really believed it was necessary. Mind you the political outcome wasn't to be ignored either. All in all, a very good day.

As he passed through the lobby he didn't notice what was happening in the corner of the lobby. Nor for that matter did anyone else, as intended. One of his entourage and a stranger, walked past each other and the exchange of the large envelope happened so fast that not even the CCTV cameras would have seen it.

At just about the same time that the President of the United States was reading a digest of the Senators committee report, prepared for him by his staff, Paulo Mandero was being even more thorough and reading the whole thing. The document had been faxed through to him that morning by his contact in Washington. Once again, Paulo was amazed by the power of money. He knew he shouldn't be after all these years but it still staggered him how easy it was to buy a politician from any country. Compared to some, American ones weren't even that expensive.

He put the heavy report down and considered the recommendations carefully. If and it was a big if, the recommendations were actually implemented, it could mean real problems for his business. However, knowing in advance would be a great advantage, especially over his rivals. On reflection, his new toy currently resting in its secret dock was likely to prove a godsend. What really worried him however, wasn't the fact that the Americans were going to spend a great deal more money on their Coast Guard. That would take years to come into effect. No, it was the idea that they would unleash their military, with orders to ignore international borders and laws that could be a real problem. For the first time, the damned Americans looked like they were prepared to play dirty. He briefly considered whether it would be worth leaking the report to his own government or even the press but immediately rejected the idea. Never give away any advantage and this foreknowledge was just that. No, he would keep his powder dry and watch developments

He then turned to the other document that had accompanied the report. This was the information he had commissioned from some of his friends in the press, into the public background of the Senator, who lead the anti-drug committee. It was surprisingly thin. The man seemed to have led a charmed life. There was no evidence of youthful indiscretions, no predilection for any illegal joys of the flesh. For a God botherer of his standing that was most unusual. They were nearly always the worst. It probably only meant that he had good security. It was a real shame though, there didn't seem to be any ready levers that could be used if things turned nasty. He turned to the last page and looked at the photographs. His face broke into a smile, the best lever of all looked out of the page at him.

A week later, sunlight streamed through gaps in the curtained windows of the master suite of the Senator's yacht,

Daddy's Girl and illuminated the two naked forms lying on the bed.

Jon woke with a start and immediately realised he had a hangover and an erection. Rolling over, he took in the naked form of Jacky, lying on her back with her legs apart, snoring gently. The sight did little to help his problem. A true blonde, the sunlight was picking out the soft golden hairs on her arms and around her very perky nipples. Looking further down, the soft triangle of hair between her legs, matched the fan of blonde hair on the pillow.

She opened her eyes and saw him looking. 'Morning Jon, enjoying the view?'

Jon immediately realised, by the teasing, gentle tone of her voice, that this was a different girl from the one he had gone to bed with last night. A fantastic dinner in a very expensive restaurant had been followed by an invitation to spend the night on the boat. As soon as they walked over the gangway and Jacky had unlocked the door to the main saloon, she became a changed girl. Something had clearly affected her but Jon couldn't work out what it was. She had become nervous, then tearful and finally aggressive. They both drank too much wine and in the end he had taken her to bed purely to try and settle her down. It had started off as making love and ended up almost as rape, as she suddenly tried to fight him off. Only, that was clearly not what she actually wanted and every time he tried to pull away, she would fight just as hard to keep him inside her. They had collapsed exhausted, after an hour and Jacky had immediately fallen asleep while Jon was still trying to figure out what on earth had just gone on.

She smiled up at him and pulled him down on top of her, her hands exploring urgently. And then, all too soon, they were lying back in a sweaty heap and Jon was still wondering why this easy going, loving woman could suddenly turn into an aggressive bag of nerves at a moment's notice.

'So, why Daddy's Girl?' he asked staring at the ornate ceiling. 'I bet you didn't choose it.'

Jacky had a delightful laugh. 'You betcha. He named her without telling me and refused to change it once I found out. Imagine how embarrassing it can be on the radio.'

'Yes, it was a bit strange when we rescued your father but I had other things on my mind at the time.'

'Me too. So, why is your ship called Chester?'

'Oh, that's quite boring, our class of ship are all named after places beginning with a letter 'C'. So there's Coventry and Cumberland as well as us.'

'Yeah, that's pretty ordinary but wasn't your last ship called Prometheus? That sounds more interesting, more romantic.'

'Yes, she was a Leander class frigate. They're all named after Greek legends, like Andromeda, Euryalus, Penelope, that sort of thing.'

Jacky rolled over on her elbow and looked at him. 'So, what's the legend about Prometheus? I guess I should know but can't seem to remember.'

'Ahah, he was the Greek hero who stole fire from the Gods.'

'Go on, tell me the whole story.'

Settling back in the pillow Jon thought for a moment, realising he didn't really know it all himself, still he probably knew enough.

'Right, well, Prometheus was a Titan, that's a hero. In those days, only the Gods on Mount Olympus knew the secret of how to make fire. So being a hero, good old Prommy decides to sneak up the side of the mountain one dark night and see if he could pinch some for all his chums down below, who were getting really desperate for a decent barbeque. Anyway, he creeps in and sees a nice fire burning and all the Gods are asleep, shagging or tormenting mere mortals, so there's no one around. He grabs some fire and makes his way down the mountain. And I bet you don't know what he said as he climbed down?' Jon asked with a twinkle in his eye.

'No go on,' said Jacky in anticipation.

'Fuck, that's hot, ouch, bloody hell it's burning, ouch!'

Jacky hit him in the ribs, while laughing at the same time. 'Oh, I should have seen that coming, got me there you sod.' She rolled over and kissed him. 'And what happened next?'

'Ah, well that's the not nice bit. The Greek Gods were a bit into original forms of revenge. When Zeus, the King of the Gods, found out, he had Prometheus chained to a rock and every day an eagle flew down and pecked out his liver. Unfortunately for our dear fire thief, it then grew back and the whole thing was repeated day after day.'

'Oh, that's horrible,' said Jacky looking quite sad.

'Hey, it's only a myth, it's not real you know.'

'I know, but life can be so cruel,' and a shadow passed over her face for a second.

Jon realised that maybe there was something in this lovely girl's past that was the cause of her irrational behaviour but before he could decide whether to probe further, she jumped out of bed and made for the shower.

'Come on you lazy Englishman, lets shower each other and take the boat out. You told me you had the day off, so let's make the most of it.'

With the moment passed, Jon realised he would have to wait. Meanwhile Jacky was beckoning him from the shower cubicle and what male on the planet would refuse such an offer?

## Chapter 13

The Operations room of HMS Chester was dark and quiet except for the muted sound of the ship's staff talking into the microphones of their headsets. Surrounding the centre space, were a number of identical consoles all showing glowing screens. Each was dedicated to an operator who was monitoring various sensors; sonar, radar and electronic surveillance. There were also different consoles for the operators of the various weapons systems. The Captain sat on a high seat so that he could overlook all the stations and monitor what was happening. He also had his own dedicated console in front of him so he could control and fight his ship.

However, the Captain wasn't paying any attention. He was turned around in his seat and talking to Jon and Brian.

'So what do you think? We picked it up at a reasonable range, about half an hour ago. The tail thinks its Soviet but we've not got anything in the library with these characteristics.'

'Well I'm glad the towed array guys have an idea, Sir,' said Jon. 'I've had a look and I've never seen anything quite like it. How fast did they say they thought it was going?'

'Apparently, from the rate of change of bearing they were getting and assuming a rough range of about eighty miles, then the speed was almost fifty knots.'

'Jesus,' interjected Brian. 'I don't think we've got anything that fast in the West, at least nothing that I've been cleared to know about.'

'Nor me,' replied Captain Peterson. 'Of course, at that speed, he would have been completely blind. I know we're well out in deep water now but it strikes me that whoever he is, he's pretty overconfident.'

'Maybe he didn't expect us to be here, it's normally a fairly quiet part of the world,' replied Brian. 'This part of the Caribbean isn't normally used by the US navy and we're here for a one off trial. Maybe they're doing the same. Talking of which, will the American sub be here any time soon Sir? They could be of great help.'

'No, they've been delayed and won't be here until sometime tomorrow so we're on our own I'm afraid. Now look, the reason I haven't sent you lot hairing off down the bearing to try and localise this guy is that I don't want to spook him. With our tail out we're stooging along very quietly, so even if he has heard us, he probably doesn't know we're a warship. I would really like to get some visual identification, even a sighting of his masts.' He was interrupted by a sailor handing him a signal. Reading quickly, a look of satisfaction appeared on his face. 'We sent Fleet a signal about this as soon as we picked him up and they've been very quick to reply. It seems they're pretty sure we're the first western warship to have encountered one of the new Soviet Alpha class subs. They're apparently made of titanium and so have an incredible diving depth, they're also bloody fast as we've already seen. Right, so any ideas on how to localise him and get some form of sighting?'

Jon responded first. 'One of the problems for us Sir, is that up to about fifteen hundred feet, a submerged submarine can actually hear a helicopter, so we don't want to get too close. We could send Nellie out using her Jezebel sonobuoys, at well above that height and get a fairly accurate location but as soon as the Lynx appears or Nellie goes into the dip with active sonar, to get an accurate final position, the game will be up.'

'I've an idea Sir,' Brian interjected. 'I was out here a few years ago and the water can be incredibly clear. We actually found a Yank submarine by eye, even though he was at periscope depth. When we were on top we could see an incredible amount of detail.'

'Go on, what are you suggesting?'

'Well, if we send the Sea King out along the towed array bearing and try to get a localisation with the passive buoys, we then might be able to spot him from above. It won't give us away and he won't be expecting us. With a good lens on the camera, we should get some pretty good intelligence even if we then do spook him.'

'One minor issue Brian,' said Jon with a slight grin. 'If you look outside, it's still dark,' and then turning to the Captain. 'I assume we only have a limited window to stay in contact if this guy is going so fast Sir?'

'He's well to the south still and my guess is that he's heading for Cuba. We've long suspected that they pop in there on occasions. There's certainly nowhere else friendly around here. He seems to be doing a sprint and drift, high speed for half an hour or so when he's effectively blind and then slowing down and popping up to periscope depth for a look around. It wouldn't be normal procedure on passage but maybe he's just practising. We should be able to stay in contact for at least another four hours, even longer if he reverts to a sensible cruise speed.'

Jon thought for a second. 'Well Sir, if we get airborne in Nellie and put a sonobuoy barrier ahead of him and then back off a bit we should be able to get a reasonable position as he transits between the buoys. If the ship can keep us informed when he slows down, we can get the Lynx to pounce on him as he comes up to periscope depth. It'll take some careful timing but we might be able to photo him for some time before he sees us.'

'When can you get airborne?'

'We should be able to launch the Sea King in an hour and we should put the Lynx on immediate deck alert to respond when called. It will still be dark then but dawn is about five thirty, so by the time we've got some buoys in the water, it will be getting light.'

'Right, that's the plan then. Get your boys up and launch as soon as you can.'

Two hours later Brian and Leading Aircrewman Thompson were sitting in the dark, blacked out cabin of Nellie. Tommo was monitoring eight passive sonobuoys that had been dropped in a line across the estimated track of the submarine. In the front, the twins were enjoying the view of a spectacular Caribbean sunrise while flying slowly, to conserve fuel. They were at six thousand feet and well out of any detection range of the submarine they were hunting.

'Something coming up now,' said Tommo staring at the paper 'waterfall chart', on the plotter in front of him. The thermal paper was starting to show distinct lines which represented the various frequencies that the buoys were detecting, from the hydrophones they had lowered into the sea below them. 'Bloody hell he's noisy. If the bearing the ship gave us is accurate, he's still quite a few miles away from the barrier.'

'Well, if he's doing fifty knots then he's got to make a lot of noise.'

'Yeah, I'm getting a lot of general cavitation lines but a hell of a lot of machinery frequencies as well. This data alone should be really useful for the boffins back at home Sir.'

'Right, well according to the ship, he's only been at this speed for five minutes or so. If we launch the Lynx now, then by the time they get here it should be about time for him to come up for look see. We've probably only got one shot at this, let's hope we get lucky.'

Fifteen minutes later, Jon in the Lynx could see the Sea King ahead of him as he joined up in loose formation. 'Nellie this is Eric, ready to pounce,' he radioed, as he settled in behind the larger machine. They would normally be using encrypted aircraft call signs on the radio. However, this time they had decided to use their names to confuse anyone listening just in case they alerted the submarine.

'Eric, this is Nellie, we're just getting a doppler shift on buoy number six, looks like he's going to transit fairly close. I'm taking you under positive control, vector onto two seven three and descend to two thousand feet.'

With a terse 'Roger', Jon turned the Lynx and started to descend. Turning to Mike, his Observer, 'Mike, climb out of the seat and get ready with the camera.'

'Rightyho Boss,' replied Mike, as he undid his straps and climbed in to the rear of the aircraft, where he pulled the special Hasselblad camera out of its box and checked it over. 'Ready when you are,' he called back over the intercom. 'I just need to open the cabin door and I'm on it.'

'Don't open it yet, wait until I'm visual and I've slowed down.'

The radio came to life again. 'Eric, we have a transit on buoy six, close enough that we reckon we know where he is. Come right ten degrees, slow down to sixty knots and descend to two hundred feet. He should be coming up any time now.'

With excitement mounting, Jon descended down to two hundred feet. The almost featureless blue sea was now rushing past them, even though they were now only flying at sixty knots.

'OK Mike, you can open the door now and keep your eyes peeled.'

They flew on, in tense silence for a few minutes, while Brian continued to pass them small course alterations and estimates of range to the contact. In the end, much to Jon's chagrin, because no doubt it would cost him vast quantities of beer, it was Mike who spotted it first.

'Periscope visual at one o'clock, about five hundred yards.'

Sure enough, there was the white feather plume of a submarine's periscope, just ahead of them. Jon grunted acknowledgement and accelerated towards it. In the cabin, Mike had already started taking photographs. Within seconds and long before the submarine Captain could react, they had slowed down and were directly overhead. Below the Lynx was the black teardrop shape of a nuclear submarine. Jon immediately realised that this was different from anything else in the Soviet arsenal. Its shape was unlike anything else he had seen and it was a lot smaller than he expected. It was quite amazing how much detail could be seen and Jon just hoped that the filter they had fitted to the lens of the camera would allow that detail to be recorded.

The submarine had clearly detected them because within moments the periscope mast slid down and the black bulk simply disappeared as it slipped deeper into the ocean.

In the back Mike was exultant. 'Hey Boss, I shot off almost four film cartridges. That should give the intelligence boys something to chew on.'

'Damn right. Well I guess he's not coming back up now he knows he's been rumbled, guess we can go home.'

In the Sea King there was jubilation as well. 'Well done everyone,' called Brian over the intercom. 'Not only have we got some major intelligence, we've also proved the two aircraft concept in an actual operational scenario. Tea and medals all round when we get home.'

'Hang on Sir,' said Tommo. 'Look, I've got something odd here. I'm getting something else, right out to the west. If I didn't know better I'd say it was a diesel submarine. It's quite an odd signature as well, quite faint but definitely there.'

'Any idea of how far away?'

'At least ten miles further than our barrier Sir.'

'Right, well we've not got enough fuel to go and investigate and anyway there are other navies operating out here, I guess it will be one of them. Let's go home.'

Phil Masters was sweating despite the cold air in the control room. He had just seen a Sea King helicopter in the far distance as he swept the horizon with the periscope. They had been running at periscope depth with the snorkel up and diesels running long after the sun had risen. Not the least because they still didn't have decent batteries on board and so he was being forced to use the engines far more than he would have liked. The sighting of the helicopter mercifully heading away from them was a harsh reminder that they were still vulnerable. He was well aware of the anti-submarine capabilities of NATO helicopters and warships. The H3 or Sea King was used by many nations. If he had been in a British nuclear submarine he wouldn't have been worried at all. In this museum piece it was a different matter. He would have to have a straight talk with Paulo when they returned.

## Chapter 14

The hotel in Medellin was rated at five stars but Paulo couldn't for the life of him work out why. It was a little shabby definitely not in the best part of town. However, it was perfect for the purpose of the meeting he was attending. When the invitation had arrived he was at first amused at the cheek of it and then in parts worried and curious. The top five drug cartels in Columbia had never attempted to get together in one place before. It was a recipe for distrust turning to violence. However, the guarantees that had been offered seemed robust enough and in the end curiosity had got the better of him. He suspected that it was the same for the others. Each attendee had been allocated one complete floor of the hotel and could bring as much security as he wished. The only time the principals would be together would be at the meeting this morning. Paulo had a pretty good idea what it was all about and smiled to himself, hoping he was right.

Manuel's massive bulk suddenly filled the doorway to the sitting room where Paulo had been taking his ease.

'All in order Boss, It was very quiet last night and the boys report that everyone is keeping their heads down.' He gave a snort. 'Even that pig Rivera seems to have been behaving. Mind you the number of hookers that he had last night will probably have worn him out.'

Paulo snorted in derision. 'Don't count on it. What about the Marcellos?'

'They arrived early this morning, so everyone is here. We should be getting the invite any time soon.'

Just as if someone had been listening to their conversation, the telephone rang and Paulo picked it up. He listened for a second and then nodded silently and put it down.

'Right get your team together. We go down in five minutes.'

The hotel's small conference room was crowded. Although only five families were present it had been agreed that five guards could accompany each principal and so the room was almost filled, especially as no one wanted to sit too close to each other. Paulo had to admire the logic. Should anyone want to wreak vengeance it would be almost impossible for them not to be caught in the crossfire as well. No, that wasn't the real worry. If the authorities wanted to, they could take out just about the whole of the country's drug aristocracy at one stroke. Mind you that would hardly be in their interest as it was that aristocracy that paid their pensions.

Paulo looked around. The Marcello brothers sat on the far right surrounded by their men. Phillipe was the oldest and the brains of the family. His thin, pock marked face was in stark contrast to his fat brother who was already sweating despite the air conditioning. Paulo wondered whether it was due to amount of his own product he had taken last night. Rumour had it that he wouldn't last much longer, addiction and venereal disease were apparently vying for the privilege.

Adolpho Rivera sat in front of Paulo. Only the back of his sleek, groomed head could be seen. Paulo had no time for the man. He was too flamboyant and too stupidly cruel. It was known that his workers were in almost open revolt. Paulo wouldn't be at all surprised if one day soon, they exacted some form of vengeance on him for the way they were treated and the way he treated their daughters. Paulo wasn't worried. He already had contingency plans for when the man was gone. They were almost neighbours, so it would be simple to take over his real estate before anyone else blinked.

Dario Gomez off to the left was a different matter all together. Like Paulo he looked and acted like a true professional businessman. He had built his empire up out of nothing and was viciously ambitious. Paulo respected him and despised him in equal measure. As if he knew he was being scrutinised Dario turned and locked eyes with Paulo, acknowledging his presence with a curt nod before turning back towards the front of the room.

The door at the front opened and the fifth principal entered. Paulo was surprised to see he didn't have any bodyguards with him. Enrique Delgardo was an old man, although he still moved with the sprightly step of someone much younger. His full head of hair was white and his face was lined but a hard alert intelligence still shone from his piercing, blue eyes. He didn't wait on ceremony and started to talk into the silence that his entrance had caused.

'Thank you all for coming gentlemen. Frankly I never thought that the day would come when we would all be able to share a room together, maybe it is a sign of the times. Or maybe some or all of you are simply biding your time. I strongly advise you to desist any such thoughts, remember I control this hotel.'

The implied threat was reacted to in several ways but the only overt sign was when Philippe Mandero forcibly grabbed his brother and made him sit down. Angry words were exchanged but not loud enough to reach Paulo's ears.

'Enough, we are here for a reason. I suspect that some of you may already know this,' he continued and stared briefly at Paulo as he continued. 'My contacts in the States have reported some very disquieting news and it affects us all. If we are to have any success then need to work together to counter it. As you are no doubt aware the Americans seem to have no scruples when it comes to interfering with the politics of the countries of Central America. You only have to look at what they have done in Nicaragua and El Salvador. I have received intelligence that they may try something similar here. The difference is that they will be targeting our industry rather than our politics.'

A general murmur started around the room at these words. For forms sake Paulo reacted along with the rest although of course, he already knew all about the situation.

'One of the excuses they will use, will be our continuing internal guerrilla war.' As he said it he looked at several members of the audience intently. 'Funding such activity may be seen as good for business but it could give them the legitimacy they need.'

The meeting descended into chaos with everyone shouting at once. Paulo wasn't surprised. Tensions had been high before the gathering, probably fuelled by the poor prices that most were getting for their drugs. Of course, this was mainly because he was currently able to supply large quantities well in excess of his competitors.

Once the initial uproar had settled slightly and Enrique had been able to present his evidence, there was at last, an amount of reasoned debate. Paulo was unconcerned; he had known all this for some time and had already come up with several contingency options. He was amused to see how the others reacted though and hardly surprised when after almost an hour no one could come up with any ideas about what to do. However, as the debate raged, one thing became clear to him. Enrique's attempts to get some form of concerted action were doomed. There was no way this group of self centred idiots would ever work together. He could see how everyone was trying to work out how they could gain an advantage even as they espoused a common line. He wasn't surprised; after all it was exactly what he was doing.

Eventually an exasperated Enrique took the floor again and summed up. 'Right well you've all been warned. I have to say I'm disappointed but hardly surprised that we can't agree on some concerted response but maybe something will work out as time goes by.'

The meeting broke up in general confusion as the various bodyguard teams tried to usher their charges safely out. Paulo decided to stay put and wait until he was the last, rather like he used to do on a passenger aircraft in the old days when he didn't have his own. All the idiots would stand up and fight to get off the plane even though it always took ages for the luggage to appear on the carousel. He would wait, probably reading his book and take his leisurely leave once the cabin was empty. He would do the same now.

Just as he was indicating to his men that it was indeed time to depart, Enrique came back in. Once again he was on his own.

'Paulo, would you do me the honour of a private talk? You have my word that no harm will befall you.'

Paulo had been half expecting something like this and indicated to Manuel that he and his team should leave them alone. He held up his hand firmly when it looked like Manuel was about to object and the guards trooped silently out.

The two men sized each other up. Paulo spoke first. 'There had to be some other reason for your invitation, there was never any chance that that bunch of fools would agree on anything. I take it you have something in mind?'

'Always the perceptive one,' Enrique sighed. 'Take a seat, we need to talk.'

The two men sat and Enrique continued. 'You're right of course, there's just too much animosity and competitiveness between us but I needed an excuse to get everyone together. Paulo I'm dying. Cancer apparently and I don't have much time left, a year at the most. My wife is already gone, my son is a complete imbecile and I have no other family. I used today as a test. To be frank, I don't like you. You are too cocky and have a vicious streak but there again maybe you could say that about all of us. However, it was clear to me that you already had some foreknowledge of what I had to say. So you've had the foresight to get sources in the US. Also you seem to be thriving when the rest of us appear to be having difficulties.' Seeing the look on Paulo's face he held up his hand. 'No I don't want to know what you're up to. But out of all of them, you seem to be the most intelligent. I also hear you look after your people better than most and that means a lot to me. So here's the deal. When I go, I will ensure my men know that I want them to answer to you. I can't guarantee that some of the others won't make a play but that will be your problem. What do you say?'

'I could, of course, say that I would be best placed to take over anyway. As you say, your son is hardly in your league. But I thank you, at least this way we should avoid a war just when the Americans are looking for an excuse to become involved.'

Enrique nodded in acknowledgement of his remarks and held out his hand. 'Good, I want to spend my last months in peace, so you can start by taking on my Caribbean operation, it's only a small market as you know but it will place you in a good position once I go.'

## Chapter 15

Jon squinted out of one eye as he lifted his head from the sun lounger by the large swimming pool. He was dressed in his swimming costume and had a large frosted glass in one hand.

'Er Brian, unless I am greatly mistaken, isn't that WEO up a palm tree?'

Brian, who was similarly dressed on the lounger next to Jon, looked over to the other side of the pool. 'Yes I can confirm that our illustrious Weapons Engineer Officer is once again attempting to climb to the top of a coconut tree.'

There was an almighty splash. 'And yes, the silly bugger has fallen off it once again. That's the second time. You'd think he'd have the sense to give up.'

'I blame the gin and tonics and he's a very determined man you know. Did you see how much gin went into each glass?'

'Must be something to do with the heat. Hey, is this a great place or what?' said Brian lifting his head and looking around. To their right was a large, white, hacienda style house, with several outbuildings and leading away from a veranda to the front of them was the massive swimming pool. The whole ensemble was clearly the home of someone with money and taste. The extensive gardens were laid out with great care and several coconut palms were gently swaying in the tropical breeze. One of the trees, either by accident or design, leant over at a forty five degree angle, right over the pool. It was this one that the luckless Weapons officer was trying to climb yet again.

'Bet he doesn't make it,' observed Jon but just as he finished speaking there was yet another splash as the latest attempt on the summit of the tree failed.

'Can I get you two another drink?' It was the voice of their host, Mrs Jenny Symes. She was approaching them with a large jug, clearly containing more of the lethal mixture she had been serving all lunchtime. She was probably one of the least attractive women Jon had ever met. A mature lady, in her mid forties, she actually had a reasonable figure which filled out her white bikini rather well but nothing would ever compensate for her features. That's not to say that someone hadn't tried and the results of what must have been quite expensive and comprehensive facial surgery, only seemed to accentuate the worst of her looks.

Jon looked at his glass for a second. 'Sorry Jenny, I'm fine but it's really great of you to look after all of us like this.' Brian nodded as well.

'It's no problem Jon,' she smiled in a rather stiff way. 'Having the wardroom of a British warship for the afternoon is my treat. You've no idea how limited the social life in Nassau can become after a while. Some fresh blood is always welcome.' She said this with an almost feral look in her eyes. 'Anyway, if you'll excuse me, I'll see if there are any other glasses that need refilling.'

Despite the cosmetic surgery, Jon and Brian had to admire the way her buttocks swayed in the little bikini bottoms as their host made her way over to the next group of officers.

'Bloody lucky the Ops officer trapped her at the party the other day. Mind you she seems to be fairly catholic in her approach to men. She was clearly eying you up,' observed Brian.

Jon snorted. 'No way hosay. One mad American female at a time.'

'Ah, but she's not American. She's Swedish and her late husband left her extremely well provided for. He was apparently in the brewing trade and he left her the lot. She was telling me that apart from this millionaire's hideaway, which she lives in over the winter, she has extensive property in Sweden and the UK, as well as the aforesaid brewing company of course.'

'Hang on just a second. You mean she's a rich, blonde, Swedish girl, who is a bit of a nympho and owns a brewery?'

Brian couldn't help a roar of laughter. 'Oh yes and isn't that what you've always said you fantasize about?'

'Bugger. What a shame she looks like she's been in a train smash.'

'Well Ops always says the maxim of 'go ugly early' is the best way to trap. He was obviously right this time.'

'I heard that,' came the voice of Derek, the aforementioned Operations Officer from behind them, as he plonked himself down on the end of Jon's lounger. 'She may not be the most gorgeous totty around but as you say she has just a few redeeming features. So hands off, I know what you bloody WAFUs are like.'

Jon held his hands up in surrender. 'Hey mate, she's all yours and despite the redeeming features, just be prepared to win the Grimmy Trophy when we leave the Bahamas next week.'

'Bollocks to you then. Anyway, you know I might just need to keep in touch with the lovely Jenny when we leave. She makes a mean gin and tonic and strangely she looks even more beautiful the more you have.'

'They're officially called beer goggles old chum. Of course in this case we need to change that to gin goggles but the effect is the same.' Brian observed in a slightly slurred voice. 'Jesus, they are strong though.'

Ops could see that Jon was about to fall asleep and even Brian with his legendary hollow legs was starting to show the effect of the massive drinks. 'Oh, I needed to mention before we all get far too pissed, we've had an assessment of our photos of that sub and the sonar traces back in from the analysis guys at home, so we need to get together tomorrow morning, before we sail, to have a look.' He stopped speaking as Jon's eyes had already closed. Brian nodded and took another swig from his glass. There was another massive splash from the pool and a cheer from the watching throng around who clearly appreciated dogged determination when they saw it.

Nine o'clock the next morning, Jon mustered his aircrew in a clear space in the hangar, as Nellie was on the Flight Deck being worked on and the Ops officer joined them with a sheaf of papers in his hand.

'Morning campers, does anyone feel as crap as I do? Bloody good party yesterday. Thank Christ we sail at midday, my liver couldn't take much more.' There were bleary eyed nods of agreement from everyone and not a few ribald comments about rich Swedish Nymphomaniacs. Ops waved them away but with a smug grin. 'Right to business you pissheads, we need to look at this lot for a moment because Father and the powers that be at home are really pleased about your little photography trip the other day.'

Ops then went on to explain that it had indeed been one of the new Soviet Alpha class submarines and the intelligence gained from the photos had been excellent, particularly of the masts which hadn't been seen before. The biggest surprise had been to find an Alpha so far from home. Until then it had been assumed that they were designed as interceptors, operating with a tiny crew and designed to foray from their bases as and when an opportunity for attack arose. To find one so far away from the Soviet mainland had been a total surprise to all the intelligence analysts and was causing a great deal of rethinking to take place.

'Now the sonar traces are even more illuminating apparently,' Ops continued. 'It would appear she has a very unusual reactor and no one is quite sure how it works, although the clever money is on it being cooled by some sort of liquid metal. If that's the case, it's far in advance of anything we've got, so the brief is to keep an eye out for him, in case we can find him again.'

Brian looked sceptical. 'Unlikely Ops, we would have given him quite a fright last time. I can't see him being caught napping like that again.'

'No you're right but apparently satellite photos have shown he is now in Cuba and he will have to leave some time. We're going to be in the area on anti-drug work for the next few months, so you never know we might just get lucky again. If the intel boys can spot when he leaves, we should be able to have some chance of working out his route and getting another intercept.'

Tommo raised his hand. 'Sir, were there any comments on the diesel sub we detected at the end of the sortie?'

Ops looked confused for a second. 'Oh yes hang on, I'd forgotten all about that but there was something, let me just look.' He rummaged through the papers. 'Ah here it is, they put a little annex at the back. Right, it seems that they were a bit confused. Apparently it was a diesel powered vessel with twin screws and probably a snorting submarine, although it could also have been a small surface vessel. I take you couldn't see anything on the surface?'

One of the twins answered. We looked but there was nothing visible, it was a fair way away.'

'I did have a little radar contact,' said Brian. 'but again it could have been anything.'

'Oh well,' said Ops. 'Put it down to experience. Mind you there is one odd thing here. One of the analysts says the engine characteristics were a bit strange, in that they were clearly from very old fashioned diesel engines. Guess we'll never know.'

## Chapter 16

The air conditioning was humming quietly in the background of the office. Outside the Washington traffic moved silently, all noise banished by the thick double glazing. The calm was shattered by the door flying open and an exultant Senator George Musgrove the Third stomped in, in triumph. He made straight for his desk and sat behind it in the large leather chair. He opened the file that he had brought in with him and started reading avidly.

After half an hour, he had made copious notes and sat back with a satisfied smile on his face. He reached over and buzzed his secretary on the intercom box.

'Mary, get hold of my daughter and tell her I need to see her as soon as she can get here.'

A muffled acknowledgement came over the machine and the Senator started reading again.

Ten minutes later Jacky walked in without knocking and her father looked up at his daughter with a smug expression plastered all over his face.

'We got it girl, we got just about the whole shooting match.'

'What? surely they can't have approved everything. That's never happened before.'

'Well not everything,' he replied consulting his notes. 'The long term funding for the Coast Guard has been trimmed a bit and phased over a longer period but just about everything else is there. In particular they have approved the Marines involvement and what's even better, they've given me oversight of their operations. Not operationally obviously but the man they've appointed will answer to me. Hey girl, this is it. At last we are in a position to do some real good. Praise the Lord.'

'Just be careful daddy, being put in charge also makes you the scapegoat if it all goes wrong.'

'Oh I know that but if you believe in something then you have to have the courage of your convictions. They've even appointed a highly recommended Marine Colonel to run the show and he's here in Washington. What say we get him over here and get started?'

Jacky knew when her father was on a roll and this was the news he had been waiting for. It was the result of years of hard work, lobbying and behind the scenes arm twisting. She could hardly stand in his way now. 'I just hope mother would approve,' she said in a wistful tone.

'Hell girl, I started all this just for her, of course she would approve. It was the scum who deal in drugs that caused her to go to the angels and now at last I'm in a position to wreak our vengeance.' His tone was fervent almost evangelical.

Jacky held her counsel. The truth was never that simple. Unfortunately her father only seemed to see things in clear tones of black and white and once he had decided on what was the truth nothing would dissuade him. She had lived with him and latterly worked as his assistant for long enough to know that.

Two hours later, a crew cut, slim, fit and arrogant looking US Marine Lieutenant Colonel was shown into the Senator's office. His hard face was all angles and topped by a slightly incongruous pair of wire frame spectacles. It was obvious there wasn't an ounce of fat on the man. Jacky took an instant dislike to him the moment he opened his mouth.

'Senator, I am Lieutenant Colonel Joshua Jones, US Marine Corps. I believe we are to do business together.'

The Senator stood and shook hands with the Colonel and then introduced Jacky. 'That's me and may I introduce my assistant and also my daughter.'

The Colonel gave Jacky a curt nod and then proceeded to totally ignore her. Her hackles rose but she decided to keep her counsel. She wanted to hear what he had to say, there would be time to put him in his place later.

Her father indicated a chair and he sat rather stiffly. 'So Colonel, I assume you have been given a brief on the task?' he asked looking appraisingly at the Marine.

'Yes Sir, but no detail as of yet. My instructions are to liaise with yourself and the Coast Guard in Florida to see what can be achieved by a more proactive approach against the drug cartels.

I also understand, we will be able to take a more gloves off approach when dealing with foreign countries.'

'Indeed, deniably of course. Jacky will provide you with all the reports and the approvals we have been given. I suggest you read them thoroughly. It will be up to you to decide on what new tactics need to be developed, there is significant funding for your activities and you should be able to request the resources you need, within limits of course.'

'And my relation with the Coast Guard Sir? Who will have overall command?'

'Good question. This is seen as a joint venture but you will have the overall responsibility for any actual operations. The Coast Guard will provide intelligence and any of their assets that you require. They however, will decide the overall strategy, you will report to their officer in charge at Opa Locka and of course I will give any final approvals for any operations.'

'Are the Coast Guard happy with that? I will be treading on their toes; I may not be that popular.'

The Senator just snorted. 'They should be grateful for what I've achieved and the resources they are now going to get.'

'Can you be a bit more specific about that Senator?'

'In the short term, there will of course be, all the local Coast Guard facilities, aircraft and personnel but it has been agreed that you will be able to call on the Marine Corp assets listed in the reports that Jacky has for you. In summary this will be personnel as required, helicopters and some amphibious craft. Oh and for the next few months there will also be HMS Chester.'

'I'm sorry, is that some foreign ship?'

Jacky decided it was time she asserted herself. 'Yes Colonel, a British warship. She is over here for the next three months on UK anti-drug tasking and she's very capable. Apart from her armament she is carrying one H3 Sea King and one Lynx helicopter.'

The Colonel looked sceptical. 'I'd rather rely on good, tested, American men and equipment if you don't mind.'

Jacky bridled at his dismissive tone. 'Well you don't have any choice Colonel. May I remind you that many of the Caribbean Islands are either British or still retain the British Queen as their head of State. Apart from anything else you will need them for any activity in those areas. Unlike a certain clusterfuck invasion of a British island only few years ago.'

'If you mean Grenada young lady. We acted at the request of other Caribbean Islands to stop communist influence spreading in the area.'

'Yes and forgot to tell the British, who's Queen was their Head of State, what we were doing, as well as making a complete pig's ear of the operation. I seem to remember we subsequently discovered that the so called communist radar experts were actually employees of a British electronics firm.'

The Senator decided it was time to step in. 'Jacky that's enough. I am well aware of your views on the Grenada incident and so now, is the Colonel.' And then turning to the man, 'despite that she has a point. It was the Lynx helicopter from HMS Chester that saved my life earlier this year and I have the utmost respect for their capability. And Jacky is also correct about the political situation. We need the Brits with us on this, so just get on with it.'

The Colonel lifted an eyebrow at that. 'I hear you Senator, you clearly rate them highly. However please allow me to make my own assessments. If as you say, I have overall tactical responsibility, then it must be my decision on who and what to deploy for any operations.'

'Fair enough Colonel, but please don't forget the political angle. My daughter is quite correct in some ways about Grenada. President Reagan himself has made it clear that he doesn't want to upset our relations with Great Britain any further.'

'Noted Sir, I understand from my superiors that this task starts immediately, so I take you will want me to head down to Florida straight away?'

'Naturally, but take a day or two to read yourself in and then I would like you to spend some time on the ground assessing the problem with the Coast Guard people. I will try to come down myself in two weeks time, work here permitting, so take that as a deadline to give me your first thoughts. If I can't make it, Jacky here can represent me in all regards, she has my complete trust.'

With the interview clearly over, Jacky handed the Colonel his sheaf of papers and he left the room.

Jacky looked at her father. 'My goodness, he was a pretty scary stereotype. I hope we've got the right man for the job.'

'Well, as I said he comes highly recommended. He flew helicopters in Viet Nam and was also involved in Grenada, which strangely, is probably why he doesn't agree with you about the invasion. I'll grant you he does seem a bit of a misogynist but that probably comes with the territory. Now let's give him some space and see how things work out.'

'Fine, do you need me in Washington anymore?'

The Senator smiled at his daughter. 'I guess you'll be wanting to head back to Port Everglades, I understand that Chester will be in at the weekend?'

Jacky grinned back. 'As usual you see straight through me. But I can also keep a watching brief on the Colonel if that's alright.'

'That's OK dear and give my regards to Jon when you see him.'

## Chapter 17

HMS Chester was steaming as fast as she could through the Caribbean swell. Her bow wave was being regularly flung high over her bridge in bright cascades as she hit the waves at over twenty seven knots. Down below in the Operations room it was dark and quiet. Everyone was having to hold on tight, especially when the bow came slamming down and shook the whole ship. Captain Peterson was sitting in his chair looking intently at the radar plot and seemingly oblivious to the ship's violent motion. Jon was standing next to him, holding on tight and also watching the drama unfold.

They had sailed from Nassau that morning for a routine trip over to Florida in order to liaise with Coast Guard before starting their next operational stint as West Indies Guard Ship and commencing anti-drug patrols. A few hours out, a Coast Guard patrol aircraft had asked them to check out a suspicious high speed contact, heading towards Florida from Andros Island. The Lynx had been launched with Steve Makepeace and Brian on board. They had soon made contact with the vessel. It was what was known in local parlance, as a 'cigarette boat'; a seventy foot long speed boat with two enormous outboard engines. Two crew could be seen but it wasn't long before the situation escalated. As the Lynx flew close to check out the boat, one of them raised what looked like a pump action shot gun and fired at the aircraft. It was a particularly stupid thing to do and had no result except to make the Lynx shear off and return to the ship for some ordnance to sort out the problem.

The Captain turned to Jon. 'I bet you wish it was you in the Lynx?'

'No Sir, quite happy for someone else to have the excitement for once and Steve needs the experience.'

The Captain grunted acknowledgement of Jon's remark. 'Good point, thank goodness for helicopters and fast ones at that. We're never going to catch the bugger the speed he's going, it's over twice what we can do. You know I just can't work out why he fired on the aircraft, there wouldn't have been much we could have done if he had just ignored us.'

'Yes Sir, I guess he just panicked but Eric is almost back there now and that rifle should sort him out.'

'Let's hope our tame Royal is a good shot.'

In the Lynx, the 'tame Royal' otherwise known as Corporal Derek Payne from the ships Royal Marine detachment, was lying on the helicopter's cabin floor completing his checks on his half inch, recoilless, Sniper Rifle before telling Brian that he was ready. Five miles in front of the Lynx, the cigarette boat was leaving a boiling white wake in the blue sea as it thundered along at over fifty knots. Every now and then it lifted almost completely clear as it hurtled over a large wave before slamming down hard, in a blast of spray. It was quite clear it had no intention of stopping.

Steve looked over at Brian. 'Do we go and let him take another pot shot at us Sir? Or can we just open fire anyway?'

'I'm not giving the bugger another chance to hit us. We've positively identified him as the same boat that shot at us half an hour ago. As far as I'm concerned he gets one warning and that's it.' He then called over the intercom. 'Corporal you can open the cabin door now. We'll fly up alongside him about half a mile away, so we're well out of range of his pop gun and then you can fire half a dozen shots across his bow. We'll see if he gets the message. I've got the camera ready in case he decides to do something even more stupid.'

Soon the Lynx had the boat broadside on to port and the rifle opened fire. Tracer rounds had been deliberately used and six shots could be seen hitting the sea just ahead of the speeding boat. There was no doubt of the message they were being given.

Suddenly there was activity below as the crewman not driving the boat started to throw white bales over the side which hit the sea with a splash and settled in the wake streaming back behind them.

'Silly twat is trying to get rid of the evidence,' observed Brian, clicking away with the camera. 'It won't help him, I'm getting it all on film. Right Corporal, no more Mr Nice Guy, take him out.'

'Aye Aye Sir,' came the cheery reply over the intercom which was soon followed by the sound of measures shots. The first two hit the starboard engine and the cover flew off. The boat immediately slewed to one side before the skipper regained control. He then started zig zagging wildly, obviously trying to spoil the aim of whoever was firing at them from the helicopter. For a moment it seemed to work then the Corporal hit the other engine and the boat slammed to an ignomious halt. The other crewman had stopped ditching bales. As the helicopter slowly approached he could clearly see the muzzle of the rifle sticking out of the door and he reached down and lifted the shotgun over his head, making a very visible effort to throw it over the side.

'I'm betting he wished he had never used that in the first place,' said the Corporal. 'Don't suppose I could give him a little scare Sir?'

'Certainly not you blood thirsty bugger. Mind you it is tempting. No, what we will do, is go and pick up one of those bales for evidence if we can, while the ship's catching us up. That boat isn't going anywhere.'

Half an hour later with Eric safely back on board and two very sheepish looking smugglers locked away, Chester set sail again for Florida. The cigarette boat had been hoisted on board as well as a large quantity of what was almost certainly Cocaine. The Captain called those involved into his cabin for a debrief.

'Well done all of you,' he announced to the team. 'We haven't officially started our anti-drug work and we've already got two of the bad guys. I suspect that the bales we recovered will be of significant value, so a good haul all round.'

'What are we going to do with the bad guys Sir?' Asked Jon. 'They were in international waters.'

'Good point, they have no documentation and are refusing to say what their nationality is, so we take them with us to the States and hand them over. It's where they were heading after all. Now, while you are all here I have some rather interesting news. Apparently the US government are starting to get really worried about the drug problem and are enhancing the Coast Guard effort with assets from their Marines. I have a signal from Fleet instructing us to cooperate with them while we are on station. It looks like they're keen not to commit another balls up like they did in Grenada the other year. Anything to do with British interests, is to involve us. However, we are also to get involved in any of their operation's if they request it.'

'This must be the initiative that Jacky's father, the God bothering Senator was working on,' said Jon. 'She was telling me all about it. He's been fighting Congress for more resources for years. It looks like he's finally had some success.'

'Yes, well we'll know all about it soon. This briefing we're attending in Opa Locka will cover all the detail. It should be interesting,' responded the Captain.

Two days later, the operations team from HMS Chester, key Coast Guard personnel and Lieutenant Colonel Jones USMC, were seated in a briefing room at the USCG facility at Opa Locka. Jon was seated with the other British staff but Jacky was sitting next to him on his left, attending as the Senator's representative. She had to sit somewhere and no one seemed to object, especially Jon, when she plonked herself next to him with a large smile on her face.

'What's this Marine Colonel like?' he whispered conspiratorially in her ear.

She grimaced. 'Just let him talk, he's been winding up the Coast Guard guys all week. See what you think.'

Just then the lights dimmed and the Coast Guard Captain took the stage, to give a brief welcome and introduction before asking Glen Thomas to take the lectern to outline the current situation.

Glen looked at his audience for a second. 'Before I start, I would like to say a word of thanks to the crew of HMS Chester. For those who didn't know they apprehended a cigarette boat, two days ago, on the way over here. I've just received the assay on the value of the contraband and it was pure Cocaine with a street value of over five million dollars. Well done Chester.'

A smattering of applause rippled around the room.

'Gentlemen, as you know we have a problem. I don't intend to go into detail. I believe that all of us here are aware of the issues. Up until now, we have only been able to interdict smugglers on the high seas or once they attempt to get into the country. However, we now have this new initiative. This means we can target two key areas that we couldn't before. Firstly, the local distribution centres such as the Bahamas and other Caribbean Islands. This should severely curtail the cartel's flexibility and hopefully force them into more risky, long transit smuggling runs from their own territory. Once we have hopefully had some success there, we will be in a position to move against the source areas directly, such as the Columbian mainland.'

A murmur of surprise echoed around the room.

Glen continued with a wry smile. 'Yes, but covertly and deniably of course. However, one thing at a time. I will now hand over to our new team member, Lieutenant Colonel Jones of the US Marines who will provide some more detail.'

Glen departed the lectern to allow the Marine Colonel to take the stage. He looked appraisingly around the room and then started talking.

'I've been here about two weeks and I guess the learning curve has been pretty steep. You guys in the Coast Guard sure do things differently. It seems to me that up until now most activity has been reactive. You are only able to wait for the enemy to attack so to speak. Gentlemen it's now time to change that and become fully proactive. Let me explain how we do things in the US Marine Corps.'

For half an hour the Colonel put up and discussed a number of slides. Jon became more and more uncomfortable and when the Colonel paused for breath he raised his hand.

'Yes Sir, I see you have a question?'

'Yes Colonel, I'm Lieutenant Commander Hunt from HMS Chester, I know we're two countries separated by a common language but I have to be honest here. Frankly I haven't understood much of what you've been saying. You seem to be using a jargon that I've never come across before. For examples what on earth do you mean by 'fighting in the urban canyon below the rim'?' There was a ripple of amusement and agreement around the room.

The Colonel looked perplexed for a moment and then slightly annoyed that anyone, particularly a foreigner would question his brief. 'Well Sir, it means fighting in an urban environment, inside the perimeter of a town or city.'

'Right, got it. Sorry Colonel I didn't mean to be rude but we need to establish a baseline understanding here, don't you agree?' Jon continued.

An angry frown started to appear on Colonel Jones's face but before he could say anything the USCG Captain stood. 'Colonel I think our British friend actually speaks for all of us here. While we really appreciate your input and the resources you are bringing, as you yourself pointed out, we don't operate in the same way as the Marines. Your tactical doctrine is very different, as is the language you use to describe it. Perhaps you could finish off your talk with a brief on those very resources and then maybe we should break down into a smaller meeting to thrash out some common doctrine and tactics, including an input from our British friends.'

Colonel Jones could see he was outnumbered and admitted to himself that maybe the Captain had a point. 'Very well Sir, to continue then, these are the resources that have been authorised if required.' He went on for another fifteen minutes before sitting down still seething slightly.

Jacky whispered in Jon's ear as a general discussion stared. 'Well done but I don't think you've made much of a friend there.'

He looked back at her. 'Well it isn't a bloody love in is it? I just hope there is more to the man than just clever words on how to kill people.'

## Chapter 18

Enrique Delgardo had been badly wrong. He didn't last a year, he didn't even make it past the month. But he had been true to his word and instructed his men to answer to Paulo once his funeral was over. Paulo knew it wouldn't be that simple but he had a head start over the other vultures and he had moved fast to place his own people within the various areas of Enrique's empire. The biggest potential problem had been the son. He seemed to think that an inheritance was all that was needed for him to be qualified to take over and manage a major drugs business. It was to Paulo's enormous amusement, when it was some of Enrique's own people who solved the problem for him. The day after the funeral, Manuel Delgardo was found floating in his swimming pool in a pool of blood, minus his testicles. Other injuries testified to one or several people, probably women, taking great delight in wreaking revenge clearly with no fear of any retribution forthcoming.

However, it wasn't all plain sailing. It was clear that many of Enrique's men thought they could strike out on their own. Paulo had sent in some of his own people to disabuse them of the notion. With the mandate from their old Boss and the reality of Paulo's men striking swiftly, order had been restored with only a few examples having to be made.

After the initial dust had settled, Paulo decided that a visit to his new Caribbean operation was the first priority. Not because it was by any means the biggest operation but because being so far away, he wanted some hands-on time with the people on the ground.

He looked down from the small cabin of the seaplane as it banked across the busy waters of Drake's Passage, the channel between Tortola and the main outlying Islands of the British Virgin Islands. The water was dotted with the sails of yachts and the bays and anchorages were full of moored vessels. The place was a sailor's paradise which also made it a smuggler's paradise. The chain had over sixty islands within its boundaries and policing them was almost impossible. Admittedly many were just tiny lumps of rock but there were more than enough for the purpose of concealing his sort of operation. It was also extremely helpful that right next door were the American and Spanish Virgins, providing an excellent route into the mainland US. In addition, one only had to travel a few miles to the south to get to the lucrative markets of the Windward and Leeward Islands, from Antigua down to Grenada.

The little plane straightened out and the pilot throttled back to start his approach to the harbour at Road Town. Soon, there was a loud thump as the floats hit the water and they were taxiing in to the jetty by the main marina. The door was opened by a sandy haired, lean faced man in his mid forties. He was wearing shorts and sun bleached T shirt.

'Mr Mandero, I'm Tony Jacobs, welcome to the British Virgin Islands.' He held out his hand and Paulo shook it, noting the firm dry grip as well as the South African twang to the man's words. 'We'll just get you bags loaded onto the boat and we'll be off.' He directed the staff unloading the bags to put them onto the fast looking workboat tied up further along the jetty.

Paulo looked around. 'What, no customs or immigration?'

Tony just grinned. 'Not for you Mr Mandero, it's all been taken care of.'

As Paulo boarded the work boat, he was privately impressed. They must have a good handle on the local authorities if he could enter and leave so easily. He was looking forward to seeing the rest of the operation.

As they sped out into Drake's Passage, Tony pointed out the various islands that they could see. Paulo was amazed at how close St John's, which was part of the US Virgin Islands chain, actually was.

'Yes Sir and it's almost impossible for the US authorities to police entry and exit. Once you're there, you're effectively in the United States and so moving things inwards is far easier.' Tony explained. 'Our favourite trick is to recruit an old couple who need retirement money and get them to act as mules on a one off trip back to the US mainland. Two suitcases owned by an elderly couple are almost impossible to intercept. They get their retirement funds and we make an enormous profit. I have a small team who trawl around the hotels over there looking for willing recruits. You'd be amazed at how easy it is.'

Paulo nodded, he had used the same technique many times himself.

Tony pointed ahead. 'That's where we're going, it's called Salt Island. It got its name from the salt flats on the far side. Off to one side, underwater, is a famous wreck. It was a mail ship called the Rhone and she went down in a hurricane in the middle of the last century. If you ever saw the film 'The Deep' it was filmed on her although they made out it was Bermuda. It means we get quite a lot of boats around here going diving on her but it's actually good cover for us.'

Paulo nodded, looking at the low flat island fast approaching. They swept into a large bay, past several moored boats and tied up to a rickety looking but surprisingly firm wooden jetty. Paulo realised that first impressions could be deceptive around this man. He realised he was going to have to tread carefully. Tony led the way up a gravel path to a simple whitewashed house. Several outbuildings surrounded the compound. The whole place looked like the private home of some rich retiree and definitely not the centre of one of the most successful drug smuggling operations in this part of the Caribbean. Paulo was becoming more and more impressed.

He was taken up to a suite of rooms that wouldn't have been out of place in a five star hotel. As it was getting late he told his host he would rather just retire for the night and they would get together first thing in the morning. Tony bade him goodnight and closed the door behind him. Paulo had just finished unpacking, when there was a soft knock at the door. His approval of his reception went up yet another notch when he saw the two identical blonde girls in the doorway. The smiles on their faces said everything. Maybe he wasn't actually that tired.

The next morning he was joined by Tony for breakfast on the veranda overlooking the bay.

'Morning Mr Mandero, I hope everything was to your satisfaction last night?' Tony asked with a grin.

'Call me Paulo please and yes more than satisfactory. May I ask? Are those two young ladies local?'

'No, they're just visiting. Please feel free to ask them to accompany you when you leave, if that is what you want.'

'You know, I might just do that. Now to business, you seem to have a very slick organisation here. I had a look at your numbers before I came over. However, we need to get a few things straightened out first. Be honest please, what are your views on the transfer of control and more importantly how are your people taking it?'

Tony thought carefully for a moment. 'You may not know the whole history of this operation Paulo. When Enrique set it up, he recruited me to run it. He was a very hands off person as long as things were running smoothly and I've made it my business to ensure that is exactly what happens. The deal was that he supplied the goods from his resources and then it was up to me how to move it onwards and make the sale. It also helped that, as a semi independent organisation, there would be less of a lead back to his business.'

Paulo could read the subtext of the statement. 'And you want to know if I will do the same?'

Tony nodded. 'Frankly we don't care who's in charge, if that's what you want to call it.' And he looked at Paulo with a frank challenge in his eyes.

'Fair enough, as I said, I've looked at your numbers and they seem pretty good. I always work on the principle that if it isn't broken then don't try to fix it. However don't be surprised if my methods of delivery are different and the quantities I ask you to move increase. Think you can handle that?'

'Yes, I was always telling Enrique that we could move more stuff but he was quite cautious and wanted to keep below the main radar. We're not the only outfit operating in this area as I'm sure you realise.'

'Fine, as long as we understand each other. Right, I think it's time we toured the real estate don't you?'

The rest of the morning was spent in a leisurely tour. There actually wasn't that much to see. There was an underground storage facility next to the main house, a boathouse and workshop near the jetty and another store with various equipment and tools. The security was excellent and Paulo noted the alert guards and even a kennel with some very savage looking dogs penned up. They went back to the veranda where a light lunch had been laid out

'Our story is that I'm a rich businessman who likes his privacy. None of the authorities seem to object,' Tony explained. 'Although we have to pay quite highly for that, as you would expect.'

Looking around, Paulo had a thought. 'Do you have a chart around here? I would just like a quick look at the sea approaches.'

Slightly mystified, Tony went to a desk and pulled out a Marine chart of the area. 'Will this do?'

'Perfect.' Paulo studied the area around Salt Island. 'Please tell me if I'm right but it looks to me as if the water is very deep right until only two miles from the shore out to the southwest. Even then it stays at over thirty metres right up to the coast.'

'Yes, there are a few shallow patches which are at twenty metres but otherwise you can get within a few hundred yards in deep water. But why on earth do you want to know? You talk like you have a submarine.' The last was said with a humorous but also searching tone.

For a moment Paulo almost decided to tell the truth. He had taken a liking to this man, both for his efficiency and his apparent trustworthiness. He had a knack of assessing people's character accurately. It was one of the reasons he was still alive and Tony was ringing all the right bells. But no, he wasn't going to risk his Crown Jewel, at least not yet.

'Ha, if only I had, no I just like to have a full picture of all the real estate. We may have to land stuff out of sight and I was just curious to see past the far side of the island.'

He could tell that Tony wasn't satisfied but tough luck, he would just have to keep wondering, for now at least.

## Chapter 19

The little room was a mess. A central table was covered in papers and charts and sharing the space were several coffee cups and a half tray of doughnuts. A large clipboard held a large scale chart of the Caribbean Sea and surrounding countries. One wall contained a white board that was covered in felt tip pen writing. On Jacky's insistence, the window was open to let out the fug of the cigarettes that Glen Thomas was smoking, even if it let in the Florida heat. The four occupants were sitting in chairs around the table. They had agreed on a closed door, no rank, bull session and had been at it for several hours.

Glen looked at his colleagues. 'So, to sum up guys, we have production here mainly on the north coast of South America. Even if the stuff is made further south it is shipped to this area for onward despatch. The cartels then either attempt to smuggle it in directly using a variety of methods; boats, aircraft and the rest. Alternatively they tranship it to distribution areas. The best ones are the Bahamas due to their proximity to Florida or The British Virgin Islands due to their proximity to US Islands. Of course there is also Cuba, Haiti and the Dominican Republic but none are quite so attractive to the cartels, not the least because of the amount of money it costs them to operate there. If we're to go on to the offensive, then either the Bahamas or BVIs are the best targets and if we succeed then we will be sending a very strong message, along with shutting down at least one conduit of supply. Now, this is where having HMS Chester around is really useful. The Bahamas are an independent country but still have the Queen of England as their head of State. The BVIs are still a UK dependency and so are even more closely tied to Britain. According to Jacky, her father has obtained diplomatic approval for operations in one or both areas as long as Chester is involved.'

Jon nodded confirmation. 'Actually it's slightly more than that, the word we have received is that we have to approve the operational plan and have to be in command of any actual operations. My guess is that if we get any publicity, we don't want another public row like the one over Grenada.'

Colonel Jones didn't look happy at that remark. 'Glen, this is an American initiative. Are you really recommending that we start out by an operation against British real estate?'

'Joshua, I've explained the situation on the ground. Yes we could go for somewhere else but all those potential targets come with their own problems, not the least that their governments would be very hostile to our actions if they came to light. With the Brits on board we stand much less chance of starting a diplomatic incident.'

Jacky who had kept her counsel, decided to intervene. 'Joshua. Chester is only here for three months and the next British warship isn't due until later in the year, so this is a unique opportunity in the short term. She is also well suited to this sort of operation especially with the mix of aircraft she's carrying. Look at how successful they've already been, even before they arrived here.'

The Colonel nodded. 'Alright, I understand but I want to talk about those aircraft in a minute.'

'So are we going to warn the relevant authorities of our plans in advance?' asked Jon. 'It seems to me we could give away any element of surprise.'

'Absolutely not. No, there will be no warning. We're pretty sure that the respective authorities are riddled with corruption. For example if you look at the Bahamian Air Defence Force; every time it goes out to buy some anti-drug running patrol aircraft, for some reason or another the deal always falls through at the last minute. However, if they do kick up a fuss, they can be told to can it by your government.'

'Fair enough,' said the Colonel. 'You make good points and despite the kicking I've had from you two over Grenada, I agree we don't want a repetition of the fallout from that. So what do you recommend Glen? Which of these two targets is the best?'

'As Joshua mentioned some time ago, we've always been reactive until now and so haven't really been interested in what happens in other countries. That's all changed now of course and we are expecting some information from our intelligence agencies and the DEA which should arrive on Monday. Once we have that we should be able to decide on our first operation.'

'Right,' said the Colonel. 'Let's talk about resources. I can get hold of at least one amphibious ship which can operate up to six Hueys, several CH Fifty Three Sea Stallions and up to six companies of Marines. It would seem we are talking about a small amphibious landing type of operation, so we won't be short of men or equipment.'

'In Chester we also have a company of Royal Marines, as well as the Sea King and Lynx,' responded Jon not wanting to be overwhelmed with American largesse.

'Yeah I know the Sea King,' replied the Colonel but what is this Lynx? Some sort of British machine I assume.'

'Colonel, what have you flown?' Jon asked.

'Well mainly the good old Huey, but that includes the attack version. Finest helicopter in the world.'

Glen flinched at the words and looked at Jon. Jon looked thoughtfully at the Colonel. 'Joshua, I got my guys to fit a set of dual controls to Eric, that's my Lynx by the way. How do you fancy a trip around the bay after lunch?'

That evening, Jon was back on board Chester, which was alongside in Port Everglades. He was briefing the Captain and command team on the day's results.

'So Sir, the bottom line is that we're now waiting for any intelligence about either the BVIs or Bahamas and then we can go. If we get nothing definite that way, Jacky is going to confirm with her father that we conduct a little sweep up the side of Andros island and see what we can bag.'

The Captain nodded. 'That all seems to make sense Jon. So how is our tame Marine behaving? Have you managed to get him to talk an understandable form of English yet?'

'Oh yes Sir, he's not a bad sort once you drill under the bullshit.'

'I hear you took him for a spin in the Lynx this afternoon, how did that go.'

Jon grinned. 'You have to understand that he's only flown Hueys up to now Sir. They have this rather primitive rotor system. Basically they only have two blades and they are on a sort of see saw arrangement on top of the rotor mast. It has some really nasty characteristics if you abuse it even mildly and the result is called mast bumping and the effect is totally catastrophic. Well that is, if you consider the rotors parting company with the airframe and decapitating the pilot in the process as being a bad thing. Anyway, I disabused him of this problem with the Lynx. At one stage he did try to grab the controls but we were upside down at the time and didn't manage it.'

Brian cut in. 'I was there when they got back Sir. I've never seen the man so quiet. I don't know what you did to him Jon but he was white as a sheet. He kept stopping and turning back to look at the aircraft and shaking his head as he walked in.'

'Chalk one up to good old Westland helicopters then,' said Jon. 'But seriously, he seems to be a convert now and is actually prepared to accept that there is some decent kit out there that isn't made in the US of A.'

The meeting went on for another half an hour and then broke up. Being a Saturday various runs ashore were being planned but Jon made his excuses as soon as he could. To no one's surprise, he had a date.

That evening, he and Jacky were finishing dinner in a local steakhouse . They had managed to keep off the topic of the forthcoming operations all throughout the meal but inevitably the conversation eventually headed that way.

'So Jacky, is your father coming down soon? I sort of wondered if he would be asking to come with us on this little operation,' asked Jon. 'Actually I'm surprised we haven't seen him at all so far.'

'He's been really caught up in Washington with other business. If you ask me, he enjoys the politics more than the reality of what occurs as a result of all his machinations. But you're right, he would want to be present and as I'm his representative, then maybe I should come along instead.' She raised an enquiring eyebrow at him.

'Bloody hell, that's a bit above my pay grade but I don't see why not. I guess you ask your dad, who asks our embassy and then we get told what to do, something like that anyway.'

'And what are the rules about girls on British ships?' she asked with a wicked grin as her leg rubbed against Jon's under the table.

Jon swallowed, 'well none of that for a start.'

A thousand miles to the south Paulo was looking at the latest report from his source. It was frustrating to say the least. Now the Senator had his approvals, he seemed to be keen to start moving as fast as he could and it would appear that the Marine assets he had requested were being made available. The big problem would be to identify where they would strike first. It could be anywhere depending on how good their intelligence was. He sighed, realising that there was little he could do until they showed their hand. At least Phil seemed happier with the submarine now that he had acquired a decent quantity of golf cart batteries. It hadn't been easy but by spreading his purchases it shouldn't have raised any suspicions, especially as all the orders had been through third parties. He had to smile, when his cousin had talked him into buying a share in that golf club, he never suspected how useful it would eventually become.

He had been really impressed with his new BVI operation, especially with its Boss and so his mind turned to how the whole thing could be improved. He decided he would get Phil to do a proving run with the sub and its new batteries and take it up there for a delivery at the same time. The quantities it could deliver would be a test of the system and he would go and supervise from the other end; a final test of Mr Jacob's capabilities. He realised he hadn't felt so energised in years.

## Chapter 20

The wardroom of HMS Chester was hushed. The ship was back at sea and the officers were all sitting down to dinner together. Their guests, Lieutenant Colonel Joshua Jones US Marines and Miss Jacky Musgrove were in attendance and everyone was being held in rapture by the story being recounted by Lieutenant Mike Hazlewood the Flight's second Observer.

'So there we were, all four divisional officers waiting for our 'guilty bastards' to appear one at a time. Father wasn't amused, he really hates it when sailors miss the ship. The first to be called was my lad, Naval Airman Jones. You know, he's the spotty one, always gobbing off.'

'Hang on, wasn't he the one who trapped those two enormous fat black ladies with the pink Cadillac when we were in Fort Lauderdale last time?' the First Lieutenant asked.

'Yup, we all thought he would be eaten alive but the little bugger really seemed to have enjoyed himself when he finally got back. Anyway, he marched up, all innocent and saluted the Captain and when asked, started in on his story.'

'Go on,' said Jon. 'We're all ears,' and he gave Jacky's hand a surreptitious squeeze under the table.

'So, his explanation was quite clever. He and his mates had been in the Holiday Inn and chatting to some American ladies of a 'certain age'. Apparently the staff were really unfair to them and as they weren't hotel residents, had taken exception to the fun they were all having and asked them to leave. It was quite late and they couldn't remember the way back to the ship, so they got a taxi. The taxi driver apparently didn't like Brits and so took them the wrong way. He dropped them off in some remote area where there were no houses and the four lads were totally lost.'

'Doesn't sound too outrageous, so far,' a voice opined.

'Ah but it gets better. As they walked down this deserted road they heard a howling noise and realised that there was a pack of wild dogs stalking them.'

'Not the women from the Holiday Inn then?' someone asked, amidst general laughter.

'No, now stop it you lot, it's my story after all. Right, so realising the danger they were in, they looked for shelter and saw a church. They managed to get in and spent the night with the 'pack of the damned' howling outside. In the morning, the rector or priest or whatever, arrived and let them out. They got a lift back to the port but by this time the ship had sailed.'

'Sounds farfetched but just possible,' observed the First Lieutenant.

'Ah but we knew the real story from the doorman at the Holiday Inn. They'd been there all afternoon drinking around the pool and chatting up the rather aged totty. However, it all got out of hand when they were persuaded by the ladies to show them all their tattoos, including those on their bums. It was at this point that they were ejected. Don't ask me how but a bit later, they managed to sneak back in. It was about five in the morning, when other guests started complaining about the noise coming from the Jacuzzi. The staff once again found our team and some ladies in various states of undress in the water. Apparently they were teaching the women certain British songs, if you take my meaning.'

'Good lads, nice to see them maintaining high standards of behaviour,' observed Brian and then looking at Jon. 'Reminds me of a certain run ashore in St Lucia few years ago.'

Jon looked pained. 'Well at least we made it back to the ship in time.'

Mike continued. 'Yes well, we're not quite sure what happened next but it seems the ladies were quite protective of our lads and proceeded to take them to their rooms for late nightcaps and probably a bit more exercise, with the result that they missed the ship sailing. Right, so it was quite clear that all four had decided on a detailed and consistent story for the Captain. Father was clearly getting quite pissed off when the third lad, one of the stokers, recounted exactly the same tale, word for word. But when the last one came in he had had enough and just before the lad got to the bit about the wild dogs, he interrupted and said 'let me guess you were attacked by a pack of wild dogs?' The sailor looked at him with this deadpan look of innocent amazement on his face and said, 'yes Sir how did you know that?' It was at that point that I lost it and even though I tried, I couldn't stop giggling. DMEO here, who was Divisional Officer for the other lads, had a handkerchief stuffed in his mouth, trying desperately to stop laughing as well. The Captain turned to us and saw what was going on and told the Master at Arms to stand the lads down. Once they had gone, I expected the biggest bollocking of my life. Instead Father just joined in the hysterics. I realised afterwards that he had been having an even bigger problem than the rest of us keeping a straight face. Anyway, once we had all managed to calm down, he called in all four and confronted them with the truth. He then gave them the most enormous dressing down and two week stoppage of leave and it was all over.'

The story kept everyone amused for the rest of the meal and for some time afterwards.

Later that evening, Jon was talking to the Colonel. Jacky was being monopolised by most of the young officers and seemed to be enjoying every moment of the attention she was getting. Jon didn't mind, he knew his girl.

'So Jon, is this typical of the Royal Navy?' asked Joshua. 'Your whole ethos is very different to ours, you even allow drinking at sea.'

'Well, we're expected to be sensible about it, for example, I never drink at sea if the aircraft are serviceable. You might have noticed I've been on orange juice all evening. But some of the other officers, if they aren't required on watch, can have a drink or two. The sailors are allowed three cans of beer a day and the Senior Rates have an allowance as well. I guess it all goes back to days gone by, when the only way to keep sailors under control was to keep them pissed as farts for most of the time. The allowance in Nelson's time was a pint of rum per man per day. God knows how anything got done.'

'In the US we've never allowed that but I guess it can lead to problems when we first get ashore and cut loose. Anyway I'm really grateful to sail with you guys and from what I can gather my Marines are enjoying the experience as well.'

'Yes they seem to have settled in and are getting on very well with our Company of Royals. Let's just not let them go ashore and have a drinking contest. I suspect the Captain would be even busier when we sailed afterwards.'

Later that night Jon said goodnight to Jacky outside her cabin. Chester was designed as a command and control ship and as such had extra senior officer's accommodation. Jacky had been assigned the Admiral's suite. Jon gave her a quick peck on the cheek as she opened the door and with an enormous effort of will managed to turn down the offer of anything further.

'Sorry Jacky, apart from anything else we have our final operations brief tomorrow and I need to prepare for it.'

She pulled a face. 'Off you go then sailor boy. See you in the morning.'

At half past eight the next morning, the ships operations team, plus the Colonel and Jacky, met in the Ops room annex. The Colonel had been going over the intelligence report that had arrived. It had been compiled by the DEA from an enormous number of sources and issued to them before they sailed. He wanted to get a consensus on his plan of action. Several ship's officers, including Jon had also read the report which was amazingly detailed.

While they waited for the Captain to arrive, Jon commented on the information they now had. 'You know, I just can't get over how much is known about these scumbags, why hasn't something been done about them before now?'

The Colonel replied. 'Well, for a start, they're all operating out of sovereign countries and that means those countries need to have the motivation to do something about them. There's no doubt that a lot of palm greasing goes on to ensure they're left alone.'

'Actually, it's not unlike Northern Ireland,' responded Jon. 'When I was flying there last time, we were always given intelligence about the local bad guys and asked to look at their houses if we flew over them, to see if they were occupied. It was bloody frustrating, we knew who they were but there seemed to be little we could do about the bastards.'

'Well just for once we should be able to be a little more active,' said the Colonel just as the Captain walked in and everyone stood up.

'Sit down everyone,' he said waving his hand down to indicate there was no need for formality. 'Right I've been through this intelligence, as I know you all have. So who wants to start with any recommendations?  Colonel, maybe you should tell us your thoughts first.'

The Colonel stood and went to the front of the small room. 'Gentlemen let me remind you of the key issues here.  This is to be a covert operation, we need to get in, make arrests, shut down the operation and get out again without arousing any suspicion, at least until we're well clear.  Wherever we decide to go, the British Government will notify the local administration at the same time that we go in, so there will be no risk of the bad guys being forewarned.  Because the raid is going to be on what is effectively British soil, the US Coast Guard and US Marines will not be involved.  Well except that my team and myself might just borrow some of your uniforms, as we've agreed.  As this is our first attempt at this; we need a target that's reasonably remote, where access is straightforward and we can make a quick exit.  To my mind there is only one place that meets all these criteria.'  He looked questioningly at his audience.

Captain Peterson broke the silence. 'Salt Island.'

'Exactly Sir, it meets all those criteria and has the advantage that it used to be under the control of Enrique Delgardo, who conveniently died a few months ago, followed suspiciously quickly by his son.  There has to be some sort of power vacuum there.  Maybe the locals are trying to run it themselves.  Either way, if we take the place out it will be sending a very clear message to the whole community.'

The Captain nodded.  'Agreed.  Work up a detailed plan and we'll see if we can get the go ahead from Washington and London.  Mind you, I'm sure they'll agree, so plan on moving on Friday, there's no moon and that should give us plenty of time to prepare.'

## Chapter 21

The battered man was bleeding profusely from various cuts on his face and torso. His face was horribly puffed up and his eyes almost shut from the bruising around them. There was another wet thump as the baseball bat struck his arm. This time, it was hard enough to break it. The man screamed again.

Tony Jacobs was sitting facing the man, straddling a similar chair to the one his victim was firmly tied to. His stony face showed no emotion as he indicated to his man with the baseball bat to stop for the moment.

'I'm going to ask you again. Who are you working for? I've always known that some of my people would seek to spread their bets once Mr Delgardo moved on. So who is it?'

The man spat blood onto the toe of Tony's shoe by way of an answer.

'Very well we'll try something else. Open the door.'

The door to one side was opened and they could all see a little blonde haired boy of about five years old. He was talking to one of Tony's men.

'Your little boy? You thought he and your wife were safely hidden on Tortola didn't you?' Tony saw the fear in the man's eyes. At last he was getting through. 'Your wife is already entertaining my men in their accommodation that is if they haven't become bored with her already.'

The man started to struggle despite his broken arm.

'Right, last chance before my men start in on the boy.' He saw the light of defiance leave the man's eyes. It always amazed Tony how a man could withstand enormous amounts of pain but caved in when a loved one was threatened.

'The Marcellos,' the man said through his bruised lips.

It took another half an hour before Tony was sure he had all the information the man knew. It was as he suspected, the Marcellos were trying to move in but as usual had left it too late. He would need to send a message to them to back off. He pulled the automatic pistol out of his pocket and shot the man through the forehead.

'Cut off his hand, the one with the ring and send it to the Marcello's with my compliments. I'm sure they'll get the message.'

'What about the boy?' One of his men asked.

'Oh, yes we're finished with him, take him back to his mother.'

Tony left the basement and Paulo got up and followed him out.

The two of them went up to the veranda for a drink. Once again Paulo was impressed with his new man. 'I did wonder whether you were ruthless enough Tony. It seems I'm not to be disappointed. I liked the touch with the boy, very effective.'

Tony smiled back. 'You do realise he wasn't his actual son?'

Paulo looked amused. 'I was wondering. Who was he?'

'Just one my men's children who happens to look a bit like that idiot's boy. His wife and kid are fine, they're of no interest to me. But that was why we ensured his vision wasn't too sharp before we opened the door.'

This time Paulo laughed out loud. 'Brilliant, I'll have to remember that for the future. Just out of interest where do you dispose of the remains?'

'Oh that's easy, there's the great Salt Pond over the rise behind the house. We have to weigh them down of course, that's why we have that concrete mixer in the tool shed but it's very convenient.'

'Of course and now onto important business, I want to talk about the delivery I've arranged. A boat will be dropping off a consignment on the beach on South Bay at about two in the morning. I want you to come with me and see how it arrives.' Paulo had decided to take Tony fully into his confidence. He needed a man he could trust for this end of his expanding operations and he was now certain that he had found his man.

HMS Chester was steaming slowly up Drake's Passage. It was a dark night with no moon although starlight was providing a little illumination. The ship had called into Road Town that day for refuelling. It was a routine activity and the presence of a British warship in these waters was quite normal, so no suspicions

# Cocaine

about her purpose should have been raised. The ship's two Rigid Inflatable Boats were about to be lowered, each containing nine fully equipped Marines with two crew from the ship's company. Nellie was ranged on deck with a further twelve Marines embarked. Eric would be ranged as soon as the Sea King launched and would take in a back up crew as well as Jacky, if it was deemed safe.

Jon and Peter, one of the twins, were flying the Sea King and Steve and Brian were in the Lynx. Jon was listening in on the ships telebrief system which allowed the aircraft to communicate to the ship via detachable wire in the aircraft's belly. He heard the Captain give the command for the boats to be launched and soon afterwards the instruction to start up the Sea King. The plan required the boats to get ashore and the Marines to operate with the element of surprise before the lumbering great noisy helicopter came in with reinforcements. No one was sure what sort of resistance to expect but they were planning for the worst and hoping for the best.

'So what do you think we're going to find?' asked Peter.

'Well I did a couple of drug interdictions when I was on a Jungly squadron some years ago,' said Jon, 'and it seems most criminals, even the really tough ones, turn to jelly when confronted with soldiers dressed in camouflage and holding machine guns. Let's just hope these Caribbean types are the same.'

Soon they had the rotors running and it was only a matter of minutes later that they were given the order to launch. As they crossed over the beach they saw the two RIBs parked on the sand and then it was time to flare the aircraft hard and land it in the compound outside the main house that they had previously identified from photographs. Jon was relieved to see that it was all as expected and there were no hazards to a safe touchdown. Within seconds the Marines had disembarked and Jon was just about to lift off again when the Colonel appeared making the cut throat sign to Jon to shut down the aircraft.

Tony Jacobs was astounded. He couldn't believe what he had just seen. He was in the little rubber dinghy that had been on the beach waiting for them when he and Paulo had arrived there half an hour ago. Paulo had kept tight lipped about what was going on despite Tony's obvious curiosity. The little dinghy had headed back out to sea and there it was. *'Jesus it was a fucking submarine, the man had a bloody great submarine,'* he thought with utter astonishment. Its conning tower was clear of the water as was the top of the casing. As they had come alongside two crew members started passing down white bales of Cocaine into the dinghy.

Paulo had turned to him 'No questions Tony until we get the load safely ashore. But I think you now realise what advantages I have.' Tony nodded, too dumbstruck to say anything. It only took minutes before they were heading back to the beach which was only a few hundred metres away. Suddenly something else caught his attention. Over the rise of land he could see lights, something was flashing red and he could hear an odd growling noise which then stopped as did the red light.

'Something's going on at the house Paulo,' he said over the noise of the outboard. They grounded the boat and after telling the crewmember to unload and bury the cargo on the beach above the surf line, they headed cautiously inland.

'I hope those bloody Marcellos' haven't decided to pay a visit,' Tony said as they made their way through the scrub.

'It's not their normal way of doing business,' replied Paulo. 'But I wouldn't put it past some other operators. But I haven't heard any sounds of resistance and that light and noise sounded like a helicopter landing. Get down and let's look over the ridge just there.

The two men dropped onto their bellies and crawled the last few yards until they could see the house and its surroundings.

Tony swore. 'Jesus, those are military helicopters, what the fuck are they doing? Look it says 'Royal Navy' on the tail of one of them.'

Before he could speak further several dark clad and armed men came around the building, herding his men before them with rifles. The men had their hands secured behind them and didn't appear to be making any attempt at resistance.

'That bloody US Senator,' hissed Paulo. 'I knew he was going to start an operation somewhere, I just never guessed the bastard would start here. Shit, I'm sorry Tony but we're completely blown here we better get out while we can.'

Tony nodded having made the same assessment. At least there was a means of escape behind them if they moved fast.

Suddenly Paulo pointed to one of the military people by the house. This one was different. It was clearly a girl and although she was dressed in black, she carried no weapons. He instantly recognised her. 'I want that girl Tony, I know that face, maybe something good can come out of this bloody fiasco after all.'

Jacky had enjoyed her trip ashore in the helicopter even though it had been quite short. The whole area had been quickly secured. The men hadn't put up any sort of a fight and had been quickly disarmed and hobbled, in seated rows on the ground by the two aircraft. The Marines were still searching the house although a quantity of drugs had already been found which completely justified the raid. Father would be delighted. Until the buildings were declared safe she had been instructed to stay clear but no one had said she couldn't have a look around the grounds. It seemed all quiet around the rear of the house and she had just decided to head back when she suddenly felt a hand clamp over her mouth. She started to struggle but was pulled viciously backwards. Something struck her hard on the head and the world went black.

## Chapter 22

Jon was feeling the adrenalin charged, afterglow of a successful mission. He caught up with Colonel Jones at the entrance to the main house.

'Colonel, how's it going?'

The Colonels face was a nightmare, streaked with green and black camouflage paint, he looked truly frightening. However, his wide grin showing his white teeth, was in stark contrast to his warlike appearance. 'The place is secure, we have fifteen prisoners and at least five kilos of what is almost certainly Cocaine. None of our people were hurt although a couple of the bad guys tried to run for it and had to be forcibly restrained. Frankly as soon as they saw us, we could have been pointing a wet lettuce at them and they would have given up.'

'I'm not surprised,' said Jon. 'You lot scare the crap out me and I know you're on my side. So, what do we do now?'

'Well, we're still searching the place and we need to have a little talk to the prisoners and then we can take them to the ship and deliver them to the authorities.'

'OK, I'm going to find Brian and check the aircraft, see you in a minute.' He walked around the grinning Marines guarding the dejected looking gaggle of prisoners sitting on the ground. The soldiers all looked just as menacing as the Colonel. Brian was sitting on the edge of the cabin door of the Lynx regarding the captured men when Jon came up.

'All well Brian? No problems getting in I take it?'

'Piece of cake old chum. Did Jacky find you? They said it was all safe here, so I brought her in along with the Doc and some support guys, should be some food and coffee around soon.'

'No, I haven't seen her where did she go?'

'Over towards the house somewhere, she can't have gone far.'

Jon was heading back towards the house when one the British Marines came up to him.

'Sorry to grab you Sir but there's something odd here and I can't see the Colonel anywhere at the moment.'

'Oh, right then, go on.'

'Well, I was detailed to start debriefing the prisoners. You know, name and that sort of thing, bloody hard to drag anything out of them. But there's something wrong. Look at the way they're dressed, none of them look particularly well off. Looking at that house I would have expected the owner to at least be reasonably smart.'

Jon looked at the sullen men sitting on the ground. 'You may well have a point there. But that means there're still some people hiding.'

'Or they've legged it Sir. All the buildings have been searched so they must be on the island somewhere.'

'Shit or they've got a boat. They can't have gone from this side, as the ship would have seen them. Right go and find the Colonel and tell him what you've told me. I'm going to get a helicopter airborne to look over on the other side of the island.'

The Marine ran off towards the house while Jon ran in the opposite direction calling for Brian and Steve as he did so. They responded to his shouts and met him by the Lynx.

'Right you two, we think there may some more bad guys who've got away. They're either hiding somewhere on the island in which case we can get the bastards or they've got a boat and have legged it out to sea. I want you to get airborne as fast as possible and search the shore and sea on the other side of the island. Tell the ship what you're up to as soon as you have the radios up. I'll get the Royals to contact the ship as well and tell them what we're worried about.'

Brian nodded and Steve was already strapping in as Jon ran back towards the house looking for the Colonel. He met him coming the other way.

'Did the Marine find you Colonel?'

'Yes I'm just going to look at the prisoners myself but I've a nasty feeling he's right.'

Just then the sound of a gas turbine winding up started to make conversation difficult. Jon raised his voice. 'I've told the Lynx to get airborne and start searching over the other side of the island. If they've got off by boat we may be able to find them. If they're still on the island then we should be able to run them to ground.'

'Good thinking,' yelled the Colonel over the sound of the Lynx rotors starting up. They stood and braced themselves against the downwash as the helicopter quickly lifted and climbed away across the island.

'By the way Colonel, have you seen Jacky anywhere? She was last seen up near the house.'

'No but she can't be far away. Anyway, I've got some questions for these thugs. Let me know if the Lynx spots anything.'

Jon nodded as the Colonel walked menacingly towards the seated men. For some reason Jon felt uneasy. Where the hell was Jacky?

The little dinghy had reached the submarine and the unconscious girl was unceremoniously hauled up the side onto the casing before being lowered down the forward hatch. Tony followed her down. Paulo had gone straight up to the conning tower where Phil was waiting.

'No time to explain Phil. Get away and submerged as fast as you can. We were raided by two Royal Navy helicopters and a load of soldiers, so they must have a ship around here somewhere.'

'Shit, right get below Paulo I'll have us out of here as fast as I can.'

Paulo looked down the hatch, to the ladder leading down into the control room and hesitated.

Phil saw the look on his face. 'Look Paulo, get the fuck down there, if we don't dive soon we're going to get caught.'

Forcing himself to make the effort, Paulo started down the ladder. Phil ordered the engines to full speed and the helm hard over. In a few minutes they were in deep water and the submarine slipped silently below the surface. A minute later, the Lynx flew overhead, oblivious to presence of the submarine but not the presence of the dinghy that had been left floating behind as there hadn't been time to deflate it and take it on board.

Later that morning, with the sun well up, Jon was feeling distinctly uneasy. It had all gone too well he should have known there would be a fuckup at some stage. He was really worried about Jacky who seemed to have simply disappeared off the face of the planet. The Marines had searched the whole island and there was no sign of her or any more druggies. Then the Lynx had reported finding a small dinghy floating just off the southern point of the island. One of the RIBs had been tasked to go around and retrieve it and was approaching the beach where Jon was standing. The RIB slowly grounded on the shingle and Jon and two of the Marines waded out and pulled their salvage ashore. Just as Jon was about to start looking carefully there was a shout from further down the beach. The Colonel was waving at Jon, so he walked down to meet him.

'Look Jon, tracks going inland, something has disturbed the sand over there and it looks like a small boat has been beached here as well.'

Just then one of the Marines called over, 'More drugs Sir. They're buried but not very well. Jesus there's a lot here.'

They went over and sure enough the Marines were pulling package after package out of a shallow depression in the sand.

'Well some good news at least but it still looks like we missed the big fish and the senator's daughter,' said the Colonel gloomily. 'Where the hell did they all go?'

'Let's go and look at that dingy,' said Jon and they trooped back down the beach where the little inflatable was now resting having been pulled clear of the water.'

'Pretty standard inflatable,' observed Jon in a disappointed tone. 'Could have been lost off a yacht or just slipped its moorings. Bugger, I had hoped it might provide some sort of clue.'

'Hold on a second,' said the Colonel who had been rooting around inside on the rubber floor. 'Do you recognise this?'

A shiver of cold ran down Jon's spine. 'Oh shit, yes, that's a St Christopher, the Patron Saint of travellers and identical to the one Jacky always wore.'

Tony Jacobs was still in awe of where he was even after a day and half at sea. He still couldn't believe he was in a serviceable Second World War U-Boat but the evidence was literally all around him. The boat's skipper had explained how it had all come about but he was still having trouble accepting it was all true.  Once they had submerged and slipped away from Salt Island, Paulo had disappeared into the Captain's cabin and hadn't been seen again.  Phil, the skipper, had explained that Paulo was severely claustrophobic and he had managed to get him to take some strong sedatives until they returned to Paulo's residence in Columbia.

Swinging through the hatch into the control room he saw that Phil had just lowered the periscope.  'Evening Captain, are we well on our way now?'

Phil turned to him, the strain of the last few days showing in his face.  'Yes, we're well clear now and as it's dark we will be raising the snorkel soon so we can charge the batteries. Thank God Paulo got us some new ones, we would never have never got so far away on the old rubbish we'd been using.'

'Talking of Paulo, is he alright?'

'He should be, it'll take about two more days to get home and I reckon I can keep him knocked out for the whole time.'

'And what about the girl, do we know anything about her?'

Phil frowned.  'I'd rather hoped you would have known what that was all about.'

'No idea, we were just about to make a hasty departure when he spotted her.  He clearly recognised her from somewhere and was absolutely adamant that we should grab her but I've absolutely no idea why.  I guess we'll just have to wait and hopefully find out when we get to his place.'

## Chapter 23

The hot debrief was carried out in one of the rooms in the main house. Chester had come into the bay and anchored. Captain Peterson had come ashore to conduct it. He looked tired and worried.

'So, to sum up, we've definitely arrested fifteen drug runners and found a significant store of Cocaine. In addition, in the basement there is a dead body with a hand missing. The hand was found in a cardboard box. There are also a couple of families living in the outlying houses There is no sign of their Boss or the Senator's daughter and we think they must have escaped by boat.'

Jon was the first to answer. He was feeling sick inside. This was not how they planned it. 'Yes Sir, the Lynx continued on surface search for as long as it could. There were no boats out at sea within a radius that would have been possible in the time with even the fastest of escape boats. I've checked with the ship and there were no boat movements in the area that Chester's radars were covering, in the same time bracket. They must have gone round and hidden in one of the other islands. Can we ask the authorities to check all the marinas and harbours for boats entering between three and five in the morning? It's the only way they could have escaped and so we may still be able to find them.'

'Good idea Jon,' responded the Captain. He turned to the Ops officer. 'Derek can you get on that straight away please?'

The Ops officer nodded and left the room looking for a telephone.

The Captain turned to the Colonel. 'Joshua have you got anything out of the prisoners?'

The Colonel smiled grimly. 'Yes Sir, after we discovered that mutilated body, my people were just a little less particular in their questioning if you take my meaning, not that the bastards were that reluctant to talk in the first place. It seems the Boss man was the Tony Jacobs that intelligence reported. He's South African and comes with a fairly dreadful history. He was kicked out of the South African Police for being too violent and that's saying something for those bastards. He ended up here about six years ago working for the Delgardo clan. It seems there has been some sort of power struggle to take over the operation once Enrique Delgardo died. The dead man in the basement appears to have backed the wrong horse. There is now a new Boss but none of the men here claim to know his name. However, we do have a good description and should be able to identify him easily. Apparently, he was here last night but no one admits to knowing where he was when we came in.'

'So how on earth were they tipped off? We only made the decision on the target a few days ago,' the Captain asked in a worried tone.

'I don't think they were tipped off Sir,' responded Jon. 'Firstly if they had been, they would either have put a fight or more likely they would have buggered off taking all the evidence with them. According to the Doc, that guy in the basement was alive last night. They would hardly have been torturing people only hours before they knew a raid was coming in. And then there's the drugs on the beach. It looks to me like a delivery was being made and the two men went to collect it. They must have seen or heard the helicopters and gone back to see what was going on. For some reason they saw and kidnapped Jacky and then took off in the dinghy to be collected by the boat that was doing the delivery.'

The Captain looked thoughtful. 'I think you're right Jon, it was just bloody bad luck. What the hell am I going to tell the Senator?'

They didn't have long to wait. An operational report was sent back to London and Washington and the Senator was reported to be on the next plane. At the same time the local authorities were informed of the details and the prisoners handed over to them for trial. London had made it quite clear why they hadn't been informed in advance and whatever else was said it had the effect of ensuring that there were no protests made, at least in the hearing of any of Chester's people.

They handed over the crime scene to the local Police and Chester moved across and anchored in Road Town Bay to wait developments.

Jon and Brian were on the Flight Deck which was clear of aircraft. Both helicopters were secure in the hangar, being serviced.

'Sorry about this Jon but I don't see what else we could have done.'

Jon was leaning on a raised Flight Deck netting post, gazing gloomily over at a cruise liner tied up alongside the main town jetty. 'Maybe Brian but who said it was safe for her to wander around? It was only an hour after we went in, surely someone should have kept an eye on her?'

'That's easy to say now. Hindsight is such a wonderful thing. When we landed, she wanted to go straight over to the house. We managed to keep her with us for as long as we could but when one of the grunts came over and said the grounds were secured, there wasn't much I could do to stop her. In retrospect I should have gone with her but there didn't seem to be any danger. I'm really sorry.'

'Hey it's not your fault don't ever think that. She was, Oh Christ I mean is, a very headstrong female, bloody hell I should know. But I wonder what will happen now? Presumably they took her for a reason. I can't work out how they knew but they must have recognised her. Why else take the risk of kidnapping her, the place was crawling with Marines by then.'

'My guess is there will be some sort of ransom demand coming along fairly soon. If they did recognise her or subsequently find out who she is, they will have an enormous lever over the Senator.'

'I know, I've already thought of that and no doubt the Senator will have as well. Bloody hell, his whole initiative is buggered and right after the first operation. This isn't going to look good. By the way, have you heard any news on the Police or customs reporting any boat movements over the period?'

'Yes, Ops told me that nothing was reported or seen moving. That's not to say that they didn't sneak ashore somewhere but it looks like the trail is cold.'

'You know it just doesn't make sense. A boat or ship capable of coming up from Columbia has to be a fairly substantial vessel, where the hell could they hide it? How on earth could it just disappear? Why couldn't you find it in the Lynx?'

'I've no idea Jon but believe me we looked as hard as we could. I went and spoke to the ship's radar operators when I got back. One of them said he thought there might have been a small contact just off the beach for a while but as it was in the island's radar shadow, it was intermittent and disappeared shortly before we got there. If it had been a real contact we would definitely have seen something.'

'No, hang on that's weird. It must have been a real contact as something delivered those drugs and took the men and Jacky off. So why couldn't you see it from the air?'

Brian was about to reply, when Captain Peterson appeared on the Flight Deck. They both saluted.

'Good afternoon gentlemen, standby for fireworks. The Senator is due on board any minute. I've just been radioed to say he's on his way.'

They all looked over towards Road Town and sure enough a launch appeared around the bulk of the cruise liner heading their way. Just then, the Officer of the Day appeared and confirmed that they had just received another radio call and it was indeed the Senator on the approaching boat. It sped towards the side of the ship and quickly moored alongside the stairway that was always lowered down from Chester's starboard side when she was at anchor. The bulk of the Senator quickly mounted the steps and stepped on board. Although not strictly required to, the Captain and other officers saluted the man, an action which he studiously ignored.

'Captain Peterson, take me to your cabin and kindly explain why my daughter has been kidnapped due to the incompetence of your people.' He huffed, still getting his breath back from the climb and then seeing Jon. 'And you'd better come along as well.'

The Captain hand signalled to Jon to stay put and turned to the red faced man.

'Senator Musgrove, I think you are under some sort of misapprehension here. While I regret that your daughter got herself kidnapped.' He raised his hand to stop the Senator who was about to speak. 'I will explain that remark in due course. But I command here and you do not give orders to me or my officers, is that clear.'

Taken aback by the strength of the Captain's reply, the Senator simply nodded.

'Right Sir, now we understand each other, I would be more than grateful if you would accompany me to my cabin so we can talk and Lieutenant Commander Hunt and Colonel Jones will join us when I call for them.'

The two men went into the ship leaving Jon and Brian open mouthed on the deck.

'Bloody hell, I bet no one has spoken to that overbearing, stuck up man, like that for years,' said Jon with admiration in his tone.

'Yes, well I've observed that Father has a rather short fuse when someone tries to pull rank on him. Definitely round one to us I would say.'

Several hours later and the Senator and Colonel Jones were saluted off the ship by Jon and the Captain. The Senator had insisted that the Colonel accompany him back to Washington for more debriefs. The US Marines would stay on board until the ship docked in Florida in a few weeks time. The Captain turned around as soon as the men was safely on their way. 'Right Jon, get the command team up to my cabin in half an hour, we need to talk.'

When they had all arrived, the Captain looked around the assembled team. He had ensured they had all been given a drink.

'Gentlemen, as far as I'm concerned we conducted a successful operation, well done all of you,' and he raised his glass. 'But as you all know there was one problem and it has raised a much bigger one. Jon, the Colonel and I have just spent the last few hours with Senator Musgrove. He is obviously distraught about his daughter but now accepts that it was not any one's fault. He came here with the impression that it was but we disabused him of it quite quickly. The issue will be handled by the CIA and DEA but we may be called on again to help depending on what transpires. In the interim we are to continue with our role of aiding the Coast Guard and patrolling the West Indies. Colonel Jones is returning to Florida to continue with the Senator's programme although that may be in abeyance until we get some news about his daughter.'

'Sound to me like we're being sidelined,' observed Jon bitterly. 'I thought we were meant to be actively involved until we returned home.'

'Not so Jon,' responded the Captain firmly. 'There was always going to be a review once this first operation was over. We were never going to rush from one to the next and we still need to continue with our duties here. I'm terribly sorry about Jacky, we all know you were quite close but it's out of our hands now and you will just have to accept it.'

## Chapter 24

In the middle of the night, two and a half days later, the submarine docked safely. It was only a matter of minutes before the base was pumped out and Paulo could get out of that hateful coffin. His memory of the journey was hazy. He was grateful to Phil for giving him the sleeping pills or whatever they were but vowed to himself he would never go inside that terrible machine again. It might give him the best drug smuggling tool in the world but it scared him to death.

However, once he was standing on the casing, even though he was still inside the subterranean base, he felt his anxiety melt away. Still slightly woozy from the pills, he nevertheless felt a surge of joy which was quickly replaced by a simmering anger when he recalled why he had had to be on board in the first place. The first thing he needed was a bath and a drink, probably not in that order and then he was going to have a long think about what to do about that bastard Senator.

Tony Jacobs climbed out of the hatch behind him and looked around in awe. 'Jesus Paulo what a place, what a fantastic facility. Hey, those Krauts really knew how to build to last.'

Paulo shrugged, no longer impressed by the concrete cavern around him. 'Right Tony, you, me and Phil need to talk but not just now. I'm going up to my place to have a bath and some real sleep. It's just gone midnight so I'll see you at lunchtime. Get Phil to look after you, he has a spare room in his place.'

'Sure thing Boss but what do we do with the girl?'

Paulo had completely forgotten about her but the memory returned with a rush. He smiled, 'Ah yes the girl, my secret weapon. Get Phil to tell Manuel to take her to the cellar. He will know what to do.' He left Tony standing on the submarine casing and made his way slightly unsteadily over the gangplank and up into the welcoming open darkness of a tropical night. When he got to his bedroom, despite all his good intentions, he almost fell on his bed and was only just able to shrug off his clothes before he was deeply asleep.

He woke some indeterminate time later, with the sun streaming through the windows. He realised that he had forgotten to draw the curtains. For a few sleep addled seconds he couldn't remember why he was there and then it all came back in a rush. Unusually, he discovered he had an enormous erection and then also remembered why. Slipping out of bed he headed for the bathroom, a sense of delicious anticipation filling his mind. As soon as he was dressed, he headed downstairs shouting for coffee and breakfast. He called for Manuel while he was sipping his first cup. When the hulking presence arrived, he beckoned him over to the table.

'Did you put the girl in the cellar last night Manuel?'

'Yes Paulo, she was fine.'

'Good and did she fight you?'

'Just a bit but she's not very strong. I kept an eye on her on the camera for a while and she soon went to sleep. She's awake now, just sitting on her bed.'

'Good, now here is what I want you to do,' and he gave Manuel explicit instructions before continuing on with his leisurely breakfast. It was still several hours to noon, so he had plenty of time for what he had in mind. He gave Manuel a good ten minutes, it would be all he would need. He had done this sort of things many times before. Then wiping his lips with a napkin he got up from the table and went to the back of the main hallway and opened the disguised door. Behind it was a bare concrete staircase that led down to his play area; to the soundproofed basement. The little lobby room outside the cell door was empty which meant that Manuel had done his job and left the place to him. He really didn't want to be disturbed. Paulo looked over at the remote TV monitor and looked inside the room. Excellent, this was going to be so much fun.

Paulo was sure she knew where she was and who held her captive after several days on the submarine. He opened the door as quietly as he could but it was clear the girl had detected his presence, either by the noise or draft of air and she turned her head questioningly towards him. It wouldn't help her though, she had been expertly blindfolded. Nevertheless she continued to turn her head this way and that, trying to understand what was going on. She would probably have called out but the gag in her mouth stifled any attempts she might make to talk. Her hands were bound together and tied above her head to a hook attached to the ceiling. Her legs were pulled wide apart by two ropes secured to hooks on the ground at floor level. She started to struggle against her bonds to absolutely no effect. She was completely naked.

Paulo walked all around her enjoying the sight, enjoying the moment of anticipation. Not only would she be the tool for getting that damned Senator off his back but she was stunningly beautiful and so would be the tool for providing his satisfaction, something he had been missing for such a long time. Her figure was a delight, just what he liked in a woman. She was slim with small breasts and a light downy triangle of hair between her legs. Her buttocks had the firmness of someone who took regular exercise and her long tanned legs only confirmed this.

He walked up behind her and started running his hands up and down her slim sexy body. Her skin was smooth. She flinched when he first made contact and then became rigid as his hands explored her buttocks and private places. He slapped one buttock hard and she gasped. One hand went up to cup her left breast, as the other one untied her gag. He whispered in her ear, 'we are going to have such fun my darling, as long as you do everything you are told, as long as you perform as I order.'

She hissed back at him as she started to struggle. 'Just try you bastard, I'll never give in.'

He laughed, as he savagely squeezed and twisted one nipple. 'Oh yes you will, you always do.'

She screamed at the pain and then slumped against him in surrender. 'Paulo you bastard are you going to fuck me or just stand there talking about it.'

Phil and Tony were sitting on the veranda wondering where Paulo had got to, when he walked in accompanied by the girl from the beach. She looked fresh and beautiful and had a dreamy look. Paulo grinned at the surprise on their faces.

'Gentlemen, let me introduce you to Jacky Musgrove, the daughter of Senator Musgrove the Third. Believe it or not, she's my long term girlfriend and major source of information about what her moronic father has been up to for the last few years.'

The two men looked stunned for a moment and then Phil, ever the Englishman, rose and took her hand smiling. 'I did wonder why Paulo wanted you with him, now I know why.'

Tony belatedly rose as well and also took her hand and then they all seated themselves.

'Sorry for not explaining things on the island Tony,' said Paulo. 'But there really wasn't time and I had to make a split second decision. I realised that with the raid, Jacky's usefulness as an information source was now less valuable and her presence here will allow me to put pressure on the Senator, which is more important now. Oh and I get my girlfriend back. And of course, I was in no state to explain anything more on the trip here.'

'Er, if you don't mind me asking Paulo,' questioned Phil. 'But how one earth did you two meet and why is such a man's daughter working for you?'

Jacky answered with a grim smile. 'You have to understand my father. He blames drugs for the death of my mother, whereas in reality it was his treatment of her and me for that matter, that was the problem. In his sick twisted world, God is on his side and so he can do whatever he likes and that included beating my mother and assaulting me.' This was all said with and almost sad, wistful air. 'It all started when I was eight, he would come to my room. I didn't understand what he was doing then but I soon learned, as did my mother shortly afterwards. Father's solution to keeping her in line, was to hit her. She turned to drugs as the only way out. She died several years later of an overdose. When father came to my room the day of her funeral and tried to molest me again, I kicked him in the balls and ran away. I was only fourteen. We lived in LA in those days and I was taken in by one of the street gangs, you can imagine why but I didn't care and then Paulo rescued me. One day he was dealing with my gang and saw what had been done to me and took me away. Some of the gang didn't like that but that was their problem.' She looked up at Paulo with adoring eyes.

'Yes, well, I saw something in her right from the first moment,' admitted Paulo. 'I took care of her and got her well again. Things were difficult for me back in those days, it was hardly the safest profession in the world, so I convinced her she should go back to her father. It was the only way she could get the education she so clearly wanted and also a way of her taking revenge. We meet when we can and now maybe we can stay together.' He reached out and squeezed her hand.

'So, the good Senator is a wife beater, incestful child rapist and paedophile amongst other things,' said Tony leaning back in his chair.

Jacky smiled sadly again. 'He doesn't see it that way. As I said, he prays to the Lord for forgiveness and then when he's received it, he feels free to do what he wants all over again. When I went back to him I made it very clear what would happen if he tried anything and he believed me, probably because of the knife I was holding against his balls at the time. He has amazing powers of self denial, within the day he acted as though nothing had ever happened. I've been working for him and my revenge ever since. You won't find anything about any of this in the public domain. He's very clever at covering his tracks but once I was on the inside things were much easier for me. Oh and I'm sorry about not warning you about the raid on Salt Island but the decision was only taken once we were at sea so I had no way of contacting Paulo.'

'Alright, that's enough Jacky. Now everyone, let's eat and just relax a little,' said Paulo as one of the maids brought in a buffet lunch and set it up on the table next to them along with several bottles of wine. 'We have a lot discuss.'

They talked all afternoon. Jacky updated them on the raid and how it had come about. She also explained why it was a Royal Navy frigate that had actually conducted the operation. However, she decided to keep her counsel about her relationship with the ship's Flight Commander. That was information that no one else needed to know. Once she had finished, they all sat back for a moment to consider her words.

Paulo took the time to regard his colleagues. He realised he hadn't felt so energised in years. Here was his mad English submarine Captain, a ruthless and very effective newcomer and his beautiful and incredibly brave girlfriend. Maybe it was the booze or the after effects of the tranquilisers but he suddenly felt invincible. With a team like this they could take over the world. This vague thought suddenly crystallised. He knew exactly what they needed to do.

'Right my friends, we're not going to let this sick Senator win. Jacky you are now my hostage and we are going to ransom you. How does that sound?'

She laughed. 'As long as you don't really intend to any such thing.'

'Never my love, I'm not letting you go ever again,' and he reached over and gave her hand a reassuring squeeze. 'However, we need to convince the bastard that we're not kidding. Then we can get him to shift focus onto the other cartels. Hell, we can even help him with intelligence. Within the year we could be the only operation in the country.

Phil broke in, 'There's only one problem.'

They all looked blankly at him. 'He will almost certainly know who it was on the island and therefore who took Jacky and so his first knee jerk reaction will be to come here and try to rescue her. Even if he's not that stupid it will make us far too visible. However, I remember a story from the Second World War that we could adapt. Jacky will have to become Mincemeat.'

## Chapter 25

The Senator stared moodily out of his office window at the stop-start Washington traffic below him. Taxis and commuters vied for each precious inch of tarmac or waited impatiently at traffic lights. He saw none of it. His little girl was gone and no one seemed to be able to work out where she was or whether she was even alive. With a sigh, he went and sat back behind his desk and picked up the report that had just come through and started reading it again. It was a composite of Colonel Jones's work, DEA intelligence and extra input from the CIA. The one good thing that had come out if it was that they had identified their protagonist. Paulo Mandero was known to the CIA and DEA and strangely enough also the FBI. He had first appeared on the Police and FBI radar in the US as a teenager and had operated out of Los Angeles for several years. For someone to survive in the gang culture of the time, spoke volumes for his capabilities, especially as it seemed he never joined any of them but managed to act as a middleman and drug supplier without antagonising anyone. He then disappeared and only surfaced years later, as a rich Columbian businessman, except that his business was the same as it had been in the US. It was conjecture that his experience on the streets of LA had been the education he needed to succeed in his home country. There was no direct intelligence of how he had climbed to the top but his presence at Salt Island was a clear indication of how widespread his influence had become. That he had been able to take over someone else's operation so quickly and with a minimum of fuss was worrying and said a great deal about his capabilities; almost as much as the presence of the corpse in the cellar spoke about his business methods.

The Senator stared at the grainy black and white photograph with his brow furrowed. He had seen that face before, he was sure of it although no matter how he tried he couldn't remember where or when. Of course, the obvious assumption now was that Jacky had been taken by the man to Columbia. The only problem with that theory was that none of the so called experts could account for how he had managed to get away from the BVIs in the first place. However, the first recommendation of the report was that the DEA would put a man in place on the ground to see if he could find out if Mr Mandero had returned and whether he had any uninvited guests. Should that be the case and in the absence of any sort of ransom demand, the Senator would be strongly supporting the second recommendation that an all out raid be mounted as soon as possible.

His thoughts were interrupted by the telephone. He picked up the receiver and listened intently. As the conversation continued he went white and started trembling.

'You sure, it's definitely her?'

The voice on the other end answered. 'No Sir we can't be sure, she's been in the water for several days and at least one shark has had a go at her. I'm so sorry, we don't even have enough remains to check dental records. I know it's going to be difficult but could you fly out here and help with the identification?'

He sat back in shock. He could barely hold the receiver. 'Yes of course, where should I come to?'

'Tortola Sir, she's in the morgue at Road Town.'

'I'll be there as soon as I can get a flight.'

The next day he stood before the grisly remains of a young girl. When they pulled back the covering sheet, he almost threw up there and then. With an enormous degree of self control, managed to force himself to remain calm.

'What about the clothing?' he asked the policeman who accompanied him.

'An officer from HMS Chester came over and confirmed that they are the clothes she was wearing on the night she disappeared. Can you confirm that the jewellery is hers?'

'Yes, that's her ring and that's the bracelet I gave her as a present last year. But more than that, that birthmark on the ankle is hers.'

The policeman had to look very carefully to where the Senator was pointing. Then he could see the small blemish just above the girl's foot.

'When she was little, it was bigger and she was dreadfully embarrassed about it. But anyway it's definitely her,' and he gave a heartfelt sob, as the tears finally started to flow.

The policeman covered the body with the sheet and escorted the devastated man out into the main building.

'Have we any idea what happened?' he asked shakily as they sat down outside for a moment.

'Well Sir, the Coroner could find no sign of any damage other than that caused by fish. There was no sign of physical violence or drugs for that matter. If it wasn't for the manner in which she disappeared then the Coroner would have given a verdict of accidental death. In the circumstances, he has left the verdict open for the moment.'

A wave of pure rage overcame the Senator. 'Open verdict my ass, I know who's responsible for this and I'm in a position to do something about it. The Lord will give me the strength to overcome this man. The Lord will stand by me in my vengeance.'

A few hours later he was sitting in his hotel room, a half empty bottle of whisky on the table beside him. Despite the amount he had drunk, he still felt clear headed. First his wife and now his daughter. Why was the Lord testing him like this? What had he ever done to be treated in this way?

There was a discrete knock on the door. He ignored it. The knock was louder, more insistent this time.

'OK, I'm coming.' He got to his feet unsteadily, realising that maybe the booze was having an effect after all. He pulled the door open angrily, expecting some flunky from the hotel to be there but the corridor was empty. Frowning, he looked up and down the hallway but there was no sign of anyone. He was just about to slam the door in disgust when he looked down and saw a VHS tape. Holding onto to the door frame for support he reached down and picked it up. On the front was a label with writing in an oh so familiar hand writing. 'For the attention of Senator Musgrove the Paedophile' were the words written on it in his daughter's hand. He suddenly felt stone cold sober. With a final look around, this time to make sure no one had seen him retrieve the tape, he shut the door and shakily made his way over to the television set which had a VCR below it.

With unsteady hands he managed to insert the tape and turn on the TV. He pulled a chair up and waited for the static to clear.

The quality wasn't good but that hardly mattered. The first face to appear was the smiling, smirking visage of that bastard Mandero.

'Hey Senator, good day, I hope you're having a really great time identifying the grisly remains of your beloved daughter.' He laughed.

The Senator almost put his fist through the screen at the leering face.

Mandero continued, unknowingly. 'Well I just thought I'd let you know that Jacky isn't really dead. How about that? Fooled you eh? But get this you slimy bastard, she's not coming back to you, she's with me now, aren't you darling?'

The camera moved sideways and panned back, showing a smiling, relaxed Jacky in a bikini besides a large swimming pool. 'Yes my love I'm definitely with you now. Hey Dad, betya thought I was really eaten by sharks? But look at this place, it's just like when we and Mom were on holiday. You remember I'm sure, you would visit me at night and after sodomising me would then go and beat the hell out of mum just in case she had heard what you'd been doing.' There was no trace of a smile on her face as she spat out the words. 'You know I should be sorry for putting you through such a trauma but hey that was just the start of my revenge, you fucking, wife beating, rapist. Oh and just to make sure you know this isn't some kind of put up job by Paulo, have a look at this.' She held up a copy of the New York Times. 'Look at the date daddy, I'm sure you can work out this is long after I'm supposed to have died.'

The Senator thought he had gone through every emotion possible in the last twenty four hours. He was finding out that wasn't true. Jacky was alive but any elation he should have felt was overlaid by an even greater dread.

Jacky continued. 'So why are we sending you this little love message father dearest? Well let's start with the evidence. While you thought I was working for you as your dutiful little daughter, I was in fact compiling a dossier of shit on you. Not only have I fully documented all the things you did to me and my mother but I had you followed. I have photographs and tapes of your activities with all those other little girls and boys. So basically you're totally screwed. Great isn't it!' and she smiled widely at the camera. 'I reckon there is enough evidence to have you put in prison for life and as some of the States you fornicated in have the death penalty for your crimes I might just be able to get you executed. How cool is that?' Her face suddenly clouded over. 'But you bastard, my lover Paulo here, has talked me into maybe being a little lenient with you. So maybe you should listen to what he has to say. So I'll go now. Oh and one final thing. Your Lord can't save you now. I hope you rot in hell.'

Paulo's leering face replaced Jacky's again and started talking. He heard the words and understood their meaning but felt sick to his heart as the damned man continued with his instructions. He knew he had no choice, it was either this or a complete loss of all he had worked for followed by disgrace and incarceration. It was very clear what Mandero was trying to achieve. But as he continued to speak the Senator realised he could still do good work, he would be able to get at some of the drug smuggling bastards and maybe when the time was right, he would be able to work out a way of wreaking revenge on this maniac and getting his daughter back.

'Oh and one final thing,' Paulo said. 'Just in case you're thinking that once we have moved on a bit then you can turn your attention on me. Copies of this tape and Jacky's dossier are distributed around the world in secure deposits with lawyers. All have the same instructions, which are to release the information to the world, should I or Jacky be reported dead or we fail to keep in touch with them on a routine basis. You will excuse me if I don't tell you what that is. Now one final instruction, if you accept my terms, you must ring this number within the next hour and just say the word 'Jacky' to the man who answers.' He held up a piece of paper with a local telephone number on it. 'If you don't, Jacky will get her wish and all the lovely stories of your perversions will be on the front pages of all the world's papers within hours.' The screen went blank.

For several minutes the Senator stared blankly at the wall. He reached for the whiskey bottle and without bothering to pour any into the glass, took an enormous gulp of the fiery liquid. He might as well have been drinking water. He reached for the phone and dialled.

'Jacky,' was all he said.

## Chapter 26

The mourners all stood around the coffin as it was lowered into the freshly dug grave. Jon and Joshua Jones stood next to each other, both in full dress uniform. Other officers and men from Chester, the Coast Guard and Marines stood behind them. Once the pastor had finished, a subdued Senator Musgrove threw in a trowel of earth and passed it to Jon who repeated the action. There was a gravestone next to the new one bearing the name of Jacky's mother. All too soon they were all solemnly walking away to the cars parked at the entrance to the cemetery.

Jon was still coming to terms with the fact that the vibrant, manic girl, he thought he might have been falling in love with, was dead. What was worse, was that he felt an enormous amount of guilt. Although he knew he hadn't been involved in the decision to let her come ashore and hadn't even seen her once she had arrived at the site, he couldn't shake off the feeling that he should have done something different. That he could have prevented the whole bloody tragedy.

'Come on mate, shake yourself out if it.' Brian looked at his old friend with sympathy. 'Life goes on, whether you like it or not.'

'I know but I still don't understand what happened. How she disappeared and why she died. People are even saying that it could have been nothing to do with the two druggies getting away. Do you believe that?'

'For what it's worth, absolutely not but let's face it we'll probably never know, unless we can catch this Mandero bastard of course.'

They reached the cars and got into one which would take them to the reception that the Senator had arranged at a local hotel.

The Colonel turned to Jon as they all sat down. 'We'll need to work on a plan of action once the dust settles Jon. You guys are going to be in the area for quite a while yet, who knows, maybe we can get the bastards before you head home.'

The wake was a drab affair. People were in no mood for a party and the air of frustration and anger was palpable. Jacky's relatives were still unsure of the full story as the whole operation had been classified. The military were in no doubt about who was to blame. Jacky had been popular with everyone and everyone wanted do something about what had happened to her.

Brian intercepted Jon as he was about to sink yet another large glass of beer. 'Come on old son that won't solve anything.'

'Oh yeah, who says? It certainly won't do any harm.'

'If you think I'm going to take you back to the ship pissed as a fart, in full uniform you've got another thing coming.'

'Who said I needed your help. I can look after myself you know.'

Just then the Senator came over to talk them. 'Gentlemen, thank you for coming, it means a lot.'

'She meant a lot to me Sir, as I think you know,' replied Jon. 'When are we going to go after those bastards?'

The Senator put his hand on Jon's shoulder. 'All in the Lords time son. Give it a couple of days and we'll get together to see what needs to be done.'

Two hours later, Brian managed to get Jon back to the ship. In true naval fashion despite the amount of beer he had imbibed, as soon as Jon reached the bottom of the gangway, he managed to straighten himself and walk steadily up, until he smartly saluted the White Ensign at the ship's stern. He then made his way to his cabin where he fell flat on his face on his bunk. Brian carefully removed his jacket and left him to sleep it off.

True to his word, two days later, a conference was called. Members of the Coast Guard, Marines, DEA and Royal Navy were once again in the conference room at Opa Locka. This time the Senator was present although he declined to take a front row role. Glen Thomas once again opened the debate. The atmosphere was tense. Jon was surprised that no blame seemed to be coming their way. Indeed, in the pre-conference conversations, there seemed to be nothing but praise for the way the initial raid had been conducted. Blame seemed to be reserved for Mr Paulo Mandero. No one believed for a moment that he wasn't responsible for the death of Jacky Musgrove. Retribution was top of the agenda.

It was therefore to great consternation that the DEA representative stood up after Glen's introduction and stated that he would not be their target.

'Gentlemen, I know how we all feel about recent events but we mustn't take our eye off the end game of our endeavours. We have a mandate to do all in our power to cripple the drug trade in the Caribbean. Now, since the last extremely successful operation courtesy of our Royal Navy team members, it seems we've kicked over an ants nest. Although it appears Mr Mandero had taken over the Salt Island operation, not everyone was happy with the outcome. Two brothers, Phillipe and Sebastian Marcello were apparently also lining up to take over that particular outlet. The corpse in the cellar appears to have been one of their men. We now have intelligence that the two brothers are particularly unhappy about the whole situation and are about to try something rash. It would appear they are getting somewhat desperate and are about to undertake a major run into the Gulf. They can make the stuff but are having trouble getting enough into the US to make a decent profit. They are going for a big drop with a major diversion to blind side us. The problem for them is we know about it and will be waiting. We will need to take that end out at the same time as we go in and cut off the source. Any questions so far?'

Jon couldn't contain himself. 'Yes, where's this intelligence come from? How come we know all this now? Surely, if it was the guy in the basement then he was already dead before we got to Salt Island?'

'I'm sorry but our sources need to be protected, Lieutenant Commander. You will just have to go with the flow here.'

Jon sat back but was far from satisfied.

To continue, I will now outline what we know is planned and then we can discuss resource allocation.'

Four days later and Jon was back in the air, in Eric the Lynx. The sheer joy of flying again was slowly driving away the blues that had been haunting him ever since Jacky went missing. He knew that he had been bad company over that time. He was aware that his team had made every effort to keep out of his way and that his behaviour had been unreasonable but hell, he had good reason, didn't he?

Looking out over the slowly nodding nose of the Lynx, at the deep blue sea and light blue sky, he at last felt a quickening of spirit. This noisy, vibrating, machine was his home as much as anything else and it was slowly blowing away the blues. It was also good that Brian was sitting next to him. As a team they had been operating together for over five years and Jon knew there was no one else in the world he would rather trust in an aircraft or anywhere else for that matter.

'You back with the human race now?' Brian asked, having seen the smile on Jon's face at last. It had been a long time coming.

'Shit have I been that bad? Sorry but the last few weeks have been a bastard.'

'Yes we all know that and don't worry, we all understand. But it's about time we had the old Jon back. The lads haven't had decent run ashore for ages.'

Jon snorted in derision. 'They don't need me for that. They can misbehave all on their own I've seen it often enough.'

'Fair point but having the Boss around gives them the excuse that it wasn't all their fault.'

They both laughed knowing there was a large amount of truth in the remark.

'Anyway,' said Brian. 'We're just about on our patrol line, Nellie is about fifty miles to the north and that bit over there is the coast of Florida. So we start looking.'

'Have we any detailed idea what sort of ship we're looking for?'

'The intelligence wasn't that hot but they seem to think it will be a fair size and it will be obvious what she's up to.'

'What about the Coast Guard? Did they say they could spare any aircraft for us?'

'No, apparently all the assets they've got are on standby for the Gulf operation. The one patrol aircraft they thought they might be able to spare is still tits up, waiting spares.'

Jon grunted. 'Just the good old Brits to hold the thin blue line again. Well we'll just have to catch the bastard.'

'Yes but we've got to make it look like we've taken the bait as well, otherwise they could call off the Gulf landing.'

'Yes, well I'm not sure how we actually do that but let's find the bugger first.'

The next hour was spent patrolling at six thousand feet while they investigated the few radar contacts they had. Most were small yachts or pleasure craft and even from height it was clear they weren't their quarry.

Suddenly Nellie came on the radio. 'Hey guys, we've got a contact out to the east, it's more in your area than ours, it's in your zero eight five about forty miles.'

Brian acknowledged the call and Jon turned to head east. 'That's the problem with bloody sector radars,' muttered Brian, 'It's so easy to miss something. The Sea King can see all round, we can only look over about a hundred and sixty degrees. Anyway I've got him, your heading's good Jon he's about thirty miles away.'

It didn't take long for them to spot it. 'Looks like an old tramp steamer or large fishing boat. It's in bloody awful condition though,' Jon observed. 'Mind you it's just the sort of thing you would use for an expendable, one way trip.'

They descended down to four hundred feet and Brian carefully studied the ship through his gyro stabilised monocular. With a note of excitement in his voice he told Jon to go closer. 'I can see two guys staring at us and the rear of the deck is covered in what looks like hay bales. I just hope the big US Coast Guard stickers we've put over the Royal Navy lettering on the tail convince them they're in the shit.'

'Well, they're hardly going to know the ins and outs of US military aircraft and the stickers are pretty bloody big. Hey they're taking the bait, here we go.'

As Jon flew even closer, the men on the ship started ditching the bales over the side. Soon her wake was littered with a trail of the square, light brown, bales.

'You know those are apparently made of real marijuana. God know how much they're worth and all just as a diversion.'

'Yes well, they're now under the impression that we've caught them, which of course we have. We can't monitor all the radio bands but I'll bet a month's pay that someone is on that ship is on the HF saying that they've been caught as they had planned. Double bluffs are just so much fun.'

'Right Brian, call in Nellie and let's arrest these dastardly drug smugglers and tell Opa Locka that it looks like the bait has been taken by us gullible Coast Guard types.'

## Chapter 27

Paulo Mandero whooped with delight. The news had just come in that the Marcello brothers were no longer in business. The Senator had done his job with the intelligence that Paulo had supplied and not only had their last run into Florida been intercepted but it seemed that their compound out in the hills had been destroyed. No one seemed to know how or even who had done it but apparently the place was a total wreck and the brothers had disappeared off the face of the earth. Of course Paulo knew they would surface soon but strangely it would be in the United States where they would be in custody awaiting trial for drug smuggling. The raid had been so silent that even the locals only knew something was going on when the explosions started. Damn those Marines were good, he chuckled inwardly. With his hold over the Senator, there was no reason why all his opposition shouldn't be eliminated soon and then he would have the field clear.

He also reflected that Phil's idea for Jacky had been perfect. 'Operation Mincemeat' had been a clever plan used by the British in the Second World War to deceive the Nazis into thinking that there would be an invasion of Greece rather than Sicily which was where the invasion was really planned for. They had done it by dumping a dead body at sea close to the shore, where the tides would wash it onto the beach. They dressed the body as a British officer on courier duty who had clearly been in an aircraft that had crashed. He had certain cleverly faked classified letters in his briefcase. The body was in fact that of a tramp who had died earlier but there was enough convincing evidence to fool the Germans. So it had been with Jacky; they had her clothes and jewellery and once she volunteered that she had a small birthmark, then getting a tattooist to replicate it had been easy. Finding a suitable body hadn't been that hard either. A tour of some of the brothels in the local area had turned up a girl of suitable build and colouration. She had been invited up to Paulo's house and very soon made a very convincing corpse. The body was kept on ice and Phil had run it up to the BVI's in the motoryacht. They had even got one of their contacts to ensure it was discovered in the right place commensurate with the tides in the area. The Senator had been fooled and once his identification had been provided no one looked any further.

Jacky had then taken great delight in helping create the video for her father. It had seemed to have taken a great weight off her chest. She had been actively participating in all their plans for the future, especially when it was agreed that however far they managed to get, at some time in the future, the dossier they had compiled on her father would be released. Paulo realised, not for the first time, just how deep down her hatred burned.

'Good news then?' asked Jacky as she plonked herself down on the chair next to Paulo on the veranda overlooking the pool.

'Oh yes, the plan is working to perfection my dear,' and he went on to explain the contents of the telephone call he had just received.

'Good that's a large chunk of the opposition taken care of and what's even better, we have a record of you supplying the information to my father which can go into the dossier along with all the other filth.'

Paulo laughed. 'Yes and now we need to decide what to do next.' The only serious opposition left for us is Dario and Adolpho. They will be much more difficult for our friends in the US to take out. But I'm inclined to go for that bastard Dario he is far too clever and we don't want him working out what's really going on. I think a call to your Father is in order my dear.'

'Good and can I do it this time?'

Paulo smiled at her. 'We must wait a few days and think carefully about what to tell him but yes why not. You will have to pay a price though. As punishment, I want you to go down to the cellar and prepare yourself.'

'Yes Paulo,' she replied suddenly contrite but her expression couldn't hide the light of excitement in her eyes.

Senator Musgrove the Third was being torn apart. Having to pretend to bury his daughter, who he knew full well was alive was bad enough but what was far worse was having to take orders from that bastard Mandero. The only solace he had was that the raid to take out the Marcello's had been an outstanding success. The two brothers had been arrested in Columbia and taken to the US under the noses of the Columbian government. The information coming from the people arrested running the Cocaine into the Gulf, mistakenly under the impression that the Coast Guard were busy off the Florida Coast retrieving marijuana bales, had provided more than enough information to make sure the brothers would go to prison for a very long time. The problem now, was that at some time, probably fairly soon, the telephone was going to ring again and he knew he would have to do everything he was told.

His mind whirled with impossible ideas of revenge and deliverance but every time he thought he had found a way out, Jacky's words brought him back to earth. He knew his daughter, knew how thorough she was. If she said she had placed dossiers with various lawyers, then she had done exactly that and even if she had only half the evidence she said she had it would be more than enough to destroy him. If only he could talk to her face to face, he felt sure he could gain her forgiveness. Surely she would understand in the light of the Lord? Understand and forgive? But he couldn't admit to anyone that she was alive and so try to arrange to rescue her. Then like a blinding light he realised that was exactly what he could do. He sat down heavily in his office chair as the idea pulsed through his brain. He would have to think this through very carefully, safeguards would be needed but yes, it could work.

Just then the phone rang. It was late in the evening and his secretary had long gone home. Still shaking with the revelation of his idea, he lifted the receiver. When he heard the voice his blood ran cold.

'Hello dearest father, it's your dead daughter speaking.'

He started to say something but she cut him off. 'Don't you dare speak you bastard, just get a pen and write down what I'm about to tell you.'

Mutely he obeyed. She talked for about five minutes and before he could say any of the things he'd rehearsed in case she rang, she cut off the call, leaving him staring despondently at the dead receiver in his hand.

He looked at his notes, there was more than enough here for him to get his team to conduct another raid. It looked like it would be more difficult than the first one but no one ever expected this was going to be easy. He started to smile. With this information his idea could work. He could get her back and talk to her, beg her forgiveness and everything would be right with the world.

An hour later he felt he had covered all the angles. The deal he would be offering would be just too good to turn down he felt sure of that. He reached into his desk and took out the DEA digest that contained all the general information on the Columbian cartels. Yes, there were telephone numbers there, good. He found the right one and dialled. The phone rang for only a couple of rings before it was answered. He explained who he wanted to talk to and the phone went quiet for a minute before a new voice answered.

'Who is this? How did you get this number?'

Mr Adolpho Rivera this is Senator Musgrove, I'm sure you've heard of me, we need to talk.'

## Chapter 28

Roars of approval and beer fuelled cheering echoed around the bar. Mike Hazlewood was emulating his namesake from the sixties, although this time it wasn't on a motorbike but a 'cow on a stick' as one wag had named it. The bucking bull machine was the centre of attention for the large Wild West theme bar that the Flight team had descended on for a night of relaxation. That said, the number of the Flight who had attempted to stay on the back of the swinging, bucking machine and the amount of beer consumed clearly indicated that quiet relaxation wasn't really on the agenda.

'Come on Mike,' yelled Brian. 'Another ten seconds and it's free beer for the night.'

As if the infernal machine had heard the encouragement, or more likely its programming was deliberately ramped up to ensure free beer was not often won, it spun even faster and threw the hapless Observer onto the surrounding padding. Roars of disapproval then sounded as Mike sheepishly climbed to his feet.

'Fucking stupid thing,' he muttered as a large glass of beer was thrust into his hand. He took a giant swig and then wiped the sweat from his face with a glassy smile.

Brian turned to Jon with a savage grin. 'Your turn next Jon, everyone else has had a go.'

'Please don't take this the wrong way but fuck off Brian and actually I seem to recall that you haven't been on the sodding thing yet either.'

The argument was about to get a lot hotter with the rest of the Flight joining, in when the door opened and Jon spotted Joshua coming in.

'Thank buggery for that,' he muttered under his breath. 'Hey Joshua over here.' And he waved to catch the Colonels attention.

'Hey guys, having fun?' Joshua asked as he joined the throng. 'Anyone stayed on that thing long enough for the beer?'

Derisive comments and a few expletives were his answer.

'Right then, I guess a real Texan needs to show you weak wristed limeys how it's done.' And so saying, he put his dollar in the machine and climbed on.

The bull started up and the Colonel stayed on. It bucked and spun and the Colonel stayed on. It pitched harder, backwards and forwards and he just rode with it one hand swinging in the air above his head the other gripping the leather ring around its neck. It entered its final enraged bucking and he just gripped harder and flexed with it. The bell rang and the machine came to a stop to cheers from the boys. Climbing off to slaps on the back and universal acclaim, he waved over to the unhappy looking barman and indicated where the free beer needed to be served. Taking a large glass himself he went over to Jon and Brian.

'We need a quick chat guys, the full brief is tomorrow but there are a couple of things we need to go over if you don't mind.'

They retired to a dark corner of the bar while the rest of the Flight, inspired by Joshua's success, were lining up to try again.

He shook his head. 'If you can't do it sober you, sure as hell can't do it after a sinking a load of beer and I'm guessing your lot have a head start on me.'

'Not wrong there Joshua,' Brian responded. 'But let me guess you've done that before.'

He laughed. 'You're looking at the Orange County Under Seventeen Rodeo Champion, so I guess I maybe had a small advantage. Right let's have a quick chat and we can rejoin the party. I feel the need to cut loose.'

'So, what is it that can't wait Joshua?' asked Jon.

'It's simple. As far as I'm concerned you guys have done great. The clusterfuck at Salt Island was nothing to do with you and the whole of the second operation went as advertised. We got in and out with the two brothers, you guys responded to the diversion and the Coast Guard got the real bad guys. However, there are some assholes muttering that we shouldn't include you on the next op and I really think you will want to be there.'

'Who's muttering?' asked Brian

'Sorry I can't say. Now did the stuff we talked about come over from England and is it working?'

'What, oh yes, we got it a few days ago and it all checks out,' replied Jon.

'Good I'm going to stick my neck out tomorrow and I really need that stuff to work OK?'

'It will, we've used it before as you and I've discussed but enough of that where are we going this time? Who's the target? Jon asked.

'Mandero, Paulo Mandero, we're going to get the bastard who killed Jacky.'

They talked for a few more minutes, agreed a couple of points and then rejoined the party.

An hour later and there were still a few members of the Flight who fancied their chances on the cow but enthusiasm was waning. The Colonel was making heroic efforts to catch up with everyone in the beer consumption stakes and the mood was definitely moving on to consider where to go next. Jon was propping up the bar with Brian and the twins when there was a tap on his shoulder. He turned and saw a pretty little auburn haired girl looking at him. She had the bluest eyes he had ever seen.

'Yes, can I help?' he asked slightly puzzled.

'Are you Jon Hunt, who used to be Jacky Musgrove's boyfriend? Your ship told me you might be here.'

'Well sort of, we only knew each other a short while, I assume you know what happened? And you are?'

'Oh sorry, my name is Jenny, Jenny Harrison,' she replied looking sad. 'Look I shared an apartment with Jacky for several years and we always kept in touch. I need to talk to you, can we go somewhere quieter?'

Jon looked around. He didn't really want to leave his team but something in the girls pleading eyes convinced him he needed to hear what she had to say.

'Alright, where do you suggest?'

'There's a diner just over the other side of the car park, can we go there?'

'OK, hang on,' and turning to his friend, 'Brian mate, duty calls I need to have a quiet chat with this young lady. I'll try to catch up with you alright? I assume you'll all be misbehaving in the Pink Pussy Cat club later.'

Brian snorted. 'Yes quite probably but I'll bet we don't see you.'

'No, this is something else. See you later. Alright Jenny, lead on.'

To no few catcalls and several helpful remarks about how to conduct himself, Jon escorted Jenny out of the bar and across to the diner.

'Sorry about that,' he said as they took a seat in an almost deserted restaurant. 'It's just that a pretty girl like you coming in and whisking me away is always going to generate male envy, especially after all the booze they've had.'

She blushed. 'Don't worry I sort of took it as a compliment and anyway maybe I got the better end of the deal. I saw you at the funeral you know but it wasn't really the place to talk.'

It was Jon's turn to blush. 'I'm not sure how to respond to that but anyway that's not why we're here. What is it you wanted to tell me about Jacky?'

'Well, as I said we lived together until last year when she moved to Washington. We were real friends and used to share everything. I knew about you, she told me what you had done, rescuing her father and how you had got together. She was a lovely girl but she had a really dark side. I've never known her attracted to, let alone go out with someone like you.'

Jon was slightly taken aback. 'Well as you don't actually know me, I find it hard to understand how you can make a remark like that.'

'No look, sorry, that didn't come out right. Let me explain. Jacky was a really lovely girl but for some reason she only went out with complete bastards and I mean really rough types. When we shared an apartment you wouldn't believe some of the men she brought home. On several occasions I found her alone the next morning with bruises where she had clearly been hurt and often crying her eyes out. But a few days later the same man would be around again. I can tell just by looking at you that you're not the type to beat up their girlfriends and so I really can't understand why she liked you so much.'

'What? She told you that about me?'

'The day before she went on the operation that none of you will talk to me about, she called me. She wouldn't tell me what she was up to but she did tell me about you and how much she liked you. She sounded quite different. But look, there's one more thing and it's the real reason why I wanted to talk to you. Jacky hated her father, really hated him.'

'Hang on a second, she worked for him, she was his assistant. I didn't see them together that often but they seemed to get on alright.'

'Yes and that was the impression she usually gave. However, on more than one occasion, normally when she had had too much to drink and her latest boyfriend had left, she would open up a little. There's something in their shared past that really screwed her up and I'm sure she blamed her father for it. When she left for Washington and went to work for him, her last words to me were along the lines of that now she could finally nail the lie. I never found out what she meant by that but she definitely had her own agenda.'

'Hmm, she didn't talk about him much to me but everything else you say rings a bell I must say. Is that what you wanted to tell me?'

She looked away. 'Yes I thought you might need to know as I understand that you might still be working with her father while you are still in the States.' And then with a slightly cheeky look she continued. 'And I was curious to meet the first nice guy she ever went out with for myself.'

Jon smiled back into those deep blue eyes.

## Chapter 29

The big briefing room was starting to get very familiar to Jon and Brian. With Jacky no longer around, the Senator himself was attending but Jon had made every effort to keep clear of the man before the meeting started. He had never really liked him anyway and now that he was mulling over Jenny's words from the previous night, he was seeing the man in an even worse light.

'So, where did you end up last night Jon?' Brian asked. 'We didn't see you at the Club.'

'Sorry about that but something rather important came up. I'll tell you about it some other time.' He was about to say something more but Glen Thomas went to the rostrum to start the briefing.

'So gentlemen, I'm sure you will all be glad to know that we are now going to go after the man we missed at Salt Island.' A large photograph of Paulo Mandero appeared on the overhead projector screen. 'A relative newcomer to the senior club of drug producers, this guy seems to have been pretty successful in recent years. In fact, we still don't really know that much about him or his methods. Hopefully that will change once we have had time for a private chat. Now a quick look at the ground and then I'll hand over to Colonel Jones.' The picture changed to show a large hacienda style house set back from the sea. It had a big swimming pool and extensive landscaped gardens. There was a large jetty with two boats moored to it. 'Please note everyone, there is no beach and extensive cliffs, which means a landing is going to be difficult. Also behind the house the surrounding area is mainly forest with little room for helicopters to land. There are several villages dotted around which probably contain his staff and the workers in the jungles. Alright, that's the general picture. Colonel if you would like to explain what we're going to do.'

The Colonel took to the stage. 'Our aim is to detain Mr Mandero and take him to the US for trial. We have plenty of witnesses from Salt Island to testify against him. And before anyone asks, this has been cleared with the British Government bearing in mind the Salt Island operation was on British territory but it's one of several reasons why HMS Chester will be playing a

# Cocaine

key part in the operation.' As he made his point he looked carefully at several people in the audience, particularly the DEA representatives. 'The other aim is to destroy as much of the drug manufacturing and storage equipment that we can find. So, there needs to be two phases to the operation. The first will be a covert insertion using Chester's Lynx with a small team of nine to get Mandero. As soon as we have him we will call in the cavalry. We will have an assault ship with up six CH Fifty Three, Sea Stallion, helicopters available. They're too big to land but can fast rope our guys in to do the demolition work. We can then get them all off by boat from that jetty afterwards.'

A hand raised in the audience. 'Why use a British helicopter when we have our own?'

The Colonel smiled, he had been waiting for the question. 'Two reasons, it's actually smaller than anything we've got but still capable of carrying enough people and the only landing site is very small. The other reason which is far more important is that the Brits have developed and have experience of using aviation night vision equipment which will make getting in far easier. It's not in service with us yet but Lieutenant Commander Hunt here has already used it operationally, during the recent Falklands War, so is qualified to fly with it. Does that answer the question?'

Several nods were made, so he continued.

Brian nudged Jon. 'Used it more recently than that.'

'And we'll never be able to tell anyone,' replied Jon in a whisper.

'To continue, we know that Mandero's house is well protected. We suspect he has a couple of routine guard patrols and maybe even dogs but there will be nine of us. We will not be expected, so we have surprise and good old superior firepower on our side. Once we have secured the house we will call in the Stallions and start the heavy work while Mandero is taken out to the ships. Right, that's the broad outline for the operation. If there are no more questions we will carry on later today with the operational team, to carry out the detailed planning.'

The meeting broke up into various groups and the Colonel came over to Jon. 'Sure hope those goggles work Jon, we'll never get in without them.'

'Oh they work alright Sir, I just hope we don't make too much bloody noise and alert them as we come in.'

'Ah I've already thought of that and a small diversion might solve the problem. I need a quick word with the Senator then let's grab some lunch and talk it all through in detail.'

Senator Musgrove may have been physically present at the briefing but his mind was very far away. He was torn between doubt and certainty. Had he done the right thing? One moment he knew he had because he had no choice, the next he knew it was all going to go horribly wrong. It was only his Faith, his trust in the Lord that kept him going. He tried to remember everything that had been said and agreed during that eventful telephone call.

At first the idiot had refused to believe who was on the line and it had taken quite a lot of persuasion to convince him. Then the Senator had to sit and listen to a stream of invective. When they had finally got down to having something resembling a conversation, he almost slammed the phone down. Mr Rivera didn't seem the sharpest knife in the box but what choice did he have? He ploughed on.

'Mr Rivera, Paulo Mandero has my daughter. You may not know that, the world may not know that. They think that she's dead but I know differently. Now just listen. I want you to get her back for me. I want you to take her to a local hotel. You decide where and let me know where so we can meet. In return I can give you enough information to ensure Mr Gomez is never a threat to you anymore. On top of that I can guarantee that once I have my daughter, Mr Mandero will also be out of your hair. You will be the only power in Columbia, do I make myself clear?'

'And why should I believe you? What's to stop you bastards coming after me afterwards?'

'Because you will have enough evidence to ruin me forever, surely you see that?'

There was silence on the line for several minutes while the idea sank in. He was starting to think his desperate idea wasn't going to work when the voice returned.

'I think we can do something together Senator. We need to talk face to face but in principle we can do a deal.'

'What are you suggesting?'

'We meet in the hotel Riviera in Santa Marta, which is where we bring the girl if all goes as you say. In one week.'

He had to think quickly. 'Make it five days, as we are meeting to discuss Mr Mandero in a week.'

There was a chuckle at the end of the line. 'Fine Senator, we will see you in five days time.'

And that was what he did. Travelling as a private individual had been reasonably easy and five days later he was in his hotel room when the door was opened without ceremony and Adolpho Rivera with three burly bodyguards simply walked in.

'Don't be surprised Senator, I own the hotel after all. Now that I know it is really you we can discuss business.'

And they did, for the next two hours. The Senator was repulsed by the man but knew he had no choice. Rivera was openly contemptuous but he had to swallow his pride. Getting Jacky back was all that mattered. In the end he had to admit more than he intended about why the situation had arisen. It didn't matter, none of it mattered as long as this man could get her back. Once he had Jacky back he could explain, he could apologise and they would be reconciled, he knew it. Initially Rivera wasn't too happy when he was told that he could only move when the Senator told him too but when he explained it had to be timed with the raid that would destroy Mandero he suddenly became positively cooperative.

Suddenly his reverie was cut short. Someone was asking him a question. He had to focus hard to see who it was.

'Sorry, I didn't quite hear you.'

It was the Marine Colonel. 'Senator we need you to confirm that the political green light is on for this operation because we will have to sail in two days.'

'Oh no, it's all fine, I cleared it with the White House before coming down and the British Government have also agreed. You will get formal confirmation today or tomorrow at the latest.'

'Good, then we'll finish the detailed planning and expect to sail as anticipated. Will you be coming with us? Your daughter was always keen to attend, as you know. Or do you have a representative you want to come along?'

The question caught him by surprise and he had to think quickly. 'No, I need to be in Washington and I haven't had time to recruit a new assistant as I am sure you understand. Anyway, after your previous conduct, I'm sure you can just get on with the job. Let me wish you luck.' He didn't add that he would be heading to Columbia again in the near future. He held out his hand and the Colonel shook it before he made a swift exit. The die was cast there was nothing else he could do and the longer he stayed here the more uncertain he became.

A few minutes later, the Colonel joined Jon in the cafeteria. 'I've just said goodbye to the Senator, I thought I'd just ensure that the political green light was on and he confirmed it. But boy was he jumpy. There's something troubling that man and it's more than the loss of his daughter, he was like a kid being caught with his hand in the cookie jar.'

Jon thought for a moment and then decided to tell Joshua about his conversation of the previous night.

They discussed it for a while and then moved on. There were more pressing things to deal with in the short term. However, while they talked the Colonel mentally decided to call a friend in Washington before they left. A quick look into the man's background wouldn't do any harm.

## Chapter 30

'Jesus Christ, son, you just cannot do this with a helicopter.'

'Shut up Colonel I'm trying to fly the poxy thing and anyway I'm not your bloody son.' But Jon was laughing as he pulled Eric almost completely inverted in a zero G wingover. Some might call it a loop but that would mean he was exceeding the flight envelope of the aircraft and of course, that was something Jon would never do. Well at least not get caught doing. He pulled out at the bottom and rolled the wings level. At this height, the sun was still just lighting the sky but as they descended to four hundred feet, the light faded and a few minutes later it was almost pitch dark. The moon wasn't due to rise for another two hours and so it would be really black, very soon. Jon had put the Colonel in the Observers seat for this trip. He wanted to provide him with a practical demonstration of how good the NVG's attached to each of their flying helmets really were. He also decided to continue the Colonel's education into the manoeuvrability of the Lynx while they waited for the right conditions. They had sailed from Florida that afternoon and as they approached the Keys, the island chain at the bottom of the State, Jon used the proximity of the islands as an opportunity to give a demonstration of how effective the goggles could really be.

'Right its dark enough now. First thing we do is turn down all the internal lighting,' and Jon switched all the instruments to minimum. 'Now Colonel, pull the goggles down and have a peek.'

For a few minutes the Colonel was silent as he looked around inside and outside the cockpit. Jon continued to fly the helicopter towards the low lying island about ten miles away from them.

Finally the Colonel spoke. 'Well everything is green but this is incredible, it's like daylight.'

'Yes, we have to be careful though, there has to be some ambient light for them to work. On a cloudy night, out at sea, they are virtually useless but for our operation they should be fine. Even if it is cloudy, there should be enough light from the shore to allow them to work.'

'Well you've got me convinced.'

'Well, as a final demonstration, we'll go over to the island there and fly around over land just so you can get a full feel for their capabilities.'

On the way back to the ship the Colonel changed the subject. 'Jon, after our little chat the other day, I asked an old friend who works for the CIA these days to have a discrete look into our illustrious, evangelical, Senator's past. There was nothing obvious, he wouldn't have made the Senate if there had been. Our wonderful press would have found out during his campaign. But two things did come to light. The first was that his wife died many years ago of a drugs overdose. The investigation totally absolved him of any part in that, although there was never an answer as to why his wife was taking those sorts of drugs in the first place. However, it does possibly explain his zeal in anti-drug smuggling activities. But here's the odd thing, he flew to Columbia ten days ago. It wasn't as part of his official duties and no one knew about it until he returned, so it hasn't been possible to find out why he was there or where he went. He certainly hasn't discussed it with anyone since.'

'Now why would he do that?'

'No idea but it's odd enough that my friend will be keeping an eye on him from now on.'

The next morning Chester joined up with a US navy Assault Carrier who would be providing the 'cleanup crew' and Jon, Brian, Joshua and Captain Peterson flew over in Eric for the final mission briefing. They all gathered in one of the squadron ready rooms and the Colonel ran through the mission profile.

'Gentlemen, please note that this has to be more complicated than our last operation and timing will be critical. At twenty three hundred tomorrow night, I will launch from HMS Chester in their Lynx helicopter, with six US and two British Marines. We are all jungle warfare specialists and one of the Brits is a sniper. Lieutenant Commander Hunt here will be flying the aircraft using Night Vision Goggles and our aim is to land here, in a small clearing that has already been identified from satellite reconnaissance. We are allowing about two hours to get into position overlooking the Mandero house. Although it's only three miles, the going could be slow as the jungle thereabouts is quite dense. Because the Lynx is a fairly noisy machine, we are a going to have a diversion. At twenty three thirty, a civilian speedboat is going to pull into Mr Mandero's small marina with an engine problem. The problem will be a cracked exhaust and we've already tested just how noisy it is. If we time it right, no one will hear the helicopter approach and land. The boat is one the Coast Guard confiscated some months ago and will be manned by two Coast Guard officers. Lieutenant Thomas will be in command. The defect will be fairly easy to fix and we hope that they will be able to leave directly. They have a backup role should we need assistance and there will be arms well hidden on board. Once we are in position overlooking the house, we will split up. The Sniper team will remain in place to provide cover and stop anyone leaving as they will be able to cover the only road in and out of the area. Myself and the remaining Marines, will infiltrate the building and attempt to arrest Mr Mandero. Should there be any resistance we will meet it with appropriate force, bearing in mind that the rules are that we only fire, once fired upon. Any questions so far?'

There were none so he carried on. 'Once we have secured the area we will call in the heavy support, whose role will be to sanitise the area. We need to be out by first light, any prisoners come with us and everything needs to be deniable. Questions?'

One of the US navy officers raised his hand. 'Yes Colonel, what contingency are you planning, especially if you need reinforcements if resistance is heavy?'

'Good question, I will require at least one Stallion on immediate alert with a full company armed and ready but if it comes to calling for it, we will have failed. Their job will be to pull us out, not continue the action is that clear?'

The meeting continued for another hour and covered all the fine detail needed to conduct a military operation and when it was over, every area had been covered.

As it was winding up, Captain Peterson turned to Jon. 'Well I really hope this goes as anticipated Jon, because if it doesn't, it's a recipe for a catastrophe not to say a major diplomatic incident.'

'In my experience Sir, nothing ever goes to plan. However, the Colonel impresses me as a very flexible type and we have to start from somewhere and of course the last operation was a total success.'

The Captain grunted. 'Jon, I've been made aware of your activities in the Arctic recently as well as what you achieved in the Falklands. I think I will put my trust in you if you don't mind.'

Jon turned to his Commanding Officer, a wry smile on his face. 'No pressure then Sir.'

## Chapter 31

Jacky let out a great sigh of relief as the car sped away from Paulo's house. It hadn't been easy convincing him that she really needed to get out and do some shopping. When she had arrived she only had the clothes she was standing in. True enough, there was a large selection of female clothing in the house, as Paulo had pointed out but none of it was hers. The typical bloody male didn't seem to understand why she needed to go and buy her own things. A change of scenery after weeks of being cooped up was also a welcome change. Of course Paulo did have a point about security, especially while things were in such a state of uncertainty but as she repeatedly pointed out it was the other organisations who needed to be worried. She and Paulo had the certainty that they were invulnerable.

Nevertheless it had taken an almighty argument last night to get him to agree and in the end she had had to submit to a rigorous punishment in the basement. She grinned at the recollection. That had been fun, even if sitting on the soft leather seats of the Mercedes was causing her buttocks to throb, even now. Paulo had insisted that Manuel accompany her and that she be driven in the big German Four by Four but at least she was free for a couple of hours.

'So Manuel, do you get to go into Santa Marta very often?' she asked curious to know more about this taciturn lump of muscle who seemed to dog Paulo's steps every minute of the day.

Manuel turned to her. 'No,' he said flatly.

She sat back realising that was probably going to be the most she would get out of him and watched the scenery flash past instead. There was little to see, mainly scrub at the edge of the road and dense jungle thereafter. Although they were only eight miles out from the town, Paulo's house was the other side of a deep valley and the only road to it had to cross a bridge. Paulo had told her all about how he had to bribe to local politicians to get it modernised when he bought his property. It had the advantage of limiting access to his land as it was very much a choke point. The road had started down a series of hairpins to reach the bridge and was now steadying up to cross it, when she heard a strange noise.

At the same time a small hole appeared in the passenger window glass and Manuel slumped forward. For a split second she couldn't work out what she was seeing and then the realisation hit her as she saw the back of Manuel's head covered in blood with white splinters of bone protruding. She flung herself down behind the front passenger's seat as several more of the popping noises started up, this time from the driver's area. Suddenly, the car slammed to a halt

*'Oh Fuck we're being attacked,'* was all she was able to think before her door was wrenched open and a large muscular hand grabbed her arm and hauled her out of the car and onto the dusty road. Despite her beginning to struggle, the shock and viciousness of what was happening was just too effective to allow her to think or act coherently. With no warning, a fist went hard into her stomach, forcing all the wind out of her chest. As she gasped for air, a hand went around her face and something black and heavy was pulled over her head and tied tightly around her neck. Next she felt her hands being roughly pulled behind her and something being secured around her wrists. From the slight clicking feeling, she guessed it was a cable tie. All too soon the same thing happened to her ankles. She couldn't believe how quick it had all happened and not one word had been spoken by her assailants. She was picked up and laid down somewhere, not roughly but very firmly and she heard a vehicle door slam close to her head. At a guess she was in the back or trunk of a car.

    The next thing she heard was a double thump followed by a distant crash. That would be the Mercedes going into the gorge where it would never be found unless you were looking for it very carefully. Still whooping for breath she forced herself to calm down. If they wanted her dead then they would have shot her along with Manuel and the driver. No, this was a kidnap and they would be taking her somewhere but why her? No one knew she was with Paulo or even who she was for that matter. So this must an attempt to put pressure on Paulo. Kidnap the current girlfriend and blackmail him. But that didn't make sense either. Anyone who knew him would know that that was very unlikely to be effective.

    Suddenly there was a lurch and the vehicle started to move. From the quality of the ride and the noise, it wasn't very new or well maintained. Maybe these were just idiots out for the main chance. If they were, they would be badly surprised when they tried to blackmail Paulo. But it still didn't make sense, this was far too professional an operation, whoever had her, knew exactly what they were doing and who she was. Then it hit her, she knew what this was about and where she was going. She lay back in the dark and gathered her thoughts.

Some indeterminate time later the car stopped and she heard the door open. Rough hands grabbed her and she was slung over someone's shoulder. She tried an experimental kick but hands held her easily and pinned her legs. She went limp and the grip loosened slightly. It was soon clear they were climbing stairs and she tried to count the number of flights but soon lost count. Whoever was carrying her was very fit. His breath was hardly laboured, even when the stair climbing eventually stopped. The next thing she heard was a door opening and then closing behind her, before she was dropped onto some sort of bed or sofa. A sharp tug on her ankles and her legs were free. This was immediately followed by the same on her wrists but the hood stayed tight. Then the door opened and closed again. She sat up and felt with numb fingers around the edge of the hood. The securing loop was tied with a simple bow. It took only a matter of seconds to undo it and pull off the hood.

The light was amazingly bright for a few seconds and she blinked until she could take in her surroundings. It was a hotel room. The same sort of bland, tasteless room you would find the world over but she was pretty sure they hadn't had time to travel far, so she must still be in Santa Marta. She looked around more and realised that she was sitting on the bed. When she twisted round towards the veranda windows she saw the person sitting in the arm chair.

'Hello father, have you completely lost what little mind you ever had?'

'Now Jacky, my little darling, please don't be like that,' and he got up and walked to her. 'I need to convince you to come home. Together with the Lord we can put all this behind us.'

She stared at him with open contempt. Surely the man must realise that they were way past any chance of reconciliation?

'Have you completely lost it? Hold on a second, how did you recruit those goons to abduct me? You don't know anyone here well enough for that, I should know.' And then it hit her. 'You've sold us out haven't you, you bastard, you utter stupid bastard. Everything I said in that video is true and you have just guaranteed that it will be released. Two of Manuel's men were killed by the morons you set up to kidnap me. Don't you get it even now? You're a dead man walking.'

She could see that her words were starting to sink in. He looked guilty for a second just like a child caught stealing candy, then his expression hardened. 'Maybe so but Mr Mandero is as well after tonight, when my Marines take out his operation. Your old boyfriend is flying a team in tonight in that little helicopter of his, so by tomorrow morning Mandero will be gone.' His face took on a sickly expression. 'So you see Jacky, you have to come back to me. There's nowhere else for my little darling daughter to go now, is there?'

He was standing right before her now and Jacky's rage had been building more and more as they spoke. Almost without conscious volition she swung her right foot up between his legs and caught him squarely in the crotch. 'You stupid, stupid man,' she yelled as she tried to kick him again but he was already on his knees clutching himself with an expression of utter disbelief. However, her foot caught him in his midriff and he fell back still holding himself and gasping. She stood over him. 'And you're even more stupid than I thought because you've given me enough time to warn Paulo.'

In pain he may have been but the Senator hadn't given up. A hand shot out and caught Jacky by the ankle, pulling her off her feet and onto the floor as well. Gasping he heaved himself up just as she did the same. She was suddenly aware of just how big a man he really was.

'Now my dear, that is just not going to happen.' And he swung a massive fist at her head. His face was contorted with something more than rage and it was reflected in his coordination. Jacky easily ducked under the massive haymaker and found herself retreating backwards across the room towards the open patio windows. Her father followed her. Within seconds, she found herself out on the veranda. It had a small safety railing around it and she realised they were many stories high. Her father kept coming.

'I just pray that when you get to Hell, the first thing you see is mother's face looking down on you from Heaven and laughing at you, you fat bastard.'

The words had the desired effect, his face flushed bright red and he lurched towards her. At the last moment, she sidestepped and as he went past she dropped to one knee and with every ounce of strength left to her, grabbed his right ankle and lifted it as hard as she could.

Senator George Musgrove the Third was a big man and so not very aerodynamic but he was still travelling at over eighty miles an hour when his head smashed into the concrete patio six floors below the hotel room. His last thoughts were of angry disbelief that the Lord hadn't saved him.

Jacky didn't even wait to watch her father die. She made straight for the door. For a second she considered using the hotel telephone but immediately discarded the idea. She needed to get away. Just before she reached the door, she realised there would almost certainly be someone waiting outside. As she was looking around for anything she could use as a weapon, the screaming started from below. Clearly her father's body had already been found. On each side of the bed were standard issue bedside lights. She was glad to see they were of the fake antique brass variety. Grabbing the nearest, she wrenched the wire out of the plug just as the door started to open. Quickly making her way to the far side, she waited as a large man in a badly fitting suit entered and started calling for the Senator. She didn't hesitate, as soon as she had a clear aim she swung the table lamp at his head, as hard as she could. There was a satisfying crunch and spray of blood and the man fell like a stone. Just to be sure she hit him again when he was on the carpet. Panting with the effort she pulled his jacket to one side and sure enough there was a holstered automatic pistol. She pulled it out and checked the safety was on. A familiarity with hand weapons was one of the few things she would ever thank her father for.

Cautiously looking out into the corridor, she could see it was empty. There must be a fire escape or emergency stairs nearby. That was almost certainly how she had been delivered. However, she decided to use the lift which was only feet away. It would be faster and if anyone came after her, they would probably not expect her to go that way. When she reached the lobby there was a fair degree of pandemonium, the screaming had stopped and was replaced by shouting, presumably by someone from the hotel trying to restore some sort of order. She walked out of the hotel and no one even looked in her direction.

The problem now was that she had no money. Everything had been taken off her when she was tied up. So even if she wanted to use a public telephone she couldn't. Looking across the street she saw a taxi rank. She may not have had any cash but in Columbia she had another form of currency. Quickly climbing into the first cab, into the front passenger seat, she told the driver where she wanted to go. When it looked like the man might argue she pulled the pistol out of her trouser pocket and persuaded him it was in his best interests.

An hour later she was back with Paulo. He was extremely angry but when he had settled down just a little, he realised it was hardly Jacky's fault.

'Your father must have lost his mind, what was he thinking?'

'I think you're right Paulo, maybe we just pushed him over the edge with our video but what do we do now?'

'What we do now is get the hell out of here. Did your father say when the raid was coming in?'

'All he said was tonight.'

'Right well we have a little time then.' He picked up the phone. 'Tony, I need you and Phil up here as fast as you can, we have an emergency.'

A few minutes later and the two men arrived. Paulo told them to sit and then asked Jacky to repeat her story. Both men were aghast when she finished.

'What the fuck do we do Paulo? We can't fight these people,' asked Tony. 'Dammit we saw what they could do at Salt Island.'

'We run my friend. Phil can we use the submarine? It will be our best way out. They will almost certainly close the road, the jungle will slow us down too much and my Motor Yacht is too well known.'

Phil thought for a second. 'There's no reason why we can't get her ready in about four or five hours. I will need to get the crew together, many of them are in town or at home in the village and anyway we won't want to leave until it's dark. But Jacky what was that you said about helicopters?'

'He said they would be in the little one. That's a Lynx I think.'

Phil considered for a moment. 'That makes sense as there aren't exactly many places to land around here and they're hardly likely to try a frontal assault. So they'll land some way away and try to sneak up on us. They need to make the whole operation low key and deniable. If I remember correctly, the most you can get in the back of a Lynx is nine troops so there won't be that many to deal with. Why don't we just take them out?'

Paulo looked resigned. 'The problem my friends, is that if they fail this time, they will only try again and if we kill American soldiers it will only make them more determined. On top of that, we can't divert attention away from us, now that Jacky's father is dead. Thanks to you and your submarine Phil we have made an enormous amount of money recently. So I think it's time to retire. We'll just slip away and disappear. As much as I hate the thought of having to go in that submarine again, I have no choice. However, we won't make things easy for them. Phil go and get the submarine ready and tell me as soon as she is in a state to sail. Meanwhile, Tony and I will arrange with my people to ensure our visitors get more than they have bargained for if they arrive before we can get away.'

He turned to Jacky. 'Why don't you go with Phil my dear, pack some stuff and wait for us down in the base?'

Slightly stung by the assumption that she couldn't be of any help, she suddenly had an idea. 'Thanks Paulo but I really think you might need me up here.' And she explained why.

## Chapter 32

Lieutenant Glen Thomas, looked at his crewman and smiled. Never in his career did he expect to be travelling in a confiscated drug runner's cigarette boat, off the coast of Columbia, on a mission to take out a drug cartel at source. They were both dressed in faded jeans and T shirts and hadn't shaved for several days. They certainly looked the part of local young bucks with an expensive toy. The sixty foot boat was powered by two large inboard V8 petrol engines and capable of over sixty knots but speed wasn't what was required today. Two large nuts that held the exhaust to the manifold of one of the engines had been loosened and when they were nearer their target they would remove one and almost completely undo the other. The noise that the engine then would make would deafen anyone for a long way. The boat had been craned off the US assault ship some miles away and they didn't want the 'defect' to appear until well clear.

As soon as the headland they were approaching was on a specific bearing, he brought the boat to a stop and shut down the engines. He then nodded to his crewman to go and undo the nuts. Looking at his watch once again, he stared carefully at the sky to the north. As soon as he saw the lights of the helicopter he would start his run in. The weather was perfect, the sun had set several hours ago and the visibility was excellent. With no moon, light levels were low but the stars gave just enough to be able to see by.

Suddenly there was the flashing red light he was looking for. It wouldn't be unusual for aircraft to be operating along this coast and so standard navigation lights would be unlikely to arouse any suspicion but it was the trigger he needed. From now on their timing needed to be precise. He hit the start button for the two engines and they literally roared into life. As he opened the throttles, the noise from the broken exhaust was deafening. They headed into the small bay where Paulo Mandero had his little harbour.

In a matter of minutes, he was approaching the jetty where the massive yacht and power boat were moored. It was clear they had attracted attention, as there were several people in sight on the inner end of the pontoon. They were gesticulating and clearly shouting but nothing could be heard over the roar from the damaged engine. Looking at his watch again, Glen saw he needed only another minute or so and his job would be done, so he took his time coming alongside in as much of an incompetent manner as he could manage. His crewman threw a line to one of the men on the dock and it was caught and expertly tied off. Glen did the same with a stern line and then shut down the engines.

He jumped ashore and grinned sheepishly at the men on the dock. 'Sorry but as you can hear, we have an engine problem, we saw your boats here and hoped you could help.'

'Of course senhor we would love to help,' one of the men replied and his mouth widened into a grin. Suddenly there were half a dozen rifles pointing at them. 'You come up to the house and we will help you.'

With a sinking feeling Glen realised they had been compromised.

The identity of the dead body in the hotel in Columbia was soon flashing across to Washington. Joshua's CIA colleague was one of the first to know because he had alerted local agents to look out for the man in the first place. Quite what he was doing in such a provincial town as Santa Marta wasn't known yet but it would no doubt come out soon. However, the wheels of government agencies grind slow and it was some hours before the CIA informed the DEA, who immediately alerted the Coast Guard operations staff ashore in Florida. With Santa Marta so close to the area of the current operation, they could only assume that the mission was compromised in some way. A signal was sent immediately calling off the raid, although even as it was sent, it was accepted that it was probably too late.

Jon and Brian looked out of the window towards the lit up area of their target as they flew past. The whole area shone brightly in the NVGs, although to the naked eye it was just a few house lights. However, they weren't looking at the dock area but out to sea. Sure enough they could just make out the slim shape of the cigarette boat in just the right position.

Brian reached up and turned on the aircrafts red anti-collision light. 'Glen should see that and get going. We've got exactly eleven minutes to get on the ground.'

Jon nodded and kept on course. Shortly afterwards they coasted in well clear of the house and Jon turned the aircraft onto a more southerly heading. The clearing they wanted should be dead ahead, two miles away. They both spotted it almost at the same time. It showed up as a lighter patch in the dark jungle.

'Right, Colonel and all you guys in the back, the landing area is in sight,' Jon called over the intercom knowing that they would not be able to see a thing without the benefit of the goggles. 'We'll fly past so we can approach into wind and should be on the ground in a few minutes, so be prepared for some manoeuvring soon.'

Jon and Brian quickly completed the pre-landing checks and Jon turned into wind and started to descend. 'You know when we're training to do this sort of landing, we're taught to do two reconnaissance overflights to assess the landing zone. Guess what? That ain't going to happen tonight.'

Brian recognised the tension in Jon's voice, he had heard if often enough in the past. He also knew that Jon liked to talk to ease the pressure. 'Not a good tactical idea to give the bad guys plenty of time to see what you're up to.'

Jon laughed tensely. 'Jesus I hope there aren't any bad guys here, if there are, we're well and truly buggered. Right in we go.'

With the aid of the goggles, Jon could see that the clearing was indeed big enough but only just. He flared the aircraft and brought it to a high hover just above the jungle canopy. With Brian looking to the left and with him concentrating on his side, he brought the nose of the aircraft as close to the trees ahead as he dared, to give maximum tail clearance. He slowly lowered the collective and the aircraft descended. As they approached to ground he could see that it sloped slightly to the left but that was fine. Sloping ground landings were common enough. The right wheel touched first and as he continued to descend the helicopter rotated around it and started to lean over. The left wheel then made contact and he was able to fully lower the collective. As soon as he was sure they were firmly settled, he pulled back both engine condition levers and shut down the rotors.

As the blades came to a halt he called over the intercom. 'Free to disembark.'

His passengers didn't need a second command. Both cabin doors slid open and they jumped out to take up defensive positions around the aircraft. Jon and Brian completed the shut down checks and got out to join the others.

'All quiet,' said the Colonel. 'Did we alert anyone you think?'

'Well our timing was spot on and we saw Glen in his boat in the right place and time so we must assume it's all going to plan,' answered Jon confidently.

'Fair enough, we'll get set up here and then hit the road. Corporal, get the radio ready, everyone else get your weapons and fighting order sorted, we move out in five minutes.'

The High Frequency radio was set up next to the helicopter and tested briefly with the ships out at sea. They also tested the smaller VHF pack that they would be carrying to stay in touch with the aircrew who would be staying with the helicopter. Communications seemed good and Brian took over the role of radio operator.

'Thanks for the lift Jon, we'll call you as soon as we have the place secure and then you can come on over.' The Colonel shook Jon's hand and then suddenly Jon and Brian were on their own.

An eerie silence settled over the two of them as they sat back in the cabin of the aircraft.

'Jon do you have this strange feeling of déjà vu?' asked Brian looking around at the dense undergrowth.

'If you mean exactly like when we were on that bloody beach in Argentina, then you're spot on old chum. Hopefully, this time no one is going to fall over and break his leg though.'

Jon got out his thermos, poured them some coffee and they sat in companionable silence while they drank it. As their ears attuned to the night, they started to hear the noises of the jungle. Odd chirps and creaks made them realise there were other things out there in the dark.

They talked quietly almost as if they didn't want to disturb the wildlife. Both of them felt quite vulnerable. They were both armed with pistols and they had a nine millimetre submachine gun each but in reality knew that if the locals found them they probably wouldn't be able to use them. Time passed slowly and despite putting it off as long as he could, Jon eventually looked at his watch. 'Damn I promised myself I wouldn't do that it only makes the time drag more.'

'Go on, how long have they been gone?'

'Just over an hour, they should be there any time soon. It rather depends on what the going was like. I guess we'll know if we hear any shooting, it's not that far away.'

'Yes but let's hope we don't hear any guns, a nice radio call, saying all is well would suit me fine.'

As if his words were magic, the HF radio burst into life 'Charlie Alpha Zero, this is Foxtrot Two Nine do you read over?'

'Shit, that's the ship calling us, what can they want?' exclaimed Brian as he reached for the microphone. 'Foxtrot Two Nine this Alpha Zero over.'

'Urgent, Alpha Zero, abort the mission, I repeat abort the mission over.'

'Oh shit what's happened? Er Foxtrot Two Nine can you explain, over.'

'This is Two Nine, the mission is compromised, information only just received, over.'

'This is Alpha Zero, copied, ground forces were despatched over and hour ago, I will attempt to recall, please wait, out.'

Brian turned to Jon. 'Do you want to call them on the VHF Jon?'

Jon nodded and picked up the other microphone, 'Delta party this is Flight team do you read, over?'

Silence.

He tried again. 'Delta party, this is Flight team, do you read, over.'

There was no reply. Jon tried one more thing, 'Delta party this is Flight team, transmitting blind. Abort the mission, I repeat abort the mission, return to base. Do you copy over?'

There was still no response. Jon looked at Brian. 'What the fucking hell do we do now?'

## Chapter 33

Colonel Jones was delighted with the progress they had made. Within minutes of leaving the helicopter, they discovered an overgrown track leading in the right direction. He wasn't too surprised. Presumably the clearing had once been of some use. It was probably something to do with the people who lived in the house sometime in the past. However, it also forced his team into a narrow file which made it more difficult to maintain a defensive posture. Even so it was less than half an hour before he and is men were overlooking the target from the edge of the jungle. Their vantage point was excellent as they were on a small hill. They could see the back of the house and the road that came up from the town. In the distance, past the house to the left he could just see the dock area with the two large pleasure boats tied up. The other utility buildings were off to the right just blocking his view of the edge of the house.

He called for the two Royal Marines.

'Right, you two guys go up to the left a little more and set up your Sniper rifle. I don't want anyone coming in or out. If they're in vehicles, shoot out the tyres or engine. If they're on foot just pin them down. We don't want any casualties if we can avoid it right?'

'Yes Sir,' the Marine Corporal replied. 'Which way will you be going?'

Further down, over there for a better recce,' and he pointed to a point nearer the fence running around the whole compound. 'I want to see what sentries or patrols they have so don't expect anything to happen for a while.'

So saying he left the two men to get on with their job and indicated to is men to follow him further down the side of the hill.

Jacky had never felt so invigorated in her life as she came out of the cellar and shut the door behind her. She went up to Paulo who had been watching outside on the remote TV.

'How did it go? I only get a picture on this monitor,' he asked anxiously.

'Absolutely fantastic,' she laughed.

'They didn't suspect anything then?'

'I think the shock of seeing me alive was enough for Glen, that's the one on the right by the way, to believe everything I told him. I said that I was being kept hostage here and had seen them being brought up to the house. I bravely sneaked in to warn them about the horrible Mr Mandero. They swallowed the lot but told me not to worry as a rescue party is on its way.'

'Did they say how many?'

'Oh, much more than that. The reason for them coming in when they did was as we thought, to make a diversion and as much noise as possible to mask the sound of their helicopter landing behind us in the jungle. There are nine soldiers on board plus the pilots but they will be staying with the aircraft. The idea is for the soldiers to sneak up and surprise us before they send in a heavy squad from some ship they have offshore. They won't move until they hear from the soldiers that they have secured the house.'

Paulo thought for a moment. 'I know exactly where they've landed. There is only one possible place close by and it will take them at least forty five minutes to even get close to us.' He looked at his watch. 'I just spoke to Phil and the sub will be ready in about two hours so we've got to delay them somehow. They're going to be here very soon.'

'Why delay them?' Jacky asked. 'Surely we can do something better than that?'

Colonel Jones led his men down towards the wire fence surrounding the compound. As they descended, they lost their panoramic view and he had his men spread out either side of him. The closer they got the more careful they were but so far there had been no sign of any activity, apart from the lights shining in the house itself. There certainly didn't seem to be any foot patrols of any sort. Mr Mandero was clearly a confident man but there again the place had very limited access and he apparently owned all the land for miles around. After all it had been pretty hard to get here even with the resources they could command.

However, as he watched the quiet scene before him there was something starting to worry him. The night was quiet with virtually no wind. He called one of his men over. 'Go off to the left until you can see the dock and tell me what's going on there,' he whispered. The man nodded and crawled away.

He was back in a few minutes. 'Nothing Sir, all quiet.'

'Could you see the cigarette boat?'

'Yes Sir but there's no one around it.'

Why wasn't there? Surely if the ruse had worked then there would be people working on the engines. Maybe they had been invited up to the house. He looked at his watch. It was well after two in the morning. Maybe they Coast Guard guys had had no option but to accept some hospitality. He prayed that was the answer.

'Right listen up everyone, we cut the wire here and go in through those outbuildings. When we get to the other side, we fan out and hit the house from all sides, got it?'

There were nods all round and they made their way to the fence. One of the men started cutting the fence wire with a pair of bolt croppers as the rest waited patiently. He was just finishing when a figure appeared around the end of what looked like a large garage. It started running towards the fence. In a matter of moments they could see it was a girl and she seemed to be running away from someone or something. She was clearly in distress and kept looking over her shoulder as she ran. With a shock, the Colonel realised he recognised the face, even in the sparse illumination of the few lights that were on.

*That couldn't be right, she was dead.*

Deciding to take a risk, he called out in a low voice. 'Jacky, Jacky over here.'

The girl looked startled and hesitant, obviously not sure where the voice had come from.

'It's me Joshua Jones we've come to help. Over here, look.' And he stood half up so she could see his outline.

Without hesitation she ran to him and crouched the other side of the wire. She was breathing heavily and looked very frightened.

'What the hell girl? We all thought you were dead.'

Between gasps she responded. 'No, I was kidnapped from Salt Island, the bastards have been keeping me here ever since. Mandero had been blackmailing my father which is why I'm so surprised to see you here. The two guys in that speed boat were caught and I overheard what they said to Mandero.'

'What, how were they caught?'

'I've no idea but Paulo was suspicious and had them taken to the basement in the house, it didn't take long to get them to talk. He was talking to his guys afterwards and didn't know I was listening so I knew you would be out here somewhere. Look I've tried to get away from here but it's just not possible. The road is the only way in and the one time I tried, they caught me within minutes. So I'm free to move around the house and grounds. But this is a total surprise. Mandero thought you would be going after others with the Senator knowing I was here.'

'Too late for that, what's Mandero doing? We've clearly lost the element of surprise. In fact maybe we should just retreat and take you with us. We can always come back for the bastard later.'

'He won't be here, he's not that stupid. No this is your only chance and I would like to see him put away after all the things he's done to me.' She saw the look on his face. 'Don't ask.'

The Colonel was getting really angry now. He knew that tactically, without the element of surprise his main advantage had gone. But this man needed to be punished.

'How many men has he got? Do you know what he intends to do?'

'Not many, maybe five, most live in the village down the road. He's going to defend the main house but I can lead you to a back way in if you want, through the kitchens. You should still be able to take them by surprise. But we'd better hurry they will miss me soon.'

The Colonel thought for a moment longer. 'Alright we owe it to you Jacky, you'd better lead on.'

They followed her as she made her way between the garage and a large shed. The path was narrow but had the advantage of completely hiding their approach. Just as they reached the end, three men stood into view holding rifles levelled at them. At the same time three more men did the same behind them.

Jacky suddenly had a pistol in her hand which she swiftly held to the Colonel's head, to his shocked and total surprise.

'Sorry Joshua but you just made a basic mistake. Never lose the element of surprise and never underestimate your enemy. Now drop your weapons please.'

A cold wash of anger and outrage swept over the Colonel but with a gun at his head and his men covered, he realised he had no option. 'Do as she says men. Jacky what the hell is going on?'

'Far too complicated to explain Joshua, maybe you'll work it out one day.'

Three of the men moved in and collected the rifles while the other ones maintained a rock steady aim. They then took cable ties and cuffed the men's hands behind them before prodding them towards the house at rifle point. As they left there was a loud crash behind them and the Colonel realised they must have just smashed the radio. They were being very thorough. At least there were the two Royal Marines up on the hill, there was still hope.

## Chapter 34

'Foxtrot Two Nine please repeat your last, you were broken and unreadable.'

'Charlie Alpha Zero I repeat, pull out, we must assume that the mission is compromised, you are to pull out do you copy, over.'

'Foxtrot Two Nine, you are garbled, I cannot read you. Will call back when I have more information, out.' And Jon reached over and turned off the radio. He grinned conspiratorially at Brian. 'Bloody radios, never work when you need them to. Right get your gear let's go and find out what's really been going on.'

'Silly buggers, what's the point in pulling out if we can't get the get the grunts anyway,' said Brian. 'Right lets go.'

The two aircrew left the clearing in the same direction the Marines had before them. There was a clear trail to follow. They soon found the old path and hurried along it. By the time they were at the end they were sweating heavily and panting. So it was with some surprise that when they came out of the jungle they were confronted by two Marines with their weapons levelled at them.

'Halt or we fire,' one of them called.

'For fuck's sake Corporal it's us. The crew from the helicopter.'

'Oh, sorry Sir, didn't recognise you and you were making enough noise to wake the whole county.'

'Sorry lads, we're not trained killers like you.' replied Brian. 'Now what the hell's going on? We tried to call on the radio but there has been no answer.'

'Wish I could tell you Sir. The Colonel and his team went down there about forty five minutes ago and we've seen nothing since. We might have heard some voices a while ago but it was hard to tell. There's nothing happening at the house. We were told to make sure no one gets in or out of the gate there but no one has. But we were specifically ordered to stay here.'

'Well you can forget that now Corporal,' said Jon. 'We got a message from the ship to say the mission is compromised in some way and then when we couldn't raise you lot on the radio we were told to pull out. But bugger that, I've got a nasty feeling that the US need the British cavalry to ride over the hill to the rescue now.'

'So what do we do Sir?'

'Well, I guess there's no choice but for the four of us to go down there and try to find out what's going on. I suppose one good thing is there has been no weapons being fired but if they had been successful then we would have known by now. Do you have any idea where they went in?'

Yes Sir, down there, near that big outbuilding, we couldn't see exactly where because of that fold in the land but we would have seen them if they'd gone anywhere else.'

'Right, well I suppose common sense says we should try somewhere else, any ideas?'

'Well there's this high fence all around Sir but seeing no one seems to be moving, why don't we go down to the main entrance there and just walk in?'

Jon looked surprised for a second and then the logic seemed sound. 'Right you are, lead on Corporal, we still need to be pretty stealthy but you'd better bring that bloody great rifle of yours, you never know when we might need it.'

Inside the house the Marines had been unceremoniously ushered into the basement. The look of surprise on the Coast Guard officer's faces was only surpassed by the look of embarrassment on the Marine's. Joshua looked at Glen ruefully and just shook his head.

Jacky turned to Paulo as the door closed. 'On moment Paulo, when I spoke to the Coast Guard guys they said there were nine soldiers, two must still be out there.'

'Shit, we'll have to find out where they are.' He turned to Tony. 'You're good at extracting information, I've seen you in action. What should we do, there's very little time.'

The two men talked for a minute. Paulo turned to Jacky. 'Jacky do you know any of them apart from their officer?'

'Yes vaguely, why?'

'Do you know who's the most junior?'

'Not really but that one at the end looks the youngest.'

'Right he'll do. Tony pull him out and any one other, except the Boss man.'

Two Marines were dragged out and the door closed again.

Paulo looked at the young Marine. He could barely be out of his twenties. 'I need to know where the other two of your party are, do you understand?'

To his credit the Marine stared stonily back and said nothing. Paulo nodded to Tony who took out his pistol and placed it against the other Marine's leg and fired. The shot was deafening in the confined space and the Marine screamed and fell over with blood pumping out of a wound to his thigh.

'That, was by way of a warning young man. The next shot will be through his kneecap and the next the other one and then his elbows. Do you want to see your comrade crippled for the rest of his life?'

The Marine turned white and could see in Paulo's eyes that he wasn't bluffing. It took him a few seconds and then he blurted out. 'They're up on the hill somewhere, with a Sniper rifle, overlooking your entrance gate. Their job is to stop anyone coming in or going out and wherever you go we'll get you, you bastard.'

Paulo laughed. 'You'll have to do better than that I've been threatened by experts. Right, throw them back in and chuck a knife in after them, they can cut their bonds then and do some first aid. They won't get out of the basement in a hurry.'

He beckoned to everyone to leave and they went up to the hallway where he picked up the telephone. An auxiliary line had been installed some time ago and he was able to ring the submarine base directly. He talked for a few minutes and then replaced the receiver. 'Tony I'm sorry but the sub is still not ready and we need to take out those two remaining soldiers.'

'Don't worry I'm on it.' Tony replied and he beckoned to several of the men and they left the house by the back entrance.

'Well my dear, we will just have to wait now, fancy a drink?' They went into the large living room and Paulo opened the cocktail cabinet.

Jacky nodded. 'Surely I should go with them I might be able to try the same trick for a third time.'

'What are the chances that two grunts will recognise you?'

'No, you're right, it probably wouldn't work.' She looked relieved as she said it and as she accepted the proffered glass she realised her hands were shaking slightly. When was this day going to end?

Jon and his colleagues had reached the main entrance. There was a floodlight over the gate itself but no sign of any cameras, much to everyone's relief.

'Right can anyone see the wire to that light?' Jon asked as he looked himself. 'It's alright, I've found it.' The wire was badly stapled to the wooden post the light was mounted on. Giving it a savage yank it pulled out and he was able to rip it out of the fitting above.

It all went dark.

'Right Corporal, one at a time. We'll split up either side of the road once we're through and rendezvous at that large flower bed there.' And he pointed to the edge of the garden near the house. 'Right off you go.'

Jon took up the rear as he ran crouched towards the house in the distance. The whole thing felt surreal. Here he was playing soldiers, something he very definitively wasn't, to try and find out what had happened to a bunch of serious professionals in a country he wasn't even legally meant to be in.

When they were regrouped at the flower bed, they stopped and looked towards the house. The whole place was eerily silent. A few lights were still on, as they had been, ever since they arrived but there was still no sound or sign of movement. What on earth was going on?

'Any ideas anyone?' Jon asked.

The answer was completely unexpected and came from behind them.

'My idea is for you four to drop those weapons and surrender before we shoot you, you silly bastards,' the voice had a strong South African accent.

Jon whirled around and without thinking raised the muzzle of his machine gun. It was a mistake and something clubbed him on the side of the head. The pain was blinding and then mercifully it all went black.

An indeterminate time later Jon came round. His head felt like someone had driven a spike into it. His vision was blurred and his right ear felt twice its normal size. He tried to lift his hand to rub it but found he couldn't move it. He then found that both his hands and also his feet were immobilised. He realised he was sitting in a chair and as his vision slowly regained focus, he realised he was in some sort of living area. There was a noise behind him and person came into view.

'Hello Jon.' It was a terrifyingly familiar voice *but it couldn't be*. He focused hard and realised it was; it was Jacky back from the dead.

She could obviously read the look in his face. 'No Jon I'm not dead. You'll find out what this was all about in a day or so. Just look at the newspapers and you'll see.'

He was about to say something when she put her hand over his mouth. 'Don't talk, just listen. Paulo wanted to burn the whole place down with all of you in it. I told him not to be stupid but he does have a point, you're not exactly here with the permission of the Columbian authorities are you? But killing so many American and British soldiers is still a stupid idea. So here's what's going to happen, you will never see any of us again. But you need to get out of here fairly soon as well, although it will probably take days before the authorities become suspicious. Unfortunately all your comrades are in a secure location, so you will have to rescue them. By the time you've done that we'll be long gone. So adieu my lovely, too nice, man.' He felt her lips brush his forehead and the sound of retreating steps and then it was silent again.

He took stock. It was still dark and he could just see his watch. In its luminous glow he could see that it was about four in the morning, so only an hour and a half till the light started to return. The room was in darkness but he could just make out the bonds holding him. Good old fashioned rope by the looks of it but nevertheless quite effective. The chair was of the old, oak, dining table variety and felt very substantial. There certainly didn't seem to be any give in it. God, this was just like the bloody films. How was he going to get out? He tried jerking his whole body and was rewarded with a little movement. The effort of the movement started to get him angry. The pain it generated in his wrist coupled with the throbbing of his head was really winding him up. He looked around the room. He could see a table and the other chairs but his hands were so immobilised even if he could get to a knife he would never be able to wield it. No, the chair would have to go. That fucking, lying, twisted bitch was the cause of all this and he was damned if was going to let her get away. He started a series of hops in the chair and was rewarded with some movement towards the door. Bloody cow, that was why he was here, he was buggered if he would let her win. Suddenly he was past the door and onto a small landing. Behind him were some stairs leading down to a hallway. Harnessing his anger over the complete disaster of the whole operation and how he had been personally duped, he let it boil over to an all consuming rage and bounced the chair over the top step to plummet crashing, splintering down towards the solid floor of the hall.

*'Jesus that was just about the most stupid bloody thing I've ever done,'* he thought dazedly as everything went quiet again and a modicum of sanity returned. Lying on his back, he started to struggle in his bonds and for a second thought that all his efforts had been wasted. The chair was strong but he quickly realised that the left arm was now loose. Rocking his arm backwards hard he was rewarded by a splintering snap and the whole wooden section came free. He still couldn't undo the rope tying it to his wrist but now he could reach over to his other hand and the combined effort of both hands tore the other chair arm free as well. He now had enough purchase and dexterity to start on the knots. With a skill driven by anger and desperation he managed to undo them and within minutes was standing in the hallway panting with exertion, aching in more than one place but free at last.

## Chapter 35

Jacky looked back at the house for a final time as they rocketed around the corner in the Landcruiser, to arrive at the submarine base's entrance. She just caught the sight of a light coming on. *'That was quick, how the hell did he get free so fast? Never mind, they would be safe in a few minutes and it would take Jon some time to find, let alone set free his comrades.'* she decided not to mention anything to Paulo sitting beside her. He hadn't been keen on the idea in the first place and anyway they would be away very soon.

The car skidded to a halt and they all jumped out except the driver. Paulo said something to him and the car shot away up a dirt track in the opposite direction to the house.

'A little present to a loyal employee,' he grinned. 'We don't want the Americans thinking we are doing anything but driving out of here and when they find no vehicles at the house that will just be confirmation.'

They went in through the main door and down the ladder. Paulo nodded to the last man who stayed outside and shut the door behind them. He would cover the whole area with dirt and camouflage it before heading off back to his village.

As they made their way into the base, they could see Phil waiting for them on the dockside next to the great grey bulk of the submarine. Jacky was surprised to see that the dock was almost full of water, although the sub was clearly not yet floating.

Seeing her expression as they met, Phil explained. 'We're not leaving anyone behind and need to get away as fast as we can, so I've already partially flooded up to save time. I've rigged up a remote control for the door motors and once you two are on board, I'll activate it and jump in behind you.'

Paulo nodded but didn't speak. He was looking pale.

'Paulo, a present for you.' Phil handed him a glass of water and two white pills.

Paulo looked at them for a second and nodded gratefully. He took them and quickly swallowed both with a gulp of water. 'Right Phil, you just get us away and we'll talk once we're clear.'

With a determined look on his face he made his way down the foredeck hatch.

Jacky nodded at Phil and did the same, slipping out of sight down the hatch. Once they were clear, Phil took one final look around the base; his base and his submarine, whatever happened next, no one would be able to take the achievement away from him. All looked good so he picked up the remote control box that he had left on the deck and firmly pushed the button marked 'up'. A grinding rumbling noise started from the front of the cave and the inrush of white water immediately appeared around the submarine's bows. At the same time all the lights went out. Satisfied, Phil threw the remote as hard as he could so it and its trailing wire landed clear on the stairwell. He entered the submarine, closing the hatch firmly behind him.

Several minutes later, the base was flooded and the sleek dark grey monster slid slowly backwards out of the now flooded cave. Minutes later it was purring almost silently away from Columbia unseen and unheard by the two warships loitering just off the coast.

Jon found a light switch and blinked in the artificial glare. He was in the reception hall of the house and was immediately impressed. Mandero was a drug producing bastard but he had taste that was clear. He was surprised that he couldn't hear anything. It hadn't been long since Jacky left yet he had only heard one car disappearing. Surely there would be more? What he needed to do now was find his friends and contact the ships. The main radio was back at the helicopter but with any luck the one the Marines had been carrying might reach them as they should be closing in to shore by now. So where were the Marines? He looked around but couldn't see anything obvious. *'Shit they could be anywhere, in the house or any of the outbuildings for that matter. What was it that Jacky had said?'* He thought desperately. *'Something about a secure location and Paulo wanting to burn the place down. So wherever they were, was probably in the house somewhere.'*

Deciding on a methodical approach he discounted the upstairs rooms for his first search as they would be far less secure. He went through the whole ground floor and was mystified to find nothing, so he went upstairs only to find the same thing. Returning to the hall, he was just contemplating starting on the outbuildings when he heard a faint muffled thump from somewhere. A few seconds later it was repeated and he realised it was coming from behind him. Peering at the wall, which was in partial shadow, he realised there was the outline of a door which had been blended into the decor. Rushing over, he found it opened easily and there was a short flight of steps leading down a bare concrete passage. A light switch by the door worked and suddenly he heard the thump much louder this time. Half running down the stairs he got to the bottom to find a small room with a table and TV monitor in it. There was also another door, this time made of steel and set into a massive metal frame. The thump happened again. Jon smiled. He wondered what they had found to use as a battering ram.

The door had a simple lever handle on this side but probably nothing on the other. He decided to wait for another thump. He didn't want to open it just as it was being assaulted, that would be just too much like a cheap comedy film. The door shook again and he reached for the handle. It opened easily and he looked in on a crowd of angry, surprised faces.

'Morning men,' he grinned. 'The Royal Navy to the rescue once again.'

As soon as everyone was back out into the house and Jon had told them of events, the Colonel had his men fan out to search for their weapons. They quickly found them stacked up where they had been relieved of them. Unfortunately, as expected, the radio had been smashed beyond repair.

'We need to get in touch with the ships as soon as we can,' fretted the Colonel. 'We'd better get someone to run back to the aircraft.'

'Hang on a minute,' said Jon, as realisation dawned. 'There are two bloody great boats down there on the jetty they must have radios, we can use those. Right Corporal, get down there and find one that works, there's bound to be a Marine VHF on the bridge of both of them. Do you know what they look like?'

The Corporal looked uncertain so Brian chipped in. 'I'll go with him Jon, I know what to look for but what do we say?'

The Colonel responded first. 'We need the clean up team here as soon as possible and one aircraft to scout down the road into Santa Marta to see if they can get ahead of the cars they must be in and stop them.'

Brian nodded and ran off with the Corporal in tow. The Colonel turned to Jon. 'Right, I want the medic to look at you, there's a lot of blood down your neck and that head wound looks nasty.'

Jon put his hand to his ear. He had completely forgotten about it until the Colonel mentioned it. He suddenly realised he had a dreadful headache which he had been unconsciously ignoring in all the excitement. Feeling suddenly weak he sat down on one of the hall chairs and simply nodded.

Three hours later and some sense was emerging out of the chaos. Three Sea Stallions had winched down a company of Marines who were systematically searching the area and destroying anything to do with drug manufacture or storage. Steve Makepeace had been flown out to the Lynx in Nellie and along with Brian had taken the helicopter back to Chester. Jon was in no state to fly, not the least because there was no way he could put his helmet on and anyway, he insisted on staying to help search the house. There was no sign of any cars on the road into Santa Marta and everyone was wondering where on earth Mandero and his people had gone. Unsurprisingly the locals weren't saying anything and it wasn't part of the operation to terrorise them into giving information.

Jon was sitting in Paulo's study going through his desk to see if there were any clues there. He was frowning over some papers when Colonel Jones walked in.

'Find anything Jon? Because no one can work out where the hell they went. There were no signs of cars on the one road out of here and they couldn't have got off it in time. There are a few dirt tracks but they don't lead anywhere and anyway we've checked them all out.'

'There's something niggling at the back of my mind, Colonel, something that Glen Thomas said when we first came out here. It's one of those damn things that I'm going to stop thinking about and then it will come to me in its own sweet time.'

'I know just what you mean but what's that you've got there?'

'Ah, good question. Why do you think Mr Mandero bought a thousand golf cart batteries? I've got the invoices here.'

'No idea, does he own a golf course? I wouldn't put it past him.' Suddenly he was interrupted by one of his Marines running in holding something in his hand.

'Colonel Sir, you need to come and see this. We found a pit that wasn't very well concealed. We thought it might have drugs dumped in it but when we dug down we found skeletons and uniforms. This is the cap from one of them.' He held out some sort of black cap covered in dirt.

The Colonel looked puzzled but Jon recognised it immediately. 'You know, I'm beginning to think I may know what this is about, although it seems completely barking mad. Just let me look at this pit first and then I'll tell you what I'm thinking.'

They half walked, half ran down the track that the Marine indicated and soon were on the edge of the jungle and the cliffs. An area of about ten square metres had been scooped out of the undergrowth and several Marines were digging in it. Scattered around the edge were bits of old machinery mixed in with what were clearly human bones and scraps of uniform. Jon went over and examined the clothing. He then studied some of the bent and twisted metal.

'So Colonel, why do you think there are the buried remains of German war time sailors here? And not just that but ones that have clearly been buried quite recently, not forty years ago. Look at the condition of the clothing it's never been in the ground that long and the corpses are all mummified. That won't happen if they'd been in wet soil. Why do you think that mixed in with them are the remains of electrical equipment that is clearly of World War Two vintage. Finally why do you think that Paulo Mandero recently paid for a ridiculous amount of golf cart batteries?'

The Colonel looked nonplussed and shook his head. 'Clearly you've worked it out but you've got me I'm afraid.'

So Jon told him.

## Chapter 36

The submarine was almost silent, just the background hum of equipment. Jacky pulled the curtain back over the door to the little cabin that Paulo was sleeping in. The knock out pills certainly worked fast. She carefully made her way back to the control room taking care to avoid knocking herself out on the myriad of pipes and arcane equipment dotted everywhere. Sliding feet first through the circular watertight hatch coaming she entered the crowded space. Phil and Tony were there along with Mike Spencer the Second in Command and Manfred the old engineer, as well as the crew operating the dive planes.

'Is he out of it?' asked Tony.

'Yes,' she replied. 'Those pills are really effective.'

Tony grimaced. 'Well, they may be good at controlling his phobia but we need him to make a decision. Phil, how long before he's back in the land of the living?'

'Last time they knocked him out for about twelve hours. Damn I should have thought of that before I gave them to him. What with all the panic of getting away I just didn't think far enough ahead.'

'What are you talking about?' asked Jacky. 'Why do you need to talk to him?'

Tony gave her a patronising look. 'Because my dear, we may have got away from the Americans but we need to decide where to go now and it's his submarine and he will probably have the contacts in various places to help us.'

'Goodness, I hadn't thought of that either, I guess we were all so surprised at my father's stupidity and the speed everything happened. What do you suggest?'

Phil spoke first. 'Let's be clear on our capabilities first. We've been on battery power for six hours now, we went fairly fast at first to clear the area but now we're going at the most economical speed of only four knots to maximise out battery life.' He turned to Manfred. 'Anything you want to add old chap?'

Manfred nodded. 'When we left we were fully charged so we have almost thirty six hours at this speed before we need to start the diesels. That gives us a range of less than one hundred and fifty miles. But if we go any faster we actually have less range. We drain the batteries faster. You've got to understand that these boats aren't submarines as you know them these days, they are really submersible ships. Luckily we can run the diesels underwater using our snorkel but even so, that increases the risk of us being detected as the engines make a lot of noise and the snorkel is above the water so can be seen by eye or radar.'

Tony snorted. 'You speak as if we are at war old man. All we're trying to do is get away somewhere safe and scarper.'

Phil looked angry. 'Don't be so bloody naive Tony. Those were modern warships up there and their antisubmarine capability is a million times better than anything this sub had to cope with in the last war. They could hear us using the diesels from miles away. At the moment they don't know about us but how much do you want to bet that that they work it out quite quickly? We've got some time to get away but I need to know where to go.'

'Can we wait until Paulo wakes up?' asked Jacky anxiously.

'Is there no way we can bring him round sooner?' responded Tony.

'In maybe six hours or so we could get some sense out of him,' replied Phil. 'So here is what I suggest. Look, the Caribbean Sea is bloody deep, over a thousand metres in most places and the coasts are all relatively steep to. We can't really go to any of the popular islands to the east like St Lucia or even the BVI's.'

Tony laughed. 'No I don't think that would be a good place to go under the circumstances.'

'Right and anyway they're a bloody long way away,' Tony continued. 'As is the coast of Panama and Belize. That's not to say we can't get there but the longer we stay at sea the greater the risk. However one option, strange as it may be is Cuba. We would have to be bloody careful but I bet Castro and his lot would be happy to get their hands on this sub.'

'Absolutely not,' said Jacky. 'Can you imagine what they would do to me if they found out who I was? And anyway you know what an unstable lot they are. They're just as likely to throw all of us into jail as declare us heroes of the revolution.'

'She's got a point,' said Tony. 'I wouldn't trust that lot as far as I could spit. What are the warships likely to do? Do we know?'

'My best guess,' said Phil. 'Is that the US ones will head back up to the naval base at Roosevelt Roads in Puerto Rico. I'm not sure about the British frigate though.'

'I think I do,' Jacky replied. 'They were only deployed out here for a few months and so must be due to head home about now. My guess is that's what they'll do.'

'In which case they'll probably have to stop off at one of the islands or even Puerto Rico to refuel before going back across the Atlantic. So basically they will finish up at Paulo's place and head north once they go. They can't stay long as they don't want to be caught in the act, so my guess is they'll be off today some time. So if nothing else, we need to get out of their way. My suggestion is we head east there are several large inlets where we could beach the sub and leave her and I suspect Paulo has contacts in Venezuela anyway. We can do that until he wakes up and then give him the final decision. Anyone want to disagree?'

No one did and Phil ordered the submarine to turn right and head towards the east. 'Oh and one more thing,' he continued. 'We've never stayed submerged and not used the snorkel for periods of over twelve hours before. Not the least because our old batteries wouldn't last that long. But with these new ones we can stay down much longer as I've explained. The water temperature outside is twenty eight degrees but with all of us on board and no ventilation it's soon going to get very hot down here.'

'How hot?' someone asked.

'Well, we've seen it above thirty five even after twelve hours. So expect it to get even hotter than that.'

Once the meeting had broken up and the control room was emptier, Phil beckoned to Manfred and they went into quiet a huddle over the chart table.

'What's the status of the babies in the tubes Manfred?'

'I checked them only a week ago and they were fine. Surely you're not considering using them?'

'Last resort old friend but it's always useful to know what options you have.'

## Chapter 37

The Colonel stared in disbelief. 'A submarine Jon? Come on these are Columbian drug smugglers not the military. How would they get their hands on something like that? How would they be able to work it and for that matter where the hell would they keep it? There has to be another explanation.'

'All good questions and I don't know all the answers but you come up with something better. Let's look at the facts. They got away from Salt Island somehow and the only evidence we found was an intermittent, small radar contact that disappeared just at the right time. It was on the far side of the island so we never got to see what it was. They've managed to disappear again with no sign as to how or where they've gone. It was not that long after Jacky left me that I managed to get free and they clearly didn't leave by car and both of his boats are still tied up on the jetty. Glen will tell you that the amount of drugs coming into Florida in the last year has increased considerably and no one knows how they are doing it. That's what was bugging me earlier. He was joking when he said it but Glen even suggested the submarine idea some time ago, when we first met.'

'OK, I'll give you that they have something that we've missed but your idea is stretching things too far Jon.'

'You think so. Look, these uniforms are German war time Kriegsmarine. Here look at these badges,' and he held up the remains of a tunic. 'These were submariners, what the hell do you think they were doing here unless they came by submarine?'

'Alright then, where did they keep this mythical U-Boat of theirs? May I remind you that one of the reasons we had to conduct the operation as we did was because there are no beaches let alone submarine docks.'

'Good point but there has to be an answer.' Jon walked over to the cliff edge and looked out to sea. 'You know we picked up a strange conventional submarine signature a while ago when we were chasing a Soviet sub out there. The analysis was that it was something quite old but nothing more than that. I wonder....,' he was about to continue when he looked down at the sea by the cliffs. 'Colonel, look down there,' he exclaimed with excitement.

He looked towards where Jon was pointing. 'What am I meant to be looking at? It's just the sea and some cliffs.'

'No, look at the colour, its light blue everywhere but there, where its deep blue.' He pointed further along the shoreline. 'That must be a deep gully coming right up to the cliff. I'll bet there's a bloody great cave there which we can't see because of the overhang.'

Before the Colonel could say anything else, Jon started to run down the cliff path. When he got opposite the dark water he started to look around. The ground was mainly sand with some low scrub in patches; there was nothing to see.

'Colonel, bear with me please. Can I have those men over here for a minute? Oh and they will need their shovels.'

Mystified but willing to trust him at least for the moment the Colonel shouted to the men working on the pit to come over. Jon arranged them in a line and told them what he wanted them to do. Grabbing a spare shovel, he joined the line of them as they slowly walked down the length of the path, testing the ground as they went. A sudden shout came from the landward end and Jon shot over.

'Look Sir,' the Marine said. 'There's something very hard and metallic here and if you ask me someone has recently covered it up.'

Jon looked around and there did seem to some evidence that the ground had been recently disturbed. Grabbing his shovel, he started to scoop away the light soil covering and was quickly joined by the other Marines.

'What do you say now Colonel?' asked Jon in triumph a minute later, as he stood back to show the flat metal door hidden under the sand.

'I'd say you've discovered something Jon but I'll still reserve judgement if you don't mind.'

Jon was already pulling at the hatch and was surprised how easily it lifted. When he looked, it was clear it had been in recent use as the internal hinges were still covered in fresh grease. He peered down into darkness but all he could see was metal rungs in the wall disappearing into the gloom.

'Anyone got a torch?' he asked. Someone handed him a standard NATO green torch and he shone it down to reveal another door set vertically in the walls about twelve feet down. He was about to start down when a hand on his shoulder stopped him.

'Be careful Jon, we don't know what's down there.'

'Thank you Colonel but you were the one telling me this was all impossible a few minutes ago. Why don't you come with me and bring that nice big gun of yours as well.'

The two of them descended to the bottom of the ladder and stood side by side next to the door. Jon reached out and turned the handle and very slowly pulled it towards him. It was dark on the other side and very quiet although they could just hear the lapping sound of water coming from somewhere.

'I don't suppose this will work but it's worth a try,' said Jon as he reached for an obvious light switch on the wall inside the corridor. To his surprise, a row of lights came on and showed them a short corridor leading to what looked like a T junction. The Colonel called for two more Marines to come down and follow them in as they slowly entered the corridor.

'Well this place has clearly been used recently,' said Jon. 'Look, all this wiring for the lights is modern but this place certainly isn't, look there.' Above their head on the wall were words cut into the concrete. 'I can't read German, can you Colonel?'

'No but I recognise the words Hitler and Fuhrer when I see them. I have a nasty feeling I might just owe you an apology Jon.'

'Well let's see what's around the corner then.'

They reached the T Junction and looked both ways. To the right there were doors either side of a short corridor. To the left was where the sound of water was coming from. Taking the left turn Jon walked forward until he reached a doorway with iron steps leading downwards.

'Shit I was right,' said Jon in triumph. The massive space they could see was half full of water and Jon could just make out light filtering through from the open sea underwater in the side of the cave. Above this was a massive concrete sluice gate held up by some sort of mechanism.

'I'm guessing but it looks like they could actually shut off the cave with that door and maybe pump it out,' Jon surmised. 'That way a sub would be left dry.'

'And perfectly preserved,' the Colonel finished for him. 'Sorry Jon it looks like you were right but is there anything we can do about it, they've been gone for hours.'

'Yes but a war time U-Boat can't move that fast underwater. There may still be a chance. HMS Chester is probably one of the most advanced anti-submarine ships in the world. I would love to stay and investigate this place, it's just fantastic but I need to get back out to the ship and brief the Captain. There's still a chance we can catch this bastard.'

Two hours later Jon was back on board with the command team briefing them on his discovery. The Colonel was back ashore finishing off the job before the Marines all re-embarked on their assault ship.

'So Jon,' said the Captain. 'You found an underground base in the cliffs with working machinery and modern electrics but an inscription to Hitler on the walls.'

'Yes Sir, I know it's hard to believe but Mandero having a submarine would answer a great deal of the questions we've been asking all this time.'

The Captain looked around the operations team. 'Views anyone?'

The First Lieutenant answered first. 'Well is it against the law to own a U-Boat? So even if we could find him what could we do?'

'That's an extremely good point. But if we could prove it had been used for an international crime like smuggling drugs then I guess we would be in the right and of course we don't know if that's what they are up to at the moment. However, is there any realistic chance we could catch them. Those German machines were pretty quiet by all accounts and we don't even know where she's heading.'

Ops was looking thoughtful. 'They can't have gone too far Sir, not under battery power and at some time they're going to have to snort and when we do we should hear them from quite a distance if we have the tail out.'

'Alright, I'm going to signal Fleet and request permission to hang around for a few days at least. I'll also ask if there is any more intelligence on that diesel sub we detected while ago. Now we know it could have been a war time U-Boat they might be able to narrow down its type so we know better what we're up against. I'll also request any intelligence on people working for Mandero, maybe it will help us understand how he pulled of this trick of his. Oh and one more thing; Flight Commander?'

'Yes Sir,'

'For God's sake get down to sick bay and get that head properly stitched up.'

## Chapter 38

The temperature in the submarine was creeping up and not just the air temperature. Phil had been on the main broadcast to the crew to explain what they intended to do and some of the men weren't happy. They wanted to get ashore as soon as they could and get away. However the majority still seemed happy to wait for instructions from Paulo. Phil suspected that even now, most of them would stick by him to ensure they got paid.

Jacky went into Paulo's room and shook him again. An hour ago he had come to but was terribly groggy so she had decided to give him a little longer. This time he seemed more alert and was able to focus on her better.

'Paulo wake up, we need you to make a decision.'

'Water please. Why is it so hot?' he asked groggily.

'We've been underwater quite a while and Phil needs to know where to go.'

'Oh God that's a good point,' he smiled weakly. 'Better get him in here then.'

She handed him a glass of water and slipped out to get Phil who was in the control room. It was only a matter of seconds and she returned with him. Even so, she could see how, with the drug wearing off, Paulo was starting to panic. However, she could also see how he was forcing himself to stay calm.

Paulo,' said Phil. 'We need a decision. We need to know where you want us to go.' And he went on to briefly describe what they had done already and where they were heading. He also went over the issues with staying submerged and the fact that the warships may still be about.

Paulo swung his legs over the edge of the bed and drank the whole glass of water he had been holding.

'It seems the consensus is to get somewhere safe and then disperse and presumably get rid of the submarine, is that it?'

'Yes, well what else can we do?'

'Good point but Venezuela is probably not a good idea. I might have upset a few people there in the past.' And he laughed grimly. 'But could we get ashore in Trinidad?'

'Yes but they've probably got the most anal customs and immigration people in the world and explaining how we got in, when we try to leave could be interesting.'

'Right, well there are ways around that but why take the risk? I guess we need to get back to Columbia because that problem is going to be the same everywhere. We really don't want to draw attention to ourselves for a while.' A germ of an idea formed as he said the words. 'You know I would really like to keep this submarine, we could still use it.'

Jacky thought the drugs were still affecting his thinking. 'Oh come on Paulo, they're bound to find out about it, once the American navy knows what we're doing they'll be able to catch us easily.'

'Will they? And anyway why are they bound to find out about it? They daren't stay around my place for long and the base was very well disguised. I'm betting they are already leaving and still wondering how on earth we got away. So why don't we just wait a day or so and just go home?'

Phil was about to object when he stopped himself because the idea made a sort of sense. He still had reservations though. 'And what if they did find out? They could have destroyed the place or just be waiting for us.'

'Well, we won't know unless we look will we? How long do you think they will hang around under those circumstances?'

'I guess a few days at most, if we're fully charged we could creep in and look and even if they were still around we could avoid them. Of course seeing a ship still there will tell us if we've been rumbled and we can sneak away. And if the place is clear we can go look at the entrance or surface and put someone ashore. Even if we can't use the place again we can all go ashore and scuttle the sub. You know Paulo, the more I think about it the more it makes sense.'

'Good now give me some more of those damn pills.'

The Captain was in his cabin reading the long signal from Fleet when Jon, Ops and the First Lieutenant came in after knocking on the door. He looked up at Ops. 'Anything on Sonar Ops?'

# Cocaine

'Nothing Sir, we've had the tail out several hours now. Just flatulent whales I'm afraid.'

'Hm, no surprises there then. Well Fleet have given us three days. The Yanks have buggered off back to Roosy Roads. However, they do agree a submarine may have been used but can't spare us any surface assets for a couple of days. Apparently there is some big exercise going on but they will be giving us some maritime patrol aircraft cover. The first one is due on station in a couple of hours. We should have round the clock cover with two from then on so that might help. But frankly I'm not sure we're going to get anywhere, it's a big sea out there. If we'd picked him up straight away then we might have had a chance. Still, having asked for the time we might as well put it to good use, we always need practice. Now, as for the rest of the signal, it seems we might be up against a type twenty U-Boat which is interesting as they never made any.'

'How on earth did they find that out?' asked Jon.

'Apparently the type twenty was a bigger replacement for the 'Milch Cow' supply boats they used earlier in the war. Some were under construction when the programme was cancelled. It seems one got away. Because they were so big they used an unusual type of diesel engine, apparently someone in the Imperial War museum advised them and so they're pretty sure that the trace we saw was one of those.'

'Do we know any performance figures Sir?' Ops asked.

'Not really, they were armed with only four forward torpedo tubes and no stern tubes but they were designed to be quiet and stealthy, after all they weren't attack boats. They were also going to have a new type of snorkel but who knows what this boat has, it was never meant to have been built in the first place. Anyway, here is the really interesting thing. Guess who is Mr Mandero's professional skipper for his two boats? None other than a certain Lieutenant Phil Masters Royal Navy retired and also failed Perisher.'

'How long ago did he leave the RN?' someone asked.

'Ah, several years ago, then he worked in the City, got divorced and ended up in the Caribbean. It seems that's where he met Mr Mandero and where he's been ever since.'

'Well,' said the First Lieutenant. 'That probably explains where they got some of their expertise from and with him around they were probably able to recruit whoever else they needed. Bloody hell though, what a story. I wonder how on earth they managed to get the damned thing going after all these years?'

'If you'd seen the place they found it in you might understand,' said Jon. 'It was almost certainly kept dry and so in good condition although from the receipts I saw, they clearly had to replace all the batteries.'

He was interrupted by a knock and a rating from the communications office put his head around the door. 'Sorry to interrupt Sirs, another long signal for the Captain,' and he passed the paper in to be handed over.

The Captain read for a while and then looked strangely at Jon. 'Something very odd here Jon. It appears that the good Senator's daughter left instructions with several lawyers around the world to release a certain dossier to the press if she wasn't heard from for more than two days or she was reported dead. The contents are apparently quite damming and document the Senator's behaviour towards his wife, daughter and number of other minors over the years. If he wasn't already dead the authorities in the US would be looking for him. Any idea what the hell is going on?'

He passed the signal to Jon who studied it as he spoke. 'Well Sir, she clearly had problems. Her behaviour could be quite erratic. I met one of her friends when we were in Port Everglades last time and she told me quite a bit about how unstable she could be. The fact that she teamed up with Mandero says a lot and frankly doesn't really surprise me.'

'Are you sure she was a willing accomplice?'

'Oh yes Sir, no doubt about that. She was instrumental in deceiving Glen and Colonel Jones. But she did have some conscience. She told me she stopped Mandero burning the house down with us all in it. But reading this, it's not surprising that she ended up a mixed up kid. That bloody Senator's got a lot to answer for. This must have been some sort of insurance policy to keep the Senator off their backs. It went spectacularly wrong by the looks of it.'

'Yes well, he was found dead in a hotel in Mr Mandero's local town. It looks like quite a complicated story and I'm not convinced we'll ever hear all of it. Now this has hit the international press quite hard as you can imagine. So, just a warning gentlemen, when we next get ashore, no doubt it will come out that his daughter was associated with Chester and we will need to be careful what we say.'

## Chapter 39

Later that evening after dinner in the mess, Jon and Brian were sitting in the wardroom ante room sharing a late night drink.

'Shouldn't really be drinking Scotch,' said Jon gloomily looking into his glass. 'The Doc will go ballistic if he sees me. He's already grounded me for a week because of this lump on my head.'

'Well the lads are saying you were lucky to have been hit on the head, otherwise they might have actually hurt you.'

'Ha bloody ha. I guess these are the post trauma blues but it's so bloody depressing. Just to think that Jacky is actually alive but part of the enemy now. You know, I wonder if I had tried harder, I might have been able to help.'

'Right that's quite enough of that you silly bastard. There was nothing you could have done and you know it. Stop beating yourself up.'

'Alright, just talking out loud. So changing the subject slightly, where do you think they've headed to?'

'Well it's a big place out there and in a sub like that they could be anywhere.'

'Yes but they can't get far underwater so they will have to snort or run on the surface and then what do they do when they get where they're going?'

'Just go ashore and scuttle the sub I suppose, they're on the run after all.'

'Hmm but are they? On the run that is. Look, our little Columbian raid was meant to be deniable. The idea was to arrest them and charge them in the US like the previous one. The Yanks can't do too many of those without starting a major diplomatic incident. It was meant to be a limited exercise after all and going back to the same place twice would be far too risky.'

'So what? It doesn't help Mandero and Jacky.'

'But maybe it does. Don't forget Jacky was party to all the political machinations that set the whole thing up in the first place. She'll know how much political will there really is for all this. Now the Senator's dead and the Mandero operation failed, how much support will there be for continued operations? Why shouldn't Mandero just head home when the dust has settled? It would be far safer than trying to land in some other country and then have to get out.'

'You may have a point but didn't the Colonel disable the base before he left?'

'He told me he was going to try to blow the door mechanism to shut it all off. It was the best he could do in the time and anyway it really should be preserved for study. There must be an amazing war time story associated with it after all.'

'Bloody hell archaeology and drug smuggling. Anyway they could still get ashore by boat and fix it. Hey you could be right, it makes too much sense. Should we go and talk to Father about it?'

'Why not? It seems the most logical idea.'

Half an hour later the Captain was in agreement. 'Good thinking Jon, Brian. We were assuming he would head north to clear the coast at least and then maybe start his diesels as it got dark but if he's doing what you suggest then maybe he would do something different.'

'Yes Sir,' said Jon thoughtfully. 'If it was me I would stay quiet as long as possible and run my batteries almost flat before making any noise and then give us a few days to disappear before sneaking back with full batteries for a silent approach.'

'It'll be bloody hard to catch him then. We'll never hear him unless he uses his engines.'

'Yes Sir,' said Brian with mounting excitement. 'But we know the entrance door is down and broken so he will have to surface even if it's just to get his people ashore. That's when we can nab him.'

'Inside Columbian International waters with no evidence against him. I feel a diplomatic incident coming on chaps.'

'Shit, but surely Sir, if we work on the principle that he has a kidnapped US citizen on board as our excuse and say that we had tracked him in from international waters then we could get away with it.' Jon suggested.

'That's pushing things a bit Jon, we know she's a willing accomplice not a hostage.'

'But does anyone else know that apart from the military involved? Washington will want to keep a lid on the whole story for lots of reasons. Technically of course she died several weeks ago. So a valiant rescue attempt would be believable surely?'

The Captain still looked unconvinced. 'Sorry but you're still missing something. Just suppose we loiter clear and they surface off the base and start ferrying people ashore. What can we do about it? We can't go in and shoot at them. No, we need to think this through some more. However, that doesn't stop us getting started and seeing if we can set a trap. So the first question is, if you're right where is he now?'

A day of frustration followed. The US Orion patrol planes had been deployed along the Columbian Coast to the west and Venezuelan to the east. Chester was staying in the middle about forty miles off the coast, north of Santa Marta. Despite informed debate with the experts at home no one could really work out how long modern golf cart batteries would last. The consensus seemed to think about twenty four hours but that deadline had passed with nothing appearing either on the ships towed array or the Orion's sonobuoy barriers. Jon was spending a lot of time in the Operations room with the Captain. Not the least because it was his idea in the first place.

'How much longer before we pack it in Sir?' asked Jon despondently.

'Well Jon, all the experts agree that there's no way he can last more than two days at the absolute maximum. He slipped away about five in the morning so we're almost at the deadline now. If we don't have anything by first light we'll pack it in. I'm sorry but I certainly think you were right. The area we're covering is just too large.'

Jon was about to answer when the radio came to life. A laconic American voice on the radio identified itself Golf Hotel the eastward Orion patrol aircraft.

'Bravo Tango this is Golf Hotel, Possub low two detected on our southern barrier on buoy number eight. Assess a diesel submarine snorting. Attempting to detect a riser on my radar over.'

The air in the Ops room was suddenly electric. A possible submarine with the characteristics of a diesel boat could only be one thing. If the Orion was able to detect the submarines masts above the water with its radar then it would be a confirmed sighting and classified as a Certsub. The chase would be on. A tense silence ensued while they all waited for another report. As the minutes dragged by, the Captain looked over at the ship's plot in front of him.

'Where is the southern end of his sonobuoy barrier?' he asked the radar plotter manning the display.

The sailor pointed it out. It was close to the island of Aruba.

'Bravo tango, this is Golf Hotel, lost contact, time zero four thirty three. No riser detected. However we can confirm the contact was showing the characteristics of our target over.'

The ship acknowledged the call.

'Bugger,' said Jon with disappointment. 'We've lost him.'

The Captain wasn't upset however, he was jubilant. 'No Jon, you're wrong, we've got him. Your theory looks to be correct. Otherwise why would he still be out there near Aruba. No, my guess is that we caught the end of his charging session. It will be light soon after all. I willing to bet that he has now gone down again for the run to go home. I've got an idea how we might catch him in open water. Let's do some sums.'

## Chapter 40

The relief in the submarine when Phil ordered the boat to periscope depth that evening and after looking around through the periscope, finally ordered the snorkel raised was enormous. As soon as the diesels started, fresh air was also drawn in and the temperature started to drop. Some parts of the boat had reached over fifty five degrees and tempers had risen with the heat. Despite all the pressure, Phil had resisted the urge to do anything until darkness had fallen. Even though the area was well away from any shipping lanes and the most he had to worry about was a few yachts, he wasn't prepared to take any risks. Which was also why he had also resisted requests to charge the boat by surfacing. The radar signature of a surfaced submarine was much larger than a few masts sticking above the surface. If anyone was really looking for them, then they needed to be as careful as they could. He had explained this to Tony and Jacky earlier.

'Look, in a modern submarine we could put an Electronic Surveillance Mast up to detect any radars looking for us and easily submerge before we were detected but we don't have that sort of equipment. Our only advantages are stealth and keeping our signature to a minimum. Now, we'll run the diesels out here for eight hours. We will then be fully charged for a run back home. It's about two hundred miles and at nine knots we should arrive at about one in the morning, which should be perfect timing. That will also give us a reserve of battery life if we need to get out.'

They accepted the logic but some of the crew still needed convincing. However, the effect of cool fresh air soon had morale improving.

Jacky had been using the time for some serious thinking as well. 'Phil, I've been wondering whether we are being too cautious. We're in international waters and haven't actually committed a crime. Owning a submarine isn't on anyone's statute books as far as I know. If we're detected, especially if we are in Columbian national waters there's not actually anything a foreign navy could do about it.'

Phil looked at her sceptically. 'Are you prepared to bet on it Jacky? It was your lot that decided to ignore international law and do these raids in the first place.'

'No I'm not but I know how long the debate took to get them authorised in the first place and to authorise something like this will take considerable time and international consultation. We need to bear it in mind.'

'Fine, I will but I'm not taking any risks.'

By four thirty the batteries were full and Phil ordered the engines stopped and the snorkel lowered. The sub slipped below periscope depth and turned to the west.

Captain Peterson pointed to a chart of the southern Caribbean. 'It's simple Jon. He's out here somewhere north of Aruba. He's got two hundred miles to go and will want to arrive in the dark. It will have to be tomorrow night as he won't have the batteries for another twenty four hours. He won't hug the coast but why should he go further than he needs to? He will want to minimise his battery usage after all. So we set a trap for him here.' He pointed to a part of the coast, sixty miles to the east of Mandero's house. 'If I've got my speed time distance right, he'll pass through this line somewhere tonight at about eighteen hundred and it's the only shallow water on the whole journey. It will force him to stay at least twenty miles out from the coast. We'll get the Orions to maintain a surface search along the route in case he puts a periscope up. I'm assuming he has no radar detection equipment. I'll want Nellie airborne as well when the time comes. I know it will probably be useless but we can put a sonobuoy barrier across the track as well. However at the appointed time Nellie can start to use her active sonar. We will compliment that with the ships, twenty sixteen active sonar as well and we should have him in a vice.'

All day the ship monitored the Orions as they criss-crossed the anticipated track of their prey. Several times they reported possible risers in the right sort of place but were dissuaded from flying low to investigate. The Captain didn't want to take the risk of any chance of alerting his quarry that they were on to him.

However, the consistency of the fleeting radar contacts further convinced the ship that they were literally on the right track.

In the afternoon, Jon went down to the hangar to ensure that all was well. Nellie was already ranged on the Flight Deck ready to go and the twins, Brian and Leading Aircrewman Thompson were briefed and ready as well. He exchanged pleasantries with them but Brian could see he was troubled.

'What's up mate? Pissed off you can't fly?'

'No it's not that,' he replied. 'If this goes wrong I keep reminding myself that Jacky is on board that old relic. I've been looking at the report about her father in detail and I can understand why she went off the rails. It's her father's fault she's in that submarine, not hers.'

'We're not going to sink it mate, just get it to surface.'

'And how do we do that?'

'Come on, we've discussed this. If he won't come up once he realises we've found him, then we keep him away from the coast until his air runs out and he has to.'

'Yes and the only way to keep him away from the coast could easily be that we have to start dropping depth charges. That's why Eric has two of the buggers hanging off him as we speak.'

'Come on Jon, once we have him on active sonar, you know he won't get away, it will only be a matter of time.'

'I suppose you're right, well good luck, I'll be in the Ops room.'

An hour later and the Sea King launched. It headed twenty miles to the east and dropped a line of sonobuoys in a north south line, which would hopefully straddle their quarry's track. No one was hopeful that it would achieve anything. A submarine on electric motors was very hard to detect.

So it was with some surprise that at about the right time Tommo announced, 'I've got a faint line on buoy four. It's very weak and only showing one line but it might be him.'

Brian looked over at the paper trace showing the frequencies that the buoys were hearing and sure enough there was a faint line on one channel. He immediately warned the ship who replied to hold tight and keep watching.

'Picking it up on buoy five now Sir, he must be going between them. Looks like forty year old submarines are noisier than today's.'

Suddenly the frequency of the line started to shift. 'Doppler shift on buoy four,' he announced.

Brian needed no further encouragement, he called to the pilots, 'descend to two hundred feet, turn onto two four zero, stand by to mark dip.'

The submarine was hot again but no one minded too much as they all knew that they would be in Columbian waters soon and shortly after that they would be home. Phil had taken a few peeks through the attack periscope during the day but there had been nothing in sight. What he really missed was a decent sonar. In a modern boat he would be able to hear anything travelling on the surface from miles away. He would even be able to hear a helicopter flying if it was less than about fifteen hundred feet. In this old tub he was virtually blind. The old German hydrophones worked after a fashion but he didn't trust them at all. Still, everything pointed to a successful trip once again.

Tony came and joined him in the control room. 'So where are we sport?'

Phil took him over to the chart and showed him. 'See this shallow patch sticking out? well I've been relying on dead reckoning up till now. But we just had the step change in depth I was looking for, so that confirms our position about here. Less than seven hours to go and we'll find out what those bastards have done to Paulo's operation.'

'Don't worry about that, Paulo will get things running again pretty fast. He owns most of the countryside around him.'

'Don't I know it. But I'm not sure about the submarine. Now we've been rumbled I really don't think we'll be able to use her again.'

Tony clapped him on the back. 'Hell, maybe he'll go public and we can make a fortune taking punters around the bay. How much would people pay to travel on board a real German U-Boat?'

Suddenly a loud noise cut through the conversation. To Tony it sounded like a pulsing screech. Phil knew exactly what it was. He had heard it often enough in the past. His heart started beating hard at the same time a cold chill went down his spine.

'Fuck, fuck, fuck,' he grabbed the main broadcast. 'Hands to emergency stations stand by for manoeuvring.'

## Chapter 41

'Bravo Tango this is Nellie, Probsub high 4, bearing zero two one, range five thousand five hundred. We've got the bastard.' Brian realised that the last part wasn't exactly correct radio discipline but this was the first time he had detected a real submarine rather than one on exercise and he didn't care.

'Nellie this is Bravo Tango, Roger, closing in to acquire with twenty sixteen. Do you have a course and speed yet?'

'Standby, he's altering course heading north, speed twelve. Coming straight at you over.'

'Roger, we'll be within range in eight minutes maintain contact.'

'That'll be easier said than done,' muttered Tommo, who was now operating the active dipping sonar which was dangling on a long thin wire underneath the hovering Sea King. 'In these sonar conditions, he'll be out of range soon. Anyway, why's he turned to the north? The silly sod's running towards the ship.'

'Doesn't know she's there,' Brian responded. 'He bloody well will soon but I guess he's running for deeper water. No submariner wants to be caught in the shallows.'

Thirty metres below the surface, Phil was thinking fast. He needed deep water and the only way to go was north but that bloody Sea King had to have come from somewhere. Its ship, whatever it was, must be up there. He decided to take a risk.

'Periscope depth,' he ordered and grabbed the handles of the attack scope. As soon as they were level he risked a very quick look all round. What he saw confused him.

Mike Spencer had come into the control room looking scared and angry. 'That's a fucking helicopter sonar Phil, I've heard it enough times.'

'Don't you think I bloody know that you idiot but there's only one and it appears to have been launched off a Type Twenty Two frigate so there can only be one of them. This isn't over yet. Go and get Paulo, I don't care what you have to do but get him here and bloody conscious got it?'

Jacky had just come into the room as well and hearing the conversation went off with Mike without a word.

Phil knew he had very little time. 'What's the depth now?' he asked the helmsman.

'Two hundred metres and dropping fast.'

Thank God for that, now he had some room to manoeuvre. 'Come hard right, steer due west, set depth one hundred and fifty metres. The helmsman complied immediately but the man on the foreplanes turned to Phil.

'That's three times the depth we've tested her to.'

Suddenly the sonar noise stopped. Phil turned to the man. 'That's the helicopter moving position, there's only one and as long as we can avoid the frigate we can lose him. Now, do you want to spend the rest of your life in a fucking prison, because I don't. I've researched what this boat should be capable of and that is well within her tolerance.' He didn't add that it was at the absolute maximum of her operational clearance.

The man glared but complied and the depth started dropping. Phil got on the broadcast. 'Listen up everyone, I'm sure you all know we've been detected by now. We're going deep to try and get under the temperature layer. All compartments are to ensure you are closed up and all watertight doors are properly shut. Report any leaks if they occur.'

Phil had confidence in his men. They had practised this sort of thing many times and they were all ex professionals. Mind you it wouldn't be long before some of them would want to surface and surrender. He was half minded to himself. As he watched the depth gauge slowly creep down, he began to wonder what on earth he was doing. Then he had a brainwave. 'Turn due south, maximum speed.' He would use the window while the aircraft was moving, it might just work.

In Nellie they hadn't seen the brief exposition of the periscope but had seen the course change.

'Starting to lose contact,' called Tommo. 'He's going out of range.'

Brian immediately ordered the raising of the sonar body and a transition to a new dip position five miles further west. A few minutes later they were back in the hover and Tommo hit the transmit button on the sonar. 'Fuck, no contact Sir we've lost him.'

'No, we can't have. Lower the body to maximum.'

Tommo pushed the sonar winch handle and the sonar transducer descended to its maximum depth.

'Still nothing Sir.'

'Bugger where's he gone? He can't have gone far. Did he double back?'

'Can't have done, he'd still be in range.'

Brian called the ship, they had nothing either. This was getting ridiculous.

'Call the bottom depth helmsman,' Phil knew he had to get this right.

'One seventy and rising, one sixty,'

'Stop engines,' Phil ordered. He grabbed the main broadcast. 'This is the Captain, we are going to sit on the bottom so all hands brace for impact, I will try to make it gentle.'

'Losing control,' the planesman called. 'Speed below two knots.'

'Depth one hundred and fifty metres.'

There was a gentle shudder and the boat came to a halt. Luckily they were trimmed slightly heavy at this depth, so there would be no need to blow any ballast and alert those above to what they had done.

'Right silent routine everyone, I'm sure you've all played this game before and know the rules. We just wait here now until the bad guys get bored and bugger off.'

Nellie spent the next hour pinging fruitlessly until her fuel ran low and she had to go back to the ship. As soon as they landed Brian made his way to the Ops room leaving the pilots to shut the aircraft down. There was no point in launching again until they had worked out what the submarine had done.

The atmosphere in the Ops room was tense. Brian went straight over to the Captain. 'We definitely had him Sir, one of the best active sonar contacts I've ever seen. But I've no idea what he did, he just bloody disappeared.'

Captain Peterson smiled. 'No he didn't Brian, he's sitting on the bottom somewhere, making like a rock. If he had turned back we would have got him on the ship's sonar. You were past him and between us we would have seen him if he had gone north as well. So that leaves south and it gets shallow very quickly so he's either on the bottom deliberately or by accident and it doesn't matter. We can surmise the size of area he might be in quite easily. So this is what we're going to do.'

HMS Chester started to conduct a thorough search of the area. Her active sonar was on full power and although it didn't have very good bottom resolution it might be able to discriminate between a rock and large submarine. On top of that one other piece of equipment was being monitored very carefully and that was the ship's echo sounder on the bridge. Every hour, three small explosive charges were thrown over the side. The people in the submarine were not going to get very much sleep.

'Bastard, why doesn't he just go away?' Tony was getting very ragged. Phil knew he wasn't the only one on board. The bloody frigate had a new type of sonar that Phil hadn't encountered during his time in service and it emitted a very high pitched screech rather like someone scraping their finger nails down a black board. It was slowly driving them nuts. On top of that every hour, three loud explosions were heard. The first time it had happened Tony had almost jumped out of his skin.

'Calm down man, he's trying to provoke us. That's the standard NATO signal from a ship to a submarine to tell us to surface. What he's doing is telling us he knows what we've done and is waiting for us. As well as trying to get on our tits as well.'

'Well he's bloody well succeeding then,' was the terse reply.

Earlier on, Paulo had been eventually woken and they had explained the situation. When he was told they were sitting on the bottom. Over three hundred feet down with a British warship above them, he went almost catatonic. Phil realised he was on his own.

Manfred called from the engine room and requested to come forward. Phil approved the request and a few minutes later the old man had joined them.

'Batteries down to twenty per cent Phil but if we stay like this, running out of air will be the first problem. That or frying, with no fans. This is just the start of how hot it's going to get,' he reported. 'What are we going to do?'

'We have two choices old friend, as you well know. Surface and surrender or wait until he is as far away as we reckon he will get and then try and run for it. You never know we might make it into territorial waters and then we might just be able to argue ourselves clear.'

Manfred looked Phil hard in the eye. 'And the third option, you haven't mentioned that.'

## Chapter 42

'What third option?' Tony had picked up on the remark straight away.

'There is no third bloody option Tony. Manfred is just being silly.'

'Come on Manfred, what have you two got up your sleeve that you're not telling us?'

Manfred looked torn and then before Phil could stop him he blurted out. 'We have four operational torpedoes in the tubes. We could fight our way out.'

'What? And you didn't tell Paulo. Phil you stupid bastard. So there is a third option.'

'Don't be so fucking stupid Tony. That's a five thousand ton frigate up there with over two hundred and fifty people on board. If we sank her how many would we kill? May I remind you we haven't actually committed a crime yet. The worst they can do is charge us with smuggling and they would bloody well have to prove it first. Mass murder is another matter altogether. Anyway the torpedoes may not even work, they're over forty years old,' he said desperately.

'Manfred said they were operational,' said Tony.

'As much as we can tell but we were hardly in a position to test the fuses and warheads.'

'It doesn't matter,' this time it was Mike Spencer joining the conversation uninvited. 'Fire a couple off at her and she'll have to evade them, even if they don't go off. We can slip away in the confusion. As you said, it's not far to the coast.'

'Jesus Mike, not you as well? Have the whole crew gone fucking mad?' Just then there was the first of three loud explosions, as if to accentuate Phil's comments.

'Phil, no one on this boat wants to surrender. We're all too old to go to prison and we all have a stash of money waiting for us if we make it home. I knew about the torpedoes too you know and I've just been through the boat. There were a few dissenters but I've spoken to them. No one will object.'

'Sink the bastard,' the voice came from behind them. It was Paulo and he looked dreadful. He was sweating, yet his skin was pale and he had an almost manic expression on his face. 'You never told me about the torpedoes, why was that Phil? I promise you will regret that.'

'Paulo, the only time we might have needed them was when you weren't meant to be on board. I never envisaged something like this. Look they can't attack us physically, it's against their rules of engagement. Even if we surfaced they could try to board us but how would they do that? We could easily hold them off.' Phil realised he was starting sound desperate.

'And you are sure of this?' I don't think so. In my country, if we are threatened we shoot back. If we sink or damage that damned ship we are free. There is no debate. Just do it.' His last words were almost shouted and spittle flew from his lips.

Jacky joined in. 'If we're caught and I was beginning to think it was inevitable, then I will probably never see Paulo again. I can't live with that. Tough if some of them are killed, they are the ones who attacked us first.'

Phil was taken aback. He didn't think it worth pointing out that they actually hadn't been attacked yet. The determination in Jacky's voice was like hardened steel.

'Christ almighty, am I the only sane one left here?'

Jacky went up and put an arm around him. 'Probably Phil but we trust you, you know. Getting this machine operational was an outstanding feat and you've earned the trust of all of us over the last few days. If we can scare off this ship, yes even damage or sink her in the process so that we can get away, then that's what we should do.'

'Right, you realise she also has a helicopter that can drop torpedoes or depth charges on us if they find us.'

Mike answered. 'They won't be able to launch it if they are evading torpedoes will they? We know it must be on deck as we haven't heard its sonar for ages. Even if they can eventually launch it, we will be long gone.'

Phil looked around at the sweating determined faces and realised he had no choice. Suddenly he didn't care. He thought he had reached the pinnacle when he'd got this machine operational, never thinking it would be more than a supply boat. Now he had the chance to pit his wits against the finest his old service had to offer. Hadn't he already outwitted them once? He would do it again and prove that stupid bastard on the Perisher course how wrong he had been, all those years ago.

'Right then, we'd better get ready. It will be light soon and I will need to be able to see.'

'Gotya,' the ship's Officer of the Watch had just seen a large trace appear on the echo sounder.

'Ops room this is the bridge, we managed a run over that contact we had last time at right angles and it's definitely submarine shaped, I reckon that's him.'

'Well done bridge,' came the reply over the intercom. 'We've marked the plot. However keep up the search grid, we don't want to alert him that we know where he is.'

'Roger Ops, continuing with square search.'

Down in the Ops room there was quiet satisfaction. The Operations Officer turned to the Captain who had been there all night. 'What now Sir? I guess we just wait.'

'Absolutely right. But if he wants to get home he needs to get past that large shallow area to the south, then he can run for the coast. So we need to make sure we keep between him and it. Then he'll either run out of air or battery power and have to come up. In fact I wonder why he hasn't already. He might be able to bluff it out on the surface but can only fry down there. Who knows. Right, I want both helicopters at alert fifteen and take one depth charge off the Lynx and replace it with a Stingray. Let's be sure we cover all eventualities.'

'Are you worried he might be up to something Sir?'

'Can't see what but it's always best to cover all eventualities. I've got this nagging feeling. He's been pretty clever so far. Anyway I need some sleep. Its several hours till dawn, so I'll be in my cabin checking my eyelids for light leaks. Call me the moment anything happens.'

'Aye aye Sir.' Ops watched the Captain leave, glad that he was at last getting some sleep. The ship needed him alert and awake when something happened, as it surely would.

'Listen up everyone, this is Phil Masters. It seems we are all in agreement as to what we do next, so here is how we'll do it. First of all, I want everyone at their stations, we must be ready to react quickly. When that bloody ship is as far away as she is going to get, we will blow ballast as fast as we can. As soon as we're clear of the bottom, I will order high speed and we need to get to periscope depth as quickly as we can. Manfred the Engineer will be in the torpedo compartment ready to fire on my order. We will open the tube doors now to save time later. However, depending on how successful we are in diverting the frigate, we may need to surface and run for the coast at full speed on our diesels. If the ship manages to launch a helicopter with weapons we will actually be safer on the surface. They aren't designed to be effective against surface targets as they are too shallow. Right, all compartments call in when ready. There is enough light now, so we go when the frigate is in position.' He put down the microphone and looked and the control room crew. 'Standby.'

They nodded but said nothing except Jacky. 'I'm going to stay with Paulo, we have faith in you Phil,' and she left for the little cabin just forward of the control room.

One by one the sub reported ready and suddenly there was no reason to delay. They hadn't heard the frigate's propellers for some time now which meant she wasn't really close and the sonar was as quiet as it ever had been.

'Blow main ballast,' Phil ordered. There was a loud rushing sound as compressed air forced water out of the ballast tanks. Phil watched the depth gauge. Suddenly it started to rise. 'Stop blowing.' The boat continued upwards, he would need to flood down a bit in a minute to catch a trim but not just yet. When they were ten metres off the bottom he ordered the electric motors to give him twelve knots and waited.

'We have steerage,' reported the helmsman. 'Planes responding,' was the next report.

'Right turn to head due west, periscope depth as soon as you can. Up attack scope.' He looked through the lens of the attack periscope at dark blue water which slowly got lighter as the submarine approached the surface. Suddenly he was looking at daylight. Swinging the handles around, he did a quick three hundred and sixty degree sweep. The only thing in sight was the frigate. If they wanted to get clear they would have to get past it. She was west of him, broadside to, at about six thousand yards and luckily heading north. There was a Sea King on deck. It was looking good. This wasn't going to be a text book shoot, he didn't have time to work out his targets course and speed accurately but that didn't matter.

'Come right heading two nine zero.' As soon as the boat was pointing ahead of the frigate to give him an approximate aim off, he realised this was it. The bullshit finally stopped here.

'Fire one and two,'

There was a hissing noise.

'Good launch, torpedoes running.'

'Depth fifty metres alter course to two zero zero.' The course would keep him clear of shallow water until he could turn due south for safety. Normally he would time the torpedo run and wait for the results. This time he just wanted to get the hell out of it, praying that the torpedoes would buy them the time they needed. There was nothing left to do. Everyone in the submarine waited in tense silence.

In HMS Chester all hell broke loose. The ship's sonar had immediately detected the submarine as it left the bottom. The Captain, who had just returned to the Ops Room had ordered Nellie to scramble, although she was already half way through starting up for her planned dawn sortie. However, rather than head away towards the shore, the submarine had turned towards them.

'What the hell is he doing?' The Ops officer exclaimed.

'How long to get the Sea King launched?' asked the Captain.

'Launching now,' the Flight Deck reported.

A hush descended. They heard the roar of the helicopter through the thin walls of the ship for a few seconds as it transitioned away towards the target.

'Get the Lynx ranged,' ordered the Captain and then to everyone's surprise, 'hands to emergency stations please.'

The Ops officer gave him a puzzled look but complied. Suddenly the ship was awoken with the intermittent roar of the actions stations alarm. Followed by the main broadcast, 'HANDS TO EMERGENCY STATIONS, HANDS TO EMERGENCY STATIONS, CLOSE ALL WATERTIGHT DOORS AND HATCHES.'

# Cocaine

The Captain turned to Ops again. 'The only time a hunted submarine turns towards the hunter is if he is going to shoot back.'

Ops was about reply when the radio burst into life, the voice was urgent. 'Chester this is Nellie, torpedo tracks in the water heading towards you, they're tracking on a heading of two nine zero.'

The Captain grabbed the intercom to the bridge. 'Officer of the Watch come hard to port, head two nine zero.'

The ship started to heel over as he started to talk on the main broadcast. 'D'you here there, this is the Captain speaking. Our target appears to have teeth and has fired two torpedoes at us. We are turning to present out stern and minimise our target size. Evacuate all stern compartments if possible. As soon as possible scramble the Lynx.'

Just then, Jon came into the Ops room, grabbing onto a console as the ship suddenly straightened out and came upright. Nothing was said. There was nothing further to say. The tense seconds ticked by. They could still hear people running to their Emergency Stations outside but inside the Ops room it was dark and quiet, only the light coming from the various displays illuminated the space.

'Chester this is Nellie, Torpedoes approaching you now.'

No one bothered to answer. 'Brace for impact,' the Ops officer called over the main broadcast.

A loud whirring noise was heard going down the port side then a bang and sudden shock through the soles of their feet. But it wasn't an explosion. Jon and the Captain exchanged glances.

'Captain this is HQ1 reporting. Minor impact astern, no initial damage reported, we are checking further.'

Expressions and exhalations of relief filled the room. 'Right gentlemen, those two were duds but there's no guarantee that he won't fire again and the next ones may not be. Ops, find out where he is now and whether we can get within the ship's torpedo's range and Jon how long until the Lynx can launch?'

'I'll go down aft and check Sir but you're not intending to sink him, surely.'

'Jon, he's already fired at us and tried to sink us. If they turn to fire at us again I'm not risking my people and my ship.' There was absolutely no doubt about the Captain's resolution and

Jon knew he was right, even though Jacky was down there. He left the Ops room feeling sick and started running down to the hangar to see how they were getting on with the Lynx, just as the ship started to turn again, this time in pursuit of their quarry.

## Chapter 43

No explosions had been heard, although at about the right time they had heard a distant noise and Phil wondered whether they had at least hit the target, even if the warhead had failed. He knew that later German war time torpedoes were designed to go under a target and explode using a magnetic fuse. The ones he had were of an earlier variety and needed to physically hit the target. Maybe that was what had happened. He decided to risk a return to periscope depth. After a quick look around initially he wasn't sure what was going on. Then he saw the ship heeling into a turn to come towards him. 'Don't shoot unless you've already been shot at' was the standard rule of engagement and Phil had fired first. He knew he could expect no mercy.

Suddenly his heart hit his boots as into view came the deadly shape of a Sea King helicopter. It was only feet away, they could even hear it in the control room. He suddenly laughed. 'It's alright guys, you can hear a helicopter but the silly sods haven't armed it. I can see the weapon stations and they're empty.' He lowered the periscope and ordered them back down to thirty metres and as fast as the electric motors could take them. Soon the all too familiar sound of the helicopter's sonar could be heard, complementing the high pitched squeak coming from the frigate. He wasn't worried, they could track him as long as they liked. Although he was surprised they hadn't recalled the helicopter to arm it. Maybe they realised they had left it too late or were going to try to use the STWS, ship launched torpedo system that all frigates carried to take him out. As long as he stayed out of its relatively short range he should be alright. Once they were at the coast they could abandon the submarine and there was bugger all the Royal Navy could do about it. He started to feel a faint glimmer of hope.

In Chester they were doing a speed, time distance calculation. The Ops officer summed it up. 'We should be able to block him off unless he surfaces to get over that shallow water. But it puts us at risk of him firing at us again.

'I agree,' the Captain confirmed. 'Even so, alter course to keep us between his escape route and the shallow ground and get that bloody helicopter airborne.'

Jon was watching the Lynx being placed on its spot. He knew it would take another couple of minutes for the maintainers to spread its tail and the rotor blades. He made a decision and sneaked quickly back to his cabin and slipped into a pair of flying overalls and grabbed his flying helmet before going back to the hangar. Brian and Steve Makepeace were just about to climb in.

'Sorry Steve, my sortie.' Jon said firmly.

'Sir, I thought you were grounded?' came the puzzled reply.

'Not for this trip. Now pass me your Mae West. We need to get airborne in a hurry.'

Steve saw the determination in his Boss's eyes and realised he wasn't going to win any arguments. He mutely handed over his lifejacket.

Jon climbed in and quickly did up his straps.

'Hope that helmet will fit over that bump on your stupid head,' was all Brian said.

Jon looked at his friend with anguish in his eyes. 'Jacky's on that sub, if anyone is going to do this, it's me, alright? I can't ask anyone else to take the responsibility. Now shut up and help me get airborne.'

Two minutes later and Eric launched. Brian had been right, the tight fitting helmet had pressed right down on the gash in the side of Jon's head and it hurt like hell but nothing was going to stop him flying this trip.

Phil realised that the ship had altered course and was once again deliberately waiting for him to try to pass it, blocking his way to potential freedom. He didn't dare turn to port anymore, they could end up aground. If he surfaced now to reduce their draft and get over it, the frigate could use its four and half inch gun on him, so he had to stay underwater. He had no choice. The stupid bastards were giving him no choice.

'Standby tubes three and four,' he called. 'Come right twenty degrees, standby.' Suddenly he was back in that nuclear submarine all those years ago. It was just the same, getting this right was all that mattered. His whole life depended on the next few moments of calculation and decision but the rewards were there to be taken.

In the ship, they immediately detected the submarine's change of course. 'He's altering to fire again, instruct the Lynx to attack with Stingray.'

In Eric, they had been vectored towards the submarine, whose attack periscope could clearly be seen. There would be no need for a controlled vectored attack, where they would be directed by the Observer in the Sea King under radar control because Jon could see his target. Jon flew steadily at four hundred feet until he was five hundred yards astern of the little white feather sticking up out of the water and with a leaden heart, pushed the torpedo release button.

'Phil, PHIL!' the shout jerked him out of wherever he had been. Tony was looking at him with a strange expression.
'What? Oh shit, right.' He looked through the periscope again when two things happened almost simultaneously. A small grey helicopter shot past, in front of him. He immediately recognised it as a Lynx. *'Where the fuck had that come from,'* he thought desperately. The next thing was a noise like a wasp flying around the control room. He knew what that was as well. He also knew they were dead. *'Oh God how had it come to this?'*
'Are you going to fire the fucking torpedoes,' Tony almost screamed at him.
Phil looked at him sadly. 'No.'
It was the last thing he or anyone else in the submarine said.

The Stingray, acoustic, homing, anti-submarine, torpedo, fell clear of the side of the Lynx. As it did two things happened, the metal bands used to hold it to the weapon carrier flew free and a lanyard in the tail, pulled out, deploying a small stabilising parachute. Adopting a thirty degree nose down attitude, it plummeted into the sea in a controlled entry. As soon as it broke the surface, salt water was forced into its magnesium and silver chloride battery compartment and the pump jet at its stern started to work, accelerating it up to its operating speed of forty five knots. The sonar in the nose turned on and started looking for targets ahead as had been pre-programmed by Jon in the Lynx prior to drop. It was a matter of seconds before it acquired the submarine and tore off in pursuit. As it drew up to the submarine, it turned and made its terminal attack, hitting the casing just below the fin, directly opposite the control room. The forty five kilogram, shaped charge warhead, was designed to blast through the double hull of a modern Soviet nuclear submarine. The hull of a German wartime type twenty submarine offered no challenge at all and the blast entered the control room sending shards of red hot molten metal flying, like a swarm of angry, killing insects. It was followed micros seconds later by blasts of cooling seawater, not that there was anyone left alive to appreciate the effect. In the rest of the submarine, they lasted just a little longer. Jacky was able to grab Paulo in a last embrace before a wall of water smashed them both senseless. The last to die was Manfred in the torpedo compartment. His last thoughts were of puzzlement that the order to press the buttons on the last two of his precious torpedoes had never come through.

The submarine snapped in half and the two parts fell. They hit the sloping sea bottom and started rolling. The Caribbean Sea is very deep and the shelf they were on became steeper and steeper until it was almost vertical. The remains of U557 came to rest at a depth of over twelve hundred metres in a cloud of silt which took almost two hours to settle completely.

Jon flew past the attack periscope and turned the aircraft to watch in morbid fascination. It didn't take long. With the submarine at periscope depth, the blast from the torpedo's warhead was seen as a sickening but oddly beautiful, white plume of spray, rising from the sea. For a couple of seconds nothing happened. Then the bow of the submarine lifted almost elegantly from the surface. He could clearly see that all four torpedo doors were open. It kept rising until it was almost vertical then slipped backwards and was suddenly gone. An oil slick and a few bubbles, the only testament to its presence.

'Come on Jon, time to go home,' Brian chided.

'Yes,' he replied sadly. 'God, is the Doc going to give me a bollocking.'

## Prologue

HMS Chester was in dry dock in the US naval base at Roosevelt Roads in Puerto Rico. The potential damage of being hit underwater by a torpedo, even it had been a dud, needed checking out before a trans-Atlantic passage. Luckily a large dent was all that had been found. The general consensus was that had the warhead detonated, the ship would have lost its stern and probably have sunk.

The Captain and several of the ships officers were attending a debrief in one of the yard's conference rooms. The usual suspects were there from the Coast Guard, Marines, DEA and Washington, along with the resident British naval attaché. The circumstances of the previous few days had just been reviewed.

The British naval Captain from Washington stood to sum up. 'Gentlemen, well done for a successful operation. A severe blow has been struck against the drug smuggling capacity of several major cartels. The action against the Columbian submarine was in accordance with international law. HMS Chester was defending herself against attack on the high seas and all her crew are to be commended in how they reacted. Well done, all of you.'

He was about to sit down when Jon stood up. 'Sir, there is one other thing I would like to propose.'

Questioning faces turned towards him. 'Jacky Musgrove Sir.'

'What about her?'

'She died at Salt Island. We all attended her funeral afterwards.'

The Captain looked puzzled for a second and then Glen Thomas stood. 'That's correct Sir, she was never seen again.'

Joshua Jones also stood. 'Never seen again.'

## Authors Notes

The hurricane force storm at the start of this book is based on my recollection of just such an event when going across to the States at the start of 1982. The only real difference was that we were in a smaller 3000 ton ship, HMS Andromeda. It was just as described and the anemometer on the bridge was jammed on its maximum stop for over four hours. My problem was that I was the ship's meteorologist and so got all the blame!

We then spent some time on the AUTEC ranges in the Bahamas, flying the Lynx from the ship who was conducting Stingray trials. We were actually warned not to fly over the west coast of Andros Island in case we were shot at. We were unarmed in those days.

Wardroom cocktail parties were always a battle between the First Lieutenant and the rest of the wardroom. Being a good host and chatting up the totty were generally held to be mutually exclusive operations. We normally compromised quite well.

The 'Cow on a stick' was there. I should know I fell off the bloody thing on several occasions, as was a certain officers attempt to climb a coconut tree. I've got photos to prove it!

The story of sailors using the excuse of a pack of dogs to miss the ship is absolutely true. I was one of the unfortunate Divisional Officers who attended and had to try and keep a straight face as the same ridiculous story was repeated word for word. It was made worse by the fact that we knew exactly what had been going on in the first place.

At that time there was a British exchange officer flying with the Coast Guard from their base at Opa Locka in Florida. We hooked up with him when we were visiting down the road, in Port Everglades and flew each other's machines. Their old CH 52, a sort of single engine Sea King was a real relic and they loved the Lynx. A few years later Westlands almost sold them the Lynx as a replacement but as usual with UK industry of the time, managed to ensure the French won the contract instead.

Many of the book's smuggling stories came from those times. The story of running in marijuana into the east coast and using it as a diversion, so that harder stuff could be simultaneously smuggled in on the Gulf coast is true, as are the other stories in this book.  When you flew over the Everglades, the place was littered with the wrecks of crashed aircraft that had been deliberately flown in and crash landed at night, stuffed full of Cocaine.

We were also told, although it was never corroborated, that the Columbians had indeed found an abandoned German U-Boat and attempted to get it into some sort of working order. Apparently, it was found up a muddy creek somewhere and in too bad a condition to resurrect. It may seem farfetched but bearing in mind their use of submersibles nowadays, maybe not.  So by giving them a well preserved example, who knows what they could have achieved?

Have a look at:

www.huffingtonpost.com/2011/02/15/drug-submarine-seized-colombia_n_823445.html to see what they are capable of these days.

'Fighting in the Urban Canyon Below the Rim' is an exact phrase used by a US Marine Corps Colonel during a briefing I attended when I was on Staff course.  It was one of many and by the end of the lecture none of us had a clue what he had been on about.  The Americans seem to love to dress up simple issues with incomprehensible jargon.

Just prior to our deployment we had worked the ship up at Portland and one of the things we were required to do was operate in the western approaches on an anti-submarine exercise.  It all became real when one morning, we were flying on a surface search exercise and hit the jackpot.  We found a Soviet, Foxtrot class, diesel submarine on the surface next to a surface ship, probably an intelligence gatherer.  Conventional submarines in those days worried us a lot as they were so quiet. They could only be detected with active sonar which was very short range or when they were snorting to charge their batteries.  Andromeda came charging up and the submarine submerged and sat on the bottom where he was almost impossible to detect.  In the end we confirmed his position using the echo sounder.......

Type 22 frigates even the bigger Batch threes, never operated a Lynx and a Sea King together although there might just have been room. However the problem of localising a target found by a towed array was a real one and Sea Kings replaced Lynx on several ships as they had active sonar which could do the job. The ships could carry two Lynx so it wasn't too much of a leap to combine the two. Who knows maybe it might even have been a good idea.

Cocaine

# Arapaho

Jon and Brian fly again, this time into the cauldron of the Lebanon of the ninety eighties with a new squadron in an experimental ship:

Beirut, a city in chaos. After their embassy is bombed, the British decide on a full evacuation and call on the newly formed 844 Naval Air Squadron of Sea King helicopters led by Lieutenant Commander Jonathon Hunt, to conduct the operation.

Embarking on the experimental Royal Fleet Auxiliary 'Arapaho', the squadron almost complete their dangerous task when Jon Hunt's aircraft is shot down and he is taken hostage. Although a rescue is mounted, events move swiftly as a British Cruise ship is seized at sea bringing about a confrontation which only Jon and his squadron can resolve.

Based on real events of the 1980s and the author's own military experience, Arapaho is the fourth novel about Jon Hunt, Brian Pearce and the modern Royal Navy.